ROPED HEAT

Also by Vonna Harper:

Surrender

"Wild Ride" in *The Cowboy*

ROPED HEAT

VONNA HARPER

APHRODISIA

KENSINGTON PUBLISHING CORP.

http://www.kensingtonbooks.com

APHRODISIA BOOKS are published by

Kensington Publishing Corp.
850 Third Avenue
New York, NY 10022

All Kensington Titles, Imprints, and Distributed Lines are available at special quantity discounts for bulk purchases for sales promotions, premiums, fund-raising, and educational or institutional use.

Special book excerpts or customized printings can also be created to fit specific needs. For details, write or phone the office of the Kensington special sales manager: Kensington Publishing Corp., 850 Third Avenue, New York, NY 10022, attn: Special Sales Department, Phone: 1-800-221-2647.

Aphrodisia and the A logo Reg. U.S. Pat & TM Off.

ISBN-13: 978-0-7582-1527-7
ISBN-10: 0-7582-1527-4

First Kensington Trade Paperback Printing: June 2007

10 9 8 7 6 5 4 3 2 1

Printed in the United States of America

1

Moist heat from the wide-eyed creature's flared nostrils brushed Nari's throat and slid across the top of her breasts. Sensing the wilding was on the brink of panic, she ran her fingers over the short, rough hair covering its broad chest. Standing twice her height, it could easily kill her. Fortunately, wildings were timid grass-eaters, and she understood their unstable nervous systems.

"Listen to me, trembling one," she muttered in the melodic tone that had gentled more wildings than she could count. "You're here because you heard my song. You don't know it yet, but in your heart you want to serve me and the rest of the Baasta."

Perhaps confused by the word *Baasta*, the wilding pawed the ground.

"My breed," she explained. "My kinsmen, much as your herd, give you a sense of belonging. There are nearly two hundred of us now, living safely in timber houses we placed against the side of a mountain." Confident that the wilding wasn't about to rear, she rested her hand against the chest so she could feel the strong, quick heartbeat.

"Do you hear your own song? This constant pulsing means you're alive. And soon our hearts will beat together. No longer will you have to forage for food throughout Hevassen while meat-eaters try to feed off your flesh. Do you understand? Once you accept my people as your lords, you'll live safely." Leaning closer, she expelled her breath near the wilding's nostrils. "No longer will you be allowed to run free because we've found many uses for your kind, but we'll protect you. You'll grow fat and give birth to many babies."

Obviously not convinced, the wilding backed away, but Nari kept pace, her bare feet whispering over the late summer grass. "Look at this land we share. The ground and sky blesses Hevassan. Everything we plant flourishes. There's abundant rain, and yet it hasn't flooded since we came here. Except for the savages who are more animal than human, we have no enemies." *No longer, praise be.* "This rich gift from the Divine Eternal is home to both human and animal, an area of peace, different from so much of Punta."

At the word *peace*, she slid her fingers into the long, thick hair growing between the wilding's small ears. As the animal relaxed, Nari took in her surroundings. Wise in the ways of wildings, she'd spent yesterday riding her own beast to the nearby low country lake. Because she'd been there numerous times, she knew it was a popular watering place. Punta's twin suns had been rising when she spotted two wildings down on their front knees, necks stretched toward the water. Although she could have sung her hypnotic mind-song to both creatures, she'd chosen this young female because it was pregnant. She'd tethered her own wilding a distance away because she wanted the pregnant female to concentrate on her.

Life was indeed good, peaceful except for the savages who, according to the scouts, were currently in their caves in the northern part of Havassan. With nothing to concern herself with, she could spend the day teaching the wilding the meaning of the word *trust*. And when she returned home, she'd take her pick of the twenty-some single men, all of whom were eager to quiet the humming between her legs. At the moment she couldn't think who she might choose to fuck, let alone agree to spend the rest of her life with but—

Snorting, the wilding threw up her head. Nari shielded her eyes from the two blood-red suns and studied her surroundings. What was that faint roar? Torn between keeping her latest acquisition with her and concentrating on the sound, she tried to determine the direction it was coming from.

"Stay!" she ordered. "Take my command into you."

Although the wilding shivered, the female stood her ground. After giving her a comforting pat, Nari hurried up a nearby rise. As she did, her sleeveless hide dress rode nearly to her buttocks, increasing her awareness of her deeply tanned legs. A number of bright blue birds flew from a nearby tree, their wings and cries drowning out everything else. For a moment she was swept back to the time of the Baasta's enslavement, but they'd been free for many seasons. Free! Able to run or stand and fight as they chose. Free to make Hevassan their home.

Because to do otherwise was foolish, she carried a knife made from a night beast's thigh bone. Drawing it out of its holding bag at her waist, she gripped it in her long fingers. Because of her unique skill with wildings, she seldom hunted and had only once been involved in a battle with the savages, but she knew how to defend herself.

No, not savages!

Looking like angry insects boiling out of their home, something she'd never before seen came into view. Although she couldn't say how many there were of the sturdy, two-wheeled objects, their speed was alarming. And their direction.

Free hand at her throat, she spun toward the trembling wilding. "Hear me! No matter what happens, you must stay with me. Let me onto your back. When I command, you will run as you have never run."

Whirling back around, she ordered herself not to give in to panic. Who or whatever the newcomers were, she *had* to learn all she could about them. Gripping the knife with white knuckles, she again shielded her eyes. The newcomers were now close enough that she could see they were human and astride the screaming *things*. Taller and narrower than wagons, they had seats resembling saddles upon which the riders sat. The riders gripped chest-high horizontal bars that they turned one way or another to change direction. As for what made it possible for the *things* to move so quickly—

The furious insectlike roaring intensified. Her heart felt as if it had lodged in her throat. Biting down on a scream, she sprinted for the pregnant wilding, sheathing her knife so she'd have use of both hands. When she tried to pull the wilding's head down in preparation for jumping onto her back, the wilding reared. A hoof struck her calf, and she nearly fell.

"No! No!" She forced a calm tone. "Don't be afraid, gentle one. Your legs are swift, your back strong, your heart healthy. Take courage from those gifts. Feel my love for you and know you're safe."

Whether the wilding believed her didn't matter. What did was distracting her long enough to spring onto her broad back. As she did, pain from her injured calf made her gasp, but she hauled herself upright.

Then, although her entire being screamed at her to flee, she stared, not at the mysterious *things*, but at the newcomers astride them. She couldn't tell how many there were, perhaps thirty. All were male and wearing dark cock-cloths. Some had covered their chests with the same material, but the majority were naked from the waist up. All wore bulky belts that no doubt held their weapons.

The man in the lead was larger than most Baasta, not heavy but densely muscled. Young. Shoulders so broad and arms so thick they alone could serve as weapons. He carried himself with the pride and self-confidence of a male night beast. His ebony eyes seared into hers.

Then she noted his flowing hair. Silver!

Terror wrapped around her, and she dug her heels into the wilding's sides. "Run! For everything that's sacred, run!"

Squealing, the wilding tucked her head against her chest and leaped. When the wilding landed, Nari's head snapped back. "Run! Run for your life!" *And mine.*

Instinct took over, compelling her to urge the untamed animal toward a grove of nut-bearing trees. She managed to keep her mount going straight by pressing her hands against both sides of the solid neck, then stole another look at her pursuers.

Yes, silver hair! Centrois hair!

Even worse, the leader had already closed perhaps half the distance between them. A cry clogged her throat, but she didn't waste time or energy giving it freedom.

Swinging back around, she frantically scanned the rapidly approaching trees. Yes, a narrow opening among the heavy branches! After correcting the wilding's charge, she again glanced at the man she hated and feared with everything in her.

So close! So dangerous!

If he was angry, he hid the emotion. Instead, he appeared sure of victory. Of course! He fully believed he was only moments from capturing or killing her. Drawn deep into his gaze, she found determination—and something else.

No! She *wasn't* his possession.

Although her silent cry fed her determination to escape, reality settled over her. The Centrois were conquerors. They believed that anyone who wasn't one of them had been placed on this planet of many contrasts to serve them. The lot of a young woman like herself was simple.

If he got his hands on her, he'd make her into his lust-chattel. Unless she killed herself, or him.

"No!"

He responded by baring his teeth. *Yes*, his body language insisted. *Yes, I will have you.*

Grinding her heels into the wilding's sides, she repeatedly slapped its neck. "Run! Run as you never have."

The tall, close-bunched trees surrounded her. Trusting her mount to find its way through the maze, she again regarded her pursuer. The contraption he rode hadn't been designed for quick twists and turns. Not only did he have to nearly stop in order to change direction, but he also didn't know his way.

Praying to the Divine Eternal, she waited until she spotted an opening to her right. At the last instant, she turned the wilding into it.

The Centrois leader roared past. Cursing, he stopped, jerked his *thing* around, and started after her. Fortunately, there'd been a heavy rain two days ago, and his wheels sank into the mud. If he hadn't been so strong, he might have been thrown to the ground. As it was, he leapt off just as the thing fell onto its side. He reached into something at his waist and pointed what resembled a short, thick, shiny stick at her.

"Free!" she yelled at him.

For now, she heard as clearly as if they'd been standing side by side. *You do not yet belong to me.*

2

"**I** was wrong to think this place had only four-legged animals in it. I nearly came just watching that woman."

Intent on pulling his sun-powered moto out of the mud, the Centrois warlord Tarek barely glanced at his fellow explorer. J'ron was three years younger and full of a young man's boastfulness and hot blood. Even so, it bothered Tarek that J'ron's thinking went no further than fucking.

And yet hadn't he just had the same thought?

"Did you see her hair?" He addressed not just J'ron but the rest of the warriors who'd caught up to him.

"Red. Like Punta's suns."

Tarek nodded to acknowledge his brother's somber response and waited for Saka to continue.

"Baasta hair," Saka said, loud enough for everyone to hear. As the gasps died away, he continued. "Yes! We've found those who thought they'd escape their destiny. After all these seasons . . ."

Leaving his moto, Tarek faced his brother. "After all these seasons, we have found our father's killers."

As the others muttered acknowledgment, Saka shook his

head. Although Saka had been a small boy when the accursed Baasta had run away, the image of their mortally wounded father had been burned into his memory. It was even worse for Tarek. Just eight years old at the time, he'd broken free from his frantic mother and risked his life running through the fighting Centrois and Baasta to reach his father's side. One look at the deep knife slashes had told him everything—his father was going to die. Choking on tears that even then he knew a warrior couldn't shed, he'd looked around.

His father's killer had stood nearby, a young and handsome creature who wore a chattel's brand on his right shoulder. Even after all this time, Tarek remembered the look on the Baasta's face—not triumph and hatred, but resignation.

"I'm sorry," the Baasta had whispered. Then he'd clamped his hand to his side in an attempt to staunch his own blood flow.

Wounded. Even dying, his father had managed to slash the slave. The single cut was so deep that it had exposed a rib bone. "Die!" he had screamed in grief. "Die!"

"Brother?" Saka asked, pulling him back to the present. "What are we going to do?"

Tarek set his features so no emotions showed. How many times had he relived the horrific day that had set him on his path to become warlord? Although the answer crowded his mind, he shoved it away and drew on an image of the flame-haired female who'd just escaped. Because she wore a bare minimum of clothing, he'd easily seen that she was in her prime. His penis strained against his cock-cloth as he looked ahead to when he'd cut the hide dress off her, wrap her body in his ropes, and teach her to serve him.

There was no embarrassment in being aroused, and he wouldn't be surprised to see the same condition among his fellow warriors. They hadn't brought any lust-chattel with them, and after spending much of the summer exploring where no Centrois had ever been, they were all horny.

She had a chattel's blood and was not a laboring creature useful for construction or field work; she was destined to sexually service her master. Even with the need to keep his attention on where he'd been going—or rather had been trying to go— he'd memorized her form. Her dress was short and made for freedom of movement, which meant her lean legs had been bare. He'd clearly seen her muscled calves and thighs as she clung to the amazing creature under her. How could someone so slender ride such a large and powerful beast?

If she'd been afraid of her mount, he'd seen no sign. Instead, the way she'd leaned against it made him wonder if their hearts beat as one. Her sun-heated hair had trailed behind her as if riding on wind currents, and her every move spoke of freedom's joy.

No longer! Her days of denying her destiny were coming to an end—hers and every other Baasta. Those who resisted would die.

Even as his fingers ached with the need to bury his knife in hated Baasta flesh, he knew he wouldn't kill her. No matter how fiercely she fought, in the end she'd kneel before him, naked and broken, *his*.

"We will follow her," he ordered. "The mud will make it easy to track her."

J'ron snorted. "Has she crawled under your skin, Tarek? One look at her and you must have her?"

"I want every living Baasta, and so should you. It's our destiny, spoken by the Divine Eternal when he created Punta."

"But mostly her. Look at you." J'ron pointed. "Your cock speaks the truth."

Even as Tarek ignored the hot-blooded young warrior, he wondered if J'ron was right. As warlord, he'd claimed several lust-chattel for himself and could have more if he wanted. A man who has his choice of females shouldn't care about acquiring yet another, but this creature intrigued him.

It wasn't just the way she'd outraced him, or even her healthy body. Or even because she was a Baasta and he'd been looking for them since he'd become old enough to shoulder the weight of revenge. The female was a wild animal needing to be tamed.

Maybe someone who would die rather than submit?

He indicated the motos. "These have changed our lives. Because we've tamed the suns and taken their energy for ourselves, we are exploring places that have always been beyond our comprehension." He wanted to thank the Divine Eternal and say something about the elders who'd learned how to use the suns' heat to power equipment and other inventions such as the motos, but his men already knew that.

He spread his arms to take in their surroundings. "This land *will* belong to us. Those who killed and escaped will no longer be free. We will have our revenge!"

Shouts echoed around him. These thirty Centrois were like the night beasts who ruled with fangs and claws. None of them would be satisfied until the Baasta had been brought to their knees—or dead.

With all her heart, Nari wished she was anywhere but where she now stood—and that she didn't have to speak. But she had no choice.

Studying her family, friends, and the rest of those who made up the Baasta, she extended her arm, indicating she was ready to speak. Voices faded away as everyone looked up to where she stood on the platform reserved for public speaking or important announcements. Behind her were the many sturdy structures made with hardwood logs and placed on stone foundations where the Baasta all lived. Because the population continued to grow, new houses were always being built, and each spring the gardens expanded. Lately people had been talking about the need to develop a new village a short distance away.

When she'd returned to the village, she'd put the wilding in a corral and hurried to her parents' house, although she'd recently moved into one of her own with two other single young women. The moment she'd seen Nari, her mother had hugged her to her breast, but although she was grateful for a mother's instinct, she hadn't said anything until her father joined them. Then, pausing frequently as she struggled to come to grips with the incomprehensible, she'd told them what had happened. Her mother's face had turned white. She'd shook and opened her mouth, but only a sob had come out. Her father, his features equally pale, had nevertheless calmly reinforced what she already knew.

Everyone had to be told that after all these seasons, their former masters had found them.

"I may not have seen all of them," she explained now that the initial horrified gasps from the assembled Baasta had faded. "Those I did see were all men. They were astride *things* that weren't alive and yet moved more swiftly than my wilding. The Centrois rode them effortlessly, and if they'd been able to turn quickly, they would have overtaken me."

"How do you know they haven't followed you?" an elder asked.

"I . . . I don't. When I could no longer see him, I stopped and listened for a long time but heard nothing. Then I took the wilding to where there are many rocks and not much dirt because I didn't want to leave tracks for him to follow."

"Him?"

"Their . . . their warlord. At least I believe he was because he has the outline of two hawk heads on his chest."

Nodding, the elder explained that Centrois were given tattoos to distinguish them in various ways. The wisest were marked with owls while warriors proudly wore hawk symbols. Only warlords were given two.

Many of the younger Baasta hadn't known this because their parents had been determined to forget their pasts, but she'd wanted to learn everything she could about the breed spoken about with such hatred. Although her mother had disapproved, her father had always answered her questions.

"What was he like?" the elder's wife asked. "Centrois men always boasted about the battles they'd fought and the enemies they'd killed with good reason. They were so powerful back when—"

They're still powerful. At least he is. "He wore nothing but a cock-cloth. His muscles . . . he has the muscles of a man who takes pride in them."

"Strong."

"Yes. He sat easily on his *thing.* I thought—I hoped—it would fall over because it had only one wheel in front and another at the rear, but every time he changed direction, he placed his foot on the ground and leaned into the change. I . . . I admire his skill."

"You admire a Centrois?" someone challenged. "How can you say that?"

Trying to calm herself, she looked at those who made up her world. Except for the oldest, everyone had flame-red hair, proof that the Divine Eternal considered them one with the suns. Was the Divine Eternal responsible for silver hair as well? "What would you rather have me do? Be so terrified that I couldn't judge our enemy's strength? He knows how to fight. He's confident and takes pride in his body."

"Then the Centrois haven't changed," another elder announced. "Nari, at first light you must lead our scouts back to where you saw them. We *must* learn whether they're following you."

"First light?" a young woman with a baby at her breast demanded. "We *have* to run now! Hide."

"No." Nari's father stepped to her side. "When we escaped, we ran. But we are no longer frightened animals. Now we will fight for our freedom."

As people began debating what they should do, Nari wrapped her arm around her father's waist. Her fingers settled over the long, deep scar at his side.

"All these years," she whispered to him. "And now the past has returned."

"But we're no longer the mindless creatures we were when the Centrois enslaved us," he whispered back. "The Divine Eternal has blessed us with Hevassan, and we have learned the meaning of pride. We're no longer dependent on our *masters* for food and shelter."

"I want us to run. Not for me but for you and Mother and everyone I love—for the babies and small children."

Her father held her against him with such strength that he seemed young again. "Nari, as long as there's life in me, I'll fight to keep you and the others safe."

"No. Not alone. You—"

"Death is better than what I knew before the day I got this." He indicated the scar.

"I'll fight beside you," she insisted. "Bury my knife in Centrois flesh or die in the attempt."

He walked toward her. A faceless, voiceless man. Caught between terror and fascination, she gripped her knife and watched his approach. Fog drifted around him, and heat circled her breasts and belly with the truth. Close. Nearly touching.

She didn't move when he reached out and rested his hand on her shoulder.

Her naked shoulder.

"*Mine.*" *Although a near whisper, his voice carried power and belief.* "*You are mine.*"

"*Who . . . who are you?*"

"*Your master.*"

No, *she wanted to scream.* No, I'm free. *But his hand was so heavy, his gaze hot and hard, his body calling her to him.*

"*You don't belong here,*" *she told him.*

"*Perhaps, but I have arrived. Why didn't you run when the others did?*"

Confused, she looked around but saw only deserted houses. "*I don't know.*"

"*Ha, I think you do. You waited for me, your destiny.*"

She'd been gagged with several loops of rope that forced her mouth apart. Thinking to remove it, she tried to lift her arms, but her hands were caught behind her. Even more alarming, her elbows had been cinched together so they nearly touched.

"*There,*" *the man said, and patted her cheek.* "*Now you understand. This is what you were born to be.*"

"*No!*" *she ached to scream. Instead, she chewed on the rope and tried to make sense of what else had just changed. No longer was she standing looking at this strange and possessive man. Instead, the ground pressed against her knees. The man stood over her, his strong naked body proclaiming his superiority. Her ankles had been tied, and more restraints connecting her ankles to her wrists forced her to arch her body.*

"*This is what you want,*" *he told her.* "*In your heart of hearts, you need to be on your knees before me, wondering what I'm going to do to you, anticipating, your pussy hot and crying for me.*"

No! No! But he was right. Her cunt felt heavy. It ached.

"*How . . . how do you know?*"

The sound of her voice startled her. Taking in a shaky breath, she realized that the gag had been removed. But now she couldn't see because something soft yet secure pressed against her eyes.

"You don't need to look at my face and body," he said. *"All that matters is my cock."*

Hard male flesh stroked her cheek, and she leaned into it and smelled a man's scent. Hungry, she opened her mouth. His cock brushed her upper lip, then was gone.

"Please," she whimpered. *"Please."*

"Good. You're ready to worship my cock—and me. To turn yourself over to me."

"Nari, wake up!"

Someone was shaking her, but despite the urgency in the voice, Nari fought to stay with her dream. She'd longed for an exciting, strong lover, but she'd never imagined anything like this. Much as it frightened her, it also fascinated.

Finally she opened her eyes and looked up at her father, remembering that she'd accepted their invitation to spend the night with them. He carried a burning branch to light the area, his tangled hair telling her that he, too, had been sleeping.

"You kept crying out," he said as he sat at the edge of the layers of hay and dried grass covered by a woven blanket that served as her bed. "Moaning and whimpering. Something frightened you?"

The dream lingered even as she snuggled against her father, and when she looked at her wrists, she half expected to see rope marks on them. She hadn't been afraid, but how could she tell her father what she had been feeling when she couldn't admit it to herself?

"It must be because of what happened today," she told him. "Father, did you ever expect to see the Centrois again?"

He sighed. "I told myself we were safe here, that our long journey had taken us far enough away, but the Centrois are like night beasts. They're hunters."

Such a small creature.

Stroking her cheek, throat, and the space between her breasts caused his blood-blessed cock to swell even more than it already had. Its weight dragged, causing him to cradle and support it. He wasn't sure how long it would be before he'd force his cock into her upturned mouth, but until he'd convinced himself that his captive wouldn't bite him, he had to maintain self-control. Somehow.

"Ripe breasts," he said, and was surprised by how uncertain his voice sounded. "Right for nibbling."

If she replied, he didn't hear. Releasing himself, he leaned out over its hard length so he could take hold of her nipples. She gasped and sucked in a breath but didn't try to free herself.

Good.

"My breasts. My body." He emphasized his words by sliding his foot between her knees and forcing them apart. She had to struggle to obey his unspoken command because her ankles were tied together, and her bound wrists were snugged to her ankles.

He didn't remember tying her and had no knowledge of having blindfolded her. She'd become an erotic work of art, a naked image of submission.

Much as he wanted to see whether her pussy was wet and swollen, he continued to grip her nipples. He had no doubt he was causing her discomfort. Discomfort and arousal but not pain. Not yet.

"What does it feel like, chattel? Knowing you've lost owner-ship of your body, what are you thinking?"

"I . . . I . . ."

Her voice was a song, a bird at dawn, wind rippling over dry grasses. Mesmerized by the sound, he pressed his palms against the reddened nubs.

She sang to him.

"Beautiful, beautiful." He began making small circular mo-tions. She rocked from side to side, dancing despite the tight re-straints. He smelled her heat.

"You're a new flower. A doe eager to be mounted. How does it feel to be in heat, helpless and submissive? Eager?"

"I . . . I—"

"By all that's sacred, enough!"

Tarek surged into a sitting position. For a moment he couldn't find the line between dream and reality, but then thanks to the pale blue moon of summer, he realized his brother was standing over him. Saka nudged him again.

"If you aren't going to share that dream with me, end it." Saka pointed at Tarek's erection. If only he'd been able to run his cock into his captive's mouth!

"I can't help it," he said. "We've been without women for too long."

"I don't need those kind of memories."

Layers of meaning were behind his brother's words, but Tarek couldn't concentrate on them tonight, not with *her* scent still in his nostrils.

Her when his thoughts should be on the nearly reached goal. *Her* when nothing should matter beyond making the Baasta taste Centrois revenge.

3

After removing his weapons' belt and cock-cloth, Tarek stepped into the water. At the middle, the small lake was no more than waist-high, but by leaning over, he managed to clean off the many days of travel dirt. That done, he concentrated on rinsing his hair until dust no longer dulled its pale color. Not for the first time, he cursed the tradition that called for warriors to keep their hair shoulder length instead of cutting it short. He wouldn't have disarmed himself if his brother hadn't been standing guard.

Looking around, he noted the countless prints around the lake that obviously served as a popular watering place. Like so many things he'd seen since summer began, this area was both new and familiar, proof that Punta provided both contrast and a fundamental similarity. Before motos had been modified for extensive travel, the Centrois had only dreamed of exploring beyond familiar territory. Now, chosen because he'd proven himself as warlord, he was leading a large group of warriors. To his surprise, once they'd gotten beyond the land the Centrois had fought to control since their beginning, the warriors hadn't once had to defend themselves. Yes, they'd encountered small, isolated breeds, but those people had been peaceful.

During the season they'd been on the move, he'd seen mountains and valleys, places where the rain fell almost constantly and earth so dry he wondered if it ever felt moisture. Several of the valleys held promise should the Centrois ever decide to move, and he told himself to explore them in greater detail, but with each morning, he'd felt the need to keep traveling. His men hadn't protested because, like him, they were drawn to the excitement and adventure and even the danger of the unknown. He sometimes wondered if he was the only one whose inner battles caused him to lose sleep. Maybe, because their fathers hadn't died in their arms, the others believed with heart and soul that the Divine Eternal protected them.

"What was your dream about?" Saka asked as Tarek stepped out of the water and reached for his cock cloth.

Not for the first time since rising, Tarek examined his night thoughts. Even though being a Centrois man meant treating his lust-chattel as simple fuck objects, he hesitated.

"What is it? You've grown suddenly shy and don't want to talk about a wet dream? Did you masturbate?"

"Not right away, but I did when I couldn't get back to sleep. I came so fast you would have thought I'd never had sex."

"Are you surprised?" Saka untied his own cock-cloth in preparation for entering the lake. "There's been nothing to fuck since we left home."

And even longer for you, brother. You have slept alone since— "It isn't natural for a Centrois man to go so long without release."

Saka unabashedly wrapped his hand around his limp cock. "There's more than one way to find release."

"But a cunt's better."

"Even better is a woman you love."

Tarek reached out to squeeze his brother's shoulder, but Saka turned his back on him and stepped into the water. The lust-chattel Saka had loved had been dead for nearly a year, and yet he still mourned. Tarek wondered if his brother would go through life aching for what he could never have. Even if the female no one ever mentioned by name was still alive, she and Saka wouldn't have been able to marry. Wouldn't have been able to create a home for the infant they'd produced.

Caught in memories of when he'd held the baby being raised by a nursing chattel, Tarek absently studied his surroundings. What had the female who'd outrun him yesterday been doing here? Had she been here alone or were other Baasta around? If alone, why? And if she was part of a group, where were they? He didn't believe they were nearby since the scouts had seen no sign. Those who'd once belonged to the Centrois would never attack, but they had to have changed, maybe turned from hunted to hunters.

There was only one way to find out.

Following the female's tracks yesterday had led them in the opposite direction from where they'd been heading before encountering her; not that changing their course concerned him. What mattered was not being ambushed.

"I keep thinking about the animal she was riding," Saka said. "How did she control it?"

"I don't know. There weren't any ropes on it." Yesterday he'd seen a female leap onto the back of a strange swift creature. How had it been taught to carry her? If there were creatures like that back home, maybe there wouldn't have been a need for motos.

"Maybe she cast a spell over it," Saka ventured. "Mesmerized it."

"How? The Baasta are simple-minded. They wouldn't do anything unless they were forced."

"I say that's because, like the rest of our chattel, they didn't want to serve us. Can you blame them?"

No. "Are you done? I want to get back."

Saka stepped out of the lake and shook himself, droplets flying in all directions. When they were children, Tarek had often been frustrated by his younger brother's immaturity, but since becoming a father—and even before—Saka had started acting and speaking like an old man. Tarek had hoped that including him in the exploration would give him something other than grief to think about; even though Saka seldom spoke about the past, it remained in his eyes.

This morning, in addition to their knives, both men carried loaded sun-sticks. Securing his weapons around his waist, Tarek started toward his moto. Concentrating on his surroundings, he pondered whether this land had more to offer than where his people lived. Game was plentiful, and except for the Baasta woman, they hadn't come across any other humans. The idea of no longer having to fight the various other breeds who considered the Centrois their enemy appealed to him.

Nodding in contemplation, he asked his surroundings to speak to him. For as far as he could see, the ground was strewn with rocks ranging in size from pebbles too small to be fired from the sun-sticks to boulders large enough to conceal a predator. None of the predators they'd seen was large enough to take down a man, but—

Suddenly the hairs at the base of his skull lifted. Tense, he studied his surroundings. Joining him, Saka did the same.

"Anything?" he whispered.

Saka shrugged, then withdrew his sun-stick from its holding pouch. Sun-sticks resembled short, thick chunks of wood. They'd been designed to capture and contain the sun's strength, and when a trigger was activated, the stones stored inside it shot out the narrowest end. The rocks didn't travel all that far, but at a short distance, they struck with deadly force.

Tarek had just retrieved his own weapon when a raw howl shattered the air. He spotted a dark blur of movement coming at him. He managed to aim his sun-stick, but before he could fire, the blur struck him, knocking him backward. His head snapped back, striking something hard. His world turned red. His neck throbbed. A massive weight straddled hi.n, imprisoning him against the earth.

"Tarek!" his brother yelled.

Even as he struggled to make sense of what had happened, whoever, or whatever, was on top of him shifted position, and he found himself looking up at a near-human face. *Baasta?* No, the Baasta didn't have small burning eyes or long, protruding teeth.

Sharp pain tore his focus from the face. The creature had grabbed his shoulder. Thick, curving claws dug into his skin, but what shocked him the most was that the claws grew out of human fingers. The creature had human arms, a narrow chest, and a neck too thick for the rest of him.

Another wave of heat in his shoulder ended his attempt to make sense of what had knocked him down. Blood welled up around the claws—his blood!

As he thrashed about trying to dislodge the claws, the beast leaned down, mouth open, fangs seeking his throat.

"No!" Fear turned a bellow into a shriek. "No!"

Wet heat dampened his face. The creature pressed down, making his arms and hands go numb. He fought to keep hold of his sun-stick. The face and fangs were now so close that everything was blurring. If those fangs drew blood—

Driven by desperation and determination, Tarek surged upright and then forward. Knocked off balance, the creature flopped backward. As it tried to right itself, the claws retracted.

Tarek fired. The sound of rock striking flesh filled his ears. At first, the beast simply looked confused. Then disbelief replaced dumb questioning. Still straddling Tarek's hips, it looked down at itself to where a stream of blood was erupting from its belly. The animal-like mouth opened wider, giving Tarek a look at a double row of teeth.

Blood spurted onto Tarek's stomach, and he shoved, knocking the beast to the side and off him. Scrambling onto his hands and knees, he watched as whatever had attacked him writhed about. Its arms flopped, claws digging thin furrows in the dirt. Long and hairy legs kicked randomly. Blood continued to flow.

Saka!

Gripping his spent sun-stick, Tarek stood. His brother was only a few feet away. He, too, had been knocked to the ground, but he was on his belly, hands over his head as he tried to protect himself. Another beast straddled his waist and was clawing Saka's back.

Shoving the stick back into its bag, Tarek threw himself at Saka's attacker. Years as a warrior fueled his muscles as he wrapped his arms around the beast's neck and squeezed.

A bellow that seemed to come from inside the earth erupted from the creature. It flung itself off Saka, landing on its side and rolling onto its back with Tarek under him. Despite the weight, Tarek tightened his grip.

"Saka!"

His brother remained silent. In contrast, the beast was making loud, tortured gasps. Tarek squeezed even more. At the same time, he bent his knees in preparation for rolling the creature off him; pain sliced into his forearms.

They were engaged in a deadly battle; Tarek tried to choke the beast that might have killed his brother while the beast fought to tear the punishing arms off him. Although his nerves demanded he release the throat and do whatever necessary to get the claws off his arms, he didn't. Pain was nothing. Pain meant he was alive.

The creature's movements became more and more frenzied. It thrashed from side to side, bringing Tarek with it and nearly crushing him. Tarek shifted his grip so he could press against the windpipe with one arm. With a quick, violent twist, he managed to shake off one set of claws. Relief washed through him, replaced almost immediately by what felt like burning skewers deep in the forearm clenched around his attacker's throat.

Digging his fingers into a hairy wrist, he ripped the nails off him. Then, before the claws could find his flesh again, he reached around the oversized head. Fangs scraped his bleeding arm, but he twisted free. Even as he pressed his fingertips into the beast's eyes, it began shuddering, sobbing.

Tarek rode with the monster, one arm still between it and its life-saving breath, the other blinding it. Even when the enemy collapsed, he held on. His own muscles shook.

Saka.

Pushing the dying beast off him, he struggled to his knees. Had he ever felt this weak? After repeatedly breathing as deeply as he could, he risked standing. More time passed before he trusted himself to take a step. The monster he'd shot still twitched, but from the amount of blood it had lost, he knew it was dying. Everything he'd been taught during his rigorous journey to manhood demanded he determine whether he was still in danger, but even stronger was concern for his brother.

Saka lay on his side, his legs drawn up much like a sleeping child. Standing over him, Tarek held his breath and waited. Finally his brother's chest rose and then fell.

Tarek stood watching as the Centrois warriors examined the bodies of the two dead beasts. He'd already seen all he needed to—and more. The others might note the mix of man and animal—the naked, hairy bodies with their powerful legs and inadequate chests—and contemplate how many more there might be, but until his chest stopped burning, he couldn't put his mind to the question.

Until he'd stopped shaking.

Saka sat on the ground leaning against a large rock. His face wasn't as pale as it had been earlier, but he still appeared weak. His features were impassive, his eyes unfocused.

"What are they?" J'ron kicked the beast Tarek had shot. "Not human and yet more man than animal. I say we leave them here for scavengers to pick apart."

"Or for others of their kind to find," someone suggested.

A'tala, who was Saka and J'ron's age and often questioned the older warriors' decisions, wanted to throw the creatures in the lake, but Tarek pointed out that that would foul the water. Another young warrior wanted to burn the carcasses while yet another wondered what use could be made of the coarse hair on their backs, and two debated what their flesh would taste like.

Although he wondered if his voice or behavior would give him away, Tarek stepped to the middle of those he'd led here. He took a moment to study his companions, seeing in them courageous men who'd all seen battle and who had the fortitude to spend an entire season far from home. They were more than Centrois warriors; they were part of him. "We will leave the carcasses," he announced. "Discovering where they came from and how many there are can wait."

Skeptical gazes settled on him. He thought A'tala and J'ron might argue, but they only folded their arms across their chests.

"Before the attack, we were following the Baasta female. I say we must find her and her people before they have time to prepare."

"Prepare?" J'ron snorted. "What will they do? Throw sticks at us?"

"Maybe they'll try to drown us by pissing on us," A'tala offered.

Tarek studied J'ron and then A'tala. Had he ever been that full of himself, that quick to challenge a warlord? "We've changed since they ran away. I have no doubt that they have too."

* * *

"Are they ugly? Are their teeth long like the savages', and do they have big asses?"

Nari glanced at her cousin Reyna but didn't take her hand off the four-day-old wilding she was brushing. Despite several days of looking, the Baasta men hadn't found the Centrois, and the last thing she wanted was to talk about them. However, what she wanted and what was going to happen were worlds apart.

"No, not ugly. In fact, they're quite handsome and strong."

Reyna shuddered and went back to stroking the other newborn. Both women kept an eye on the twins' mother, who had made it clear that she wanted her babies left alone, but a wilding who grew up used to humans was calmer and easier to handle. Besides, Nari couldn't imagine ever getting tired of being around the big-eyed, spindly legged babies. Wildings went off by themselves to give birth, and it had taken her and Reyna all yesterday and most of today to find the little family. Although her parents had objected to their going off by themselves, she and Reyna were experienced in tracking down newborns. Besides, they didn't want savages or night beasts to kill the vulnerable babies before they could bring them back.

"Strong?" Reyna repeated. "Are they more powerful than Baasta men?"

"I don't know," Nari started, then decided she had to be honest. "I think so. They carry themselves like fighters, and their weapons—I wish I'd had more time to study what my pursuer had pointed at me."

"Do you?"

Still stroking the glossy coat while trying to keep the baby from nibbling on her dress and the waist-length hair she'd put in a single braid this morning, Nari faced her cousin. "I wish I'd never seen them. With all my heart, I wish they weren't here."

"What do you think our leaders will decide?"

She shrugged. "The Centrois aren't like the savages, stupid. Our fences aren't enough to keep the Centrois away."

"Do you think the Centrois are smarter than us?"

"What?"

Reyna flushed. "The Centrois treated our parents and grandparents and their parents like animals. Haven't you ever asked yourself why they let that happen? Is it because—"

"Because next to the Centrois, the Baasta are like the savages are to us?" Nari frowned. "I pray not."

"When you told everyone what happened to you, I wanted to jump on a wilding and flee. The one who nearly caught you—do you think he would have killed you?"

Nari had forced her thoughts away from the sharp-eyed man who'd come close to capturing her, but now memories swamped her. "I . . . I've never seen anyone like him. He made me think of a bear."

Reyna hugged the baby wilding's neck so tight that the creature squealed, prompting its mother to bump Reyna's shoulder with her nose. "How terrifying."

Was that what she'd felt? As she tried to calm the twins' mother, Nari probed deep for the answer. Yes, she'd been afraid, but there'd been more than that to her reaction. Insane as it was, she'd wanted him to touch her. And her dream had been about *him*.

"He's danger," she muttered. "Excitement."

"Excitement?"

"All right, sexual. Please, don't tell anyone I said that."

Reyna looked horrified. "You can't mean it."

"I don't know what I mean. By the Divine Eternal, I don't know."

You're insane, Reyna's expression said, and Nari wondered if she was right. From the time of her woman-ceremony, during which she'd learned how to judge when she could get pregnant, she'd been free to have sex with any unmarried Baasta man.

However, even though her mother and the other older women had told her how much fun sex was, she'd hesitated. The first time had been terribly disappointing, probably because the boy hadn't known any more than she did about how to make sex pleasurable. She now enjoyed spreading her legs, and climaxing was wonderful, but she wanted *more*. She just didn't know what that *more* was. Maybe if she could climb on top of a man or fuck standing up or *something*, but—

"Nari!"

Nari didn't need her cousin's warning because she, too, had heard the sound. "Run!" Even as she yelled, the wilding and her twins raced past the wildings she and Reyna had ridden, exciting and taking them with them.

Nari's calloused feet slapped the ground, making her think of drums being beaten. Unable to find a smooth pace, she ran with her arms jerking as if trying to grab something, anything. Her heartbeat increased, then started pounding. She couldn't keep enough air in her lungs. Couldn't hold down panic.

Not wanting to, she nevertheless looked back over her shoulder. Closer! Five of the *things*. One ahead of the others and coming right at her!

"Please! Please, no!"

Nearly too late to prevent a fall, she turned her attention to where she was going. Out of the corner of her eye, she spotted her cousin running at an angle away from her. She could no longer see the wildings and wasn't sure which direction she was running. *Don't head for home! Don't put your people in danger.*

But where if not toward what had always been safety and security?

The snarling roar filled her, and she raced toward a thicket. The head-high bushes became both her goal and her world. How stupid she'd been to put newborn wildings ahead of caution!

Arms now tucked close to her sides and her leg muscles

burning, in her mind she became a fleet prairie-runner. Prairie-runners had long, twiglike legs and were so slender that they didn't have enough meat on them to make killing them worth the effort.

Maybe the Centrois would decide she was worthless and let her escape.

Making a lie of her thought, the *thing* with its too-powerful rider overtook her. Him! The one who'd nearly caught her before!

Her pursuer kept pace, teasing and mocking. Then she abruptly slowed and changed direction. He kept going, and she laughed. A heartbeat later, she stopped laughing because he'd stopped and spun around, silver hair flying about his face. Catching up to her again, he charged ahead as if leading the way. Once more she swerved. Again he continued on and then corrected, returning to her.

He smiled at her—smiled! Then he passed, stopped, and faced her. She nearly ran into him.

Before she could backtrack, he launched himself at her, knocking her to the ground. His greater weight pressed her against the grass. Still, she struggled to turn over so she could punch and scratch and bite.

"Enough!" He punctuated his command by sliding lower so he straddled her buttocks. Leaning forward, he splayed his hands over her shoulders. With her arms reaching for nothing and her face buried in grass and rotting leaves, she tasted panic. He began tugging on her thick braid as if playing with her.

He was going to kill her! Or rape her. Or both.

Or even more terrifying, enslave her.

"No!" She bent her knees as far as she could and kicked. Her heels connected with his lower back, but there was no power behind her blow.

Still holding her hair, he rocked on her, grinding her breasts and belly against whatever she lay on. Her flailing arms found his thighs, and she buried her nails in his flesh. He grunted and grabbed her upper arms, the grip so tight she began to lose feeling. She thrashed her head from side to side, breathing loudly.

"Fight, Baasta chattel. Fight. It'll do you no good, but at least this way I know you're alive."

Chattel? Never!

"Dung!" she threw at him. "Eater of rotting flesh."

Capturing a wrist, he yanked her hand behind her and up. "I'll teach you what you can and can't say. What you will or won't be allowed to do."

"Animal dung!"

He forced her arm even higher. Pain exploded between her shoulder blades, but she fought him and the pain, twisting under him. He rode her as if she were a bucking wilding, prompting her to increase her struggles. Maybe he'd relaxed his hold on her arm, because it no longer hurt as much. Still she continued to tear at his thigh with her free hand, her breath harsh and hard, sweat turning her skin slick.

Reaching behind him with his free hand, he repeatedly slapped what he could reach of her buttocks. The sharp sting told her that her short skirt had ridden up during her struggle. Thoughts of what he'd do to her once she was truly helpless sent more strength to her failing muscles, and she bucked and thrashed.

Sweat ran off her sides and throat and between her breasts and legs. Her muscles trembled. He stopped slapping and pulled her other hand up between her shoulder blades. Robbed of what little leverage she had left, she collapsed and breathed in the scent of grass and dirt.

"That's all, chattel? There's no more fight in you?"

Again she tried to kick him, but this time her heels barely tapped his buttocks.

"There. The answer I was waiting for. You're mine now. Do you understand? Mine."

Determined not to say anything, she turned her head to the side and panted. He brought her hands down so they rested at the small of her back. After crossing one wrist over the other, he held them in place with a large and powerful hand. Then he released one wrist. An instant later she understood why—he was wrapping rope around the wrist he still held. Although she tried to pull free, he easily looped several strands around it.

And when he took hold of her other arm again and began lashing her wrists together, her struggles became like those of an old woman.

Caught. Like a captured wilding.

"There," he announced once her arms were secured behind her. "Now you aren't going to hurt either me or yourself."

Thinking he'd force her to stand, she wondered if she had the strength. Instead, he shifted position so he was sitting on the backs of her thighs and took his time removing her knife from around her waist. He threaded first one and then another rope loop around her waist and tied her wrists to that, making it impossible for her to move her arms.

Only then did he get off her.

Rolling onto her side a little, she tried to get her first look at him, but sweat and tears blurred her vision. She saw dark bulk. And movement.

Fear took another bite out of her when he reached for the ankle closest to him. When she kicked, he planted his forearms on her thighs and pressed down. Although she made him work for it, all too soon he'd tied another rope around her ankle, leaving a long length that he held up for her to see.

"I have to leave for a while." His tone was calm, passing along a piece of information. "And I don't want you trying to get away."

Gripping her shoulder and buttocks, he rolled her back onto her stomach. She felt him pulling her tied leg up behind her, his damnably strong fingers holding it it place. He ran rope under the loops against the back of her waist and pulled, bending her knee so her heel nearly touched her buttocks.

Then he stood.

Desperate to see what he was up to, she struggled to roll onto her side, but although the leg under her was free, the other was useless. When she tried to straighten it, she understood that he'd hobbled her.

Looking down at her, he folded his arms across his too-big chest. Through her blurred vision, she saw his confident smile.

Why not? After all, he'd captured her.

4

An emotion he'd never felt before rolled through Tarck. Despite the sounds of struggle to his left, he couldn't take his eyes off his captive. Although she was helpless, he noted nothing in the way of surrender in her defiant stare. Having survived more battles than he allowed himself to think about, he understood fear, the taste and feel of it. If he'd been hog-tied by someone larger and stronger than himself, he wasn't sure he could remain calm.

In contrast, her glare spoke of determination and courage, and he couldn't help but admire her.

"Tarek, we've both succeeded!"

J'ron's triumphant cry distracted him, and he looked in the direction the words had come from. J'ron held the other young woman against him, his arms tight around her breasts and waist. Like the woman at his feet, this captive was still dressed, but her short skirt was hiked up, revealing dark pubic hair. Although J'ron had pinned her arms against her sides, she was trying to kick back at him. The more she struggled, the tighter J'ron's hold became.

"Stop!" he ordered. "You'll break bones."

"I'll stop punishing when she's done struggling." J'ron squeezed, flattening the captive's small, high breasts. She cried out.

"No!" After another glance at his captive, he strode toward J'ron. "You're a Centrois warrior. A man, not an animal."

The others, who'd all been watching the women's capture, muttered agreement. J'ron relaxed his grip slightly, then shoved his pelvis forward, giving the woman a feel of his cock. "Don't ever call me an animal! By the time I'm done with her, she'll tell everyone what a man I am. Won't you?" He thrust again.

Much as he wanted to pull J'ron off the terrified woman, she was the younger warrior's possession. J'ron had every right to his prize, and as long as he didn't kill her, no one would protest. "She's too frightened to give a damn about your cock. If you want her to sing your praises, you have to allow her to think."

Grunting, J'ron asked A'tala to bring him some rope. Once he had, J'ron thrust the woman at A'tala to hold while he bound her arms behind her and lashed her legs together, leaving just enough distance between them that she could stand. "There," J'ron said. "At least my *property* doesn't have to grovel on the ground."

Careful not to react to J'ron's comment, Tarek turned back toward his captive. Looking down at her, he tried to think of her as *property*, but the life and energy simmering in her large eyes made that impossible. Again that strange sensation washed over him. Was his long celibacy responsible? If he hadn't gone without fucking for so long, the sight of her wouldn't have forced everything else out of focus.

And maybe she simply represented everything he'd come to hate since his father's murder?

Angry at questions without answers, he walked over to her, squared his stance, and stared down at her. Now, he was certain, he saw more than defiance from her. There was also fear and helplessness.

Good. She should fear the man who would become her master. Good. She should acknowledge her helplessness.

Just as you feared the savage who nearly killed you?

Shaking off the question, he crouched and ran his hand over her hip. She shuddered but didn't try to scoot away. Not caring whether the others saw, he slid his fingers under her skirt and touched soft flesh. "Do you remember what I said? That you belong to me."

Trembling, she tried to roll onto her back, but he pressed down, easily keeping her on her side. Her bright braid lay over her shoulder, reminding him of how the glossy bulk had felt in his hands. "Get used to my ropes, chattel. Until I've taught you all you need to know about my use for you, you'll always wear them."

"Are you afraid of me, *warrior?* Afraid I'll bury a knife in your heart?"

The others laughed, forcing him to weigh his words before responding. And as the silence held, his respect for her grew. "Is that a threat or a warning? If a threat, it has little meaning coming from someone who can't stand." He ran his fingers over her tethered leg. "And if you're warning me, I thank you." He gripped her ankle, his fingers closing around bone and tendons. "Don't expect to see a knife, let alone get your hands on one."

"How strong you are, how brave! To have conquered someone much smaller than yourself."

Fury rolled through him, then faded because he had seen the vulnerability in her eyes. "You're far from conquered, chattel."

"What do you call this?" She strained against her bonds. "If not helpless, then what?"

"Your spirit is unbroken—so far."

Although she struggled to keep her reaction private, he sensed her determination to prove him wrong—determination tempered by reality. He'd never had a conversation anything like this with a sex-chattel and hadn't so much as suspected that anything except surrender and acceptance lived in them. But this Baasta was teaching him a great deal.

Ignoring his companions, he released his hold on her tied ankle, rolled her onto her other side, and began running his fingertips over her free leg. He'd expected her skin to be dry and hardened by her physical life, but it was soft, smooth, like warm water.

This now belonged to him. She belonged to him.

At least her body did. As for her spirit . . .

Sensing her underlying tension, he had no doubt she was waiting for him to hurt her in some way and suspected she'd go to her death before acknowledging pain. A woman like that, not a chattel but a woman . . .

Confusion piled on confusion. Determined to close himself off from it, he turned his full attention to his new possession. Her calf muscle was firm, powerful. No fat lay between her skin and the underlying strength. The same was true of her thigh muscle, making him wonder which of them could run the longest. Where his muscles felt like knotted rope, hers were all of a single piece, smooth and healthy.

She shivered when his fingers traveled up from her thigh to her buttocks. She tried to look back at him. "Feel," he muttered, pressing down on her flank. "Feel my hands everywhere on you and know I can do whatever I want, whenever I want."

"No."

"No?" A smile tugged at the corners of his mouth. "What do you call this?" He lightly slapped her, the sound resonating not just in his ears but throughout his cock as well. He struggled to remember what he'd had in mind—and that his men were watching him, judging. His leg muscles threatened to cramp.

After lowering himself onto his knees, he again tapped her flank. Again she tried to turn so she had a clear view of him, but he had points to make and lessons to give. "*No* is not a word you'll use around me. You've long called yourself free, but I'll teach you different."

How? she asked with her eyes, but he had no intention of answering. A vital part of turning her into what she was destined to be depended on thrusting her into a world of unknowns, one without answers. He pressed down on her buttocks until she bore much of her weight on her breasts and belly, her head turned away from him. Her slender arms were roped with strength but were useless. No matter how she strained to lift them from the small of her back, they remained where he'd placed them. There was something unsettling about what he'd done to her, a job half finished, perhaps. He'd debated completely hog-tying her but had left the one leg free as a reminder of what she'd recently taken for granted.

Yet another wave of anger rolled over him. Like the one that had come before it, this, too, was aimed at himself, but why should he ponder what was going on inside her? He should care about nothing except himself—his plans for this living, breathing, thinking possession.

"I'd known only four winters the first time I held a spear. I turned it around and around, lifting it so the suns glinted off the blade." Leaning close, he blew a long breath along her thighs. She shivered and tried to slither away. He waited and watched, understanding the battle between desperation and acceptance. When she at length relaxed, he grabbed her skirt hem and pulled it up, exposing her buttocks. His fingers tingled; his cock jerked. *This tanned flesh, mine.* "Gripping the weapon my father had given me, I was certain I'd never hold anything that made me feel more alive. But that was before I touched my first female."

The others were still watching, but they'd stepped back, maybe because they didn't want to be touched by the energy coming from a female they had no right to. Probably they'd resigned themselves to night and the opportunity to masturbate. As for him—

Despite the warnings going off inside him, he slid a hand between her thighs. Her warmth seeped into his fingers, sheltering him and taking him too close to frustration. Hissing, she tried to lift herself off the ground. Pressing his free hand between her shoulder blades, he kept her in place. "No," he warned. "What you want doesn't matter. Only I, your master, do."

"No, never!"

Her desperation had a smell, a taste, a feel. Not sure whether he was taking advantage of it or simply acknowledging it, he worked his sheltered hand higher, nearly reaching her heated cave. Then, although maybe he'd never wanted anything more, he made himself stop.

"You're beautiful, worthy of servicing me. Think on that, chattel. In time you will be well trained, and I'll be proud of my accomplishment. No matter what I tell you to do, you'll do so. My voice will rule you. My body will become your god." *Now! Touch her clit.*

A sharp cry raked his nerves. J'ron had thrown his struggling captive over his shoulder. He started to take a step, stopped. Cursing, he squeezed a naked buttock until she squealed.

"Stop it!" Tarek pushed himself to his feet and stalked toward the younger warrior.

"She tried to bite me." J'ron stopped squeezing and started slapping. "I'll teach her—"

"No, you won't!" He grabbed J'ron's wrist.

"What about you? What were you doing?"

Tarek risked a glance back at his female. She'd managed to shift around to see what was happening. Naked concern for her companion overrode all other emotions.

"Training," he told J'ron. "Teaching her what it is to be a

sex-chattel so when her people see her, they'll understand their fate."

"Then that's what I am doing." J'ron's smile didn't reach his eyes. "Training."

"Where are you taking her?"

"Where we'll have privacy."

Privacy? Yes. Alone with his female and his emotions.

"Let him go," A'tala said. "Anything is better than looking at a female I have no right to."

"All right. But remember that a man worthy of being called a Centrois doesn't rape. He knows how to make his chattel beg to be fucked."

Fresh kill waiting to be gutted.

Nari tried to push her thought aside, but as her captor returned to her, she had no doubt what she looked like. Something about the way he'd spoken to the warrior who'd claimed her cousin had eased a little of her fear for Reyna. Obviously her captor was their leader, so when he ordered, the others obeyed. And he'd commanded Reyna's captor to stop punishing her.

Was it possible? Maybe a thread of tenderness ran through him?

Vowing to learn as much as possible about him, she fought her fear. He considered her valuable. Otherwise, he would have killed her. And as long as she lived, she could dream of escaping.

Even if it meant killing him?

He didn't speak as he crouched and untied her ankle. And except for unwrapping the rope, he didn't touch her. "Stand up," he ordered when he was done.

Frustrated by her awkwardness, she nevertheless managed to get to her knees and then stand. Doing so allowed her skirt to drop back over her hips—not that the small measure of modesty meant much because he could easily strip her naked.

What would that be like? To stand exposed before the most powerfully built man she'd ever seen?

Ignoring her, he pointed at several men. "Track the creatures the females were with. They may lead you to the Baasta."

"No!" she blurted. "They . . . they're wild. They won't—"

Strong hands she would have to become accustomed to gripped her shoulders. "Maybe you're telling the truth, but I don't think so."

Furious at having revealed so much, she stared at the ground. Although he continued to keep her dangerously close to him, his grip slackened, and pain turned into something she refused to acknowledge.

"If you find the Baasta, make sure they don't see you," he said to the five men who were getting back on their *things*. "I want no killing, yet. First, we need to determine their strengths and weaknesses."

The men he'd singled out nodded. The wilding and her newborn twins might not return to the Baasta village since new mothers kept to themselves if possible. But maybe this one preferred company and the safety of her corral to the wilderness.

Those too-strong hands were still on her, still claiming her, but he was running his fingers up and down her as if rubbing away whatever discomfort he might have caused her.

"We need meat," he said to those who remained.

"What will you be doing while we're gone?"

"What I need to."

"Need?" someone teased. "Or want."

"Maybe both."

5

Because he wanted it, she stood facing her captor. Only when they could no longer hear the *things'* strange sounds as they took off did he look down at her. As a girl, she'd broken her leg, and having to sit around doing nothing while it healed had nearly driven her crazy. Once she'd come across a bird that had gotten tangled in fishing line. When she approached, the poor thing nearly killed itself trying to escape, but she'd thrown a cloth over it, and it had calmed down long enough for her to cut the line. She'd never forget the sight of the bird taking flight.

No one would free her.

"What's your name?" he demanded.

She glared at him.

"Tell me or I'll call you *chattel*."

Stung by the hated word, she swallowed. "Nari."

"Nari? And I am Tarek, Centrois warlord; although, when I am done with you, you will call me *master*."

"Never!"

She fully expected him to shake her or throw her to the

ground. Instead, he merely returned her stare. Up close, the two hawk heads tattooed on his chest were even more imposing, the workmanship awesome. His deep-set dark blue eyes were hawk-sharp. "How old were you when your breed ran away from mine?"

A chill ran through her. "I . . . five."

"A child. Do you remember the fighting, the killing?"

"I remember sounds, crying and screaming. My mother ordering me to run."

"Did you?"

"Yes."

"Tell me, do your elders talk about what happened that day?"

"Some."

"Only some?" He sounded bitter, and his fingers dug into her again. "My life is defined by that death-dealing day, and I suspect the same is true of you. Otherwise, you and your people would not be here."

Unable to deny his wisdom, she nodded.

"There is a great deal between us, Nari. More than you know. Maybe the time will come when I'll tell you; maybe not. All that matters is this is now, and you are mine."

Don't say that, please! I can't think when you do.

"And by the time I'm done with you, you'll have handed your body over to me. Your body and your soul."

"Why?"

He didn't answer, and when he spun her around and started pushing her toward his *thing*, she acknowledged she hadn't expected him to. Because she'd been a talented seamstress, her mother hadn't been a sex-chattel, but her aunt had. The two women hadn't tried to keep their conversations from her, and as a result, she believed she knew what her aunt's life had been like. This man, this Tarek, intended to do the same to her.

Was it because he loved the power that came from having a

sex-chattel at his constant disposal, or did the reasons run deeper?

When he stood her before his *thing*, she stopped asking questions and concentrated on what he was doing. The *thing* was equipped with a large storage area that he had begun emptying. Some of the items, like his sleep-pelt and blankets, were easy to recognize while others meant nothing to her. At length he held up a slender length of leather with something hard fastened to it at both ends.

"A collar," he said.

Collar! Thanks to her aunt, she understood. Terror flooded her, and she ran. With her hands secured behind her at the waist, she ran. Her feet pounded the ground, and her blood pounded in her temples. She counted her steps to keep from thinking of anything else.

And when he overtook her, wrapped his arms around her waist, lifted her off her feet, and lowered her to the ground with her face buried in wild grasses, she tried to count her heartbeats.

"You're a fighter." He sounded surprised. After kneeling beside her, he turned her onto her back. Having to arch her back to keep pressure off her hands added to her sense of helplessness. Still, she stared at him and ordered herself not to act or feel like a frightened wild animal. To learn everything she could about him.

Rocking back on his haunches, he returned her stare, but where she made no attempt to hide her hatred of him, his eyes spoke of a gentler emotion. "My grandfathers believed the Baasta would die after they escaped because they didn't know how to survive without their masters' protection, but they were wrong." He brushed hair off her forehead, his touch gentle and lingering. "How many Baasta are there?"

"More than enough to kill you."

He laughed, the sound deep and full. Then, although he didn't need to, he again brushed her forehead. "Much has changed since our people were together. The Centrois now have weapons the Baasta cannot fathom."

No! Don't say that.

"Maybe you think I'm bragging, but have you ever seen anything like our motos?"

"Moto?" She could barely force herself to say the word.

"The machines we ride. They're powered by the suns' energy, and that power carries them through the night. As long as the suns of Punta shine, they won't tire. And their speed—you understand that, don't you?" He leaned closer as if emphasizing his point. Not daring to breathe, she continued looking up at him, praying her gaze carried defiance. But she felt so helpless, so useless.

So changed.

"What about the Baasta?" he demanded. "Are you like animals digging in the ground for enough to eat, living in holes in the dirt?"

"No!" Although she longed to tell him about the fine homes everyone took such pride in, she knew better than to reveal anything about the village. Still, much as she wanted to believe her people were safe, the risk that the Centrois would find them was great.

"What, then, chattel? Perhaps you build nests and live in trees?"

He was trying to goad her. "What about the Centrois?" she countered. "Do your homes still become fly and flea infested?"

Something dark and dangerous settled in his eyes. Believing she'd pushed him too far, she waited for his blow. Instead, he pulled her into a sitting position and held up the collar.

"There's been too much talking between us." He touched the collar to her throat. "It's time for you to learn obedience."

Was this how a wilding felt when it realized it couldn't escape? The first time she or someone else placed a rope on it, did something fundamental shift inside the beautiful creature? Did it accept that freedom and pride belonged to yesterday?

The questions fell away as he draped the surprisingly soft leather around her throat. Try as she might, she couldn't stop from sucking in a noisy breath. His mouth tightened. "You hate this, don't you?" He slid the leather from side to side. "With everything in you, you want to fight me, but I've already taught you how useless that is."

If my hands were free—

"No freedom, Nari. Nothing of your old life because it's time to embrace what I decide is your new existence."

With that, he brought the two hard ends together and snapped them in place. The collar was loose enough that she had no trouble breathing, but the solid click left no doubt—it would remain in place until he removed it. As for the ring embedded in the leather and now resting against the hollow of her throat

He hooked his forefinger through the ring and tugged on it, forcing her to lower her head. "A question before I silence you. What are those creatures you and the other female were with?"

Don't tell him anything. Fight, fight with the only weapon you have left.

Another jerk arched her neck even more. "What? Damnation, tell me!"

"Wildings." Speaking took effort.

"Wildings. Is this what you were going to do to them?" He tugged yet again. "Put ropes on them and train them?"

Stop. Please stop. "No. Not . . . the babies are too young."

"But when they become older?"

Could she refuse to speak? Perhaps, but what good would it do her? "Yes."

He relaxed his grip, but there was no forgiveness in his hold. Whatever he wanted her to do, she'd have to obey. "Think about this, Nari. You are now no different from a captured wilding."

Before a storm, the air became charged with an energy that

both frightened and excited her. The old men and women said that lightning was the Divine Eternal's way of proving His command over mere humans, but although lightning always humbled her, it also filled her with life.

She felt that way now, as if small lightning strikes were going off inside her. She was, she acknowledged, more alive than she'd ever felt.

If anything, the sensation only increased when he fastened a length of rope to her collar, his hands barely brushing her breasts after he'd finished. When he returned to his moto and brought back thin strips of leather, she could only wonder what they would feel like against her skin. Then he worked one of the strips into her mouth and secured it at the back of her head, silencing her.

"Live within yourself, wilding. For now, everything you want to say must remain buried in you. You'll speak only when I choose to let you, *if* I choose."

He had yet more leather. When he held this length to her face, she leaned away but he grabbed the rope holding her wrists and pulled her straight. "Don't move. Do you understand? Don't move."

Energy raced through her again. *Alive! Helpless and yet alive.*

"Do you understand?"

She nodded.

"Good." He sounded almost kind. Releasing the rope, he spun her away from him. Warmth from his chest heated her back. He placed an arm over her breasts and pulled her toward him. Off balance, she had no choice but to rest her back against his chest, and for a moment she wanted nothing more. Could it be that he felt the same way? Was that why his command of her breasts was so gentle?

Then he released her but left her so off balance that without use of her arms, she couldn't straighten. Something pressed against her eyes. She shook her head, but whatever it was snugged even tighter. When she'd calmed herself enough to think, she realized he was blindfolding her. Her world had already blackened, and with each wrap, the cave he'd thrust her into became all-consuming.

"Do you remember what I said?" He spoke into her ear. "That you have to live within yourself. Now, not only can't you communicate, but you can't see."

Unable to stop trembling, she fought to concentrate on his every move. All too soon, he'd knotted the strip behind her head and helped her straighten. She was in *nothing*. She'd become *nothing*. And only this man she hated with everything in her could change that.

Sensing more movement, she strained to make sense of what he was doing. She couldn't be sure but she thought he'd stood up. If he left her—

Needing him in ways she hadn't known were possible, she turned her head this way and that, trying to find something, anything. Nothing.

Terror gnawed at her. She whimpered behind her gag.

Then he touched the side of her neck, and she whimpered again, the sound a mix of gratitude and fury. When he took hold of her arms and pulled her to her feet, she had to fight to keep from trying to kick him. Her arms ached from being caught against her waist, and when he massaged them, confusion and thankfulness chased away the hate.

Perhaps sensing her discomfort, he freed her wrists from the rope around her waist. Her arms were still caught behind her, but she took heart from the small freedom. A moment later, hope turned into the weight of helplessness because he'd taken hold of her skirt hem and had lifted it to her waist. Next he tucked it under the rope there.

No matter that she didn't want to think about what she looked like, she had no choice. No matter that she didn't want to react, she did. This strong and masterful man had rendered her naked from the waist down. He'd turned her into a silent and sightless object, helpless. But he hadn't harmed her.

Yet.

In her mind she saw him standing in front of her with his arms folded across his chest, covering his tattoos, head cocked slightly as he studied her. Her legs were firm from seasons of working with wildings, and although her hips were meant for child-rearing, they were a young woman's hips. Baasta men liked her hips, thighs, and calves. When they stared at her flat belly, she knew they were imagining sliding first their hands and then their cocks between her legs.

And when she granted them access to her body and they buried their cocks deep inside her, she fed off the gift of their seed. Thanks to her mother's wisdom, she knew when it was safe to fuck and when pregnancy was possible, so there were times when no matter how hungry she was, she refused them. Yes, someday she'd allow a man to get her pregnant and then marry him, but not yet. Not until she was ready to spend the rest of her life with a single man.

"You don't have children." He spoke matter-of-factly. "Your body tells me that."

Did he expect a response?

"What about a husband. Are you married?"

She dug her toes into the grass.

Cupping his hand around her chin, he forced her to lift her head. "Are you married?"

She shook her head, then cursed herself because maybe he wouldn't have wanted her if she'd been someone's wife.

"Good." He released her chin. But before she could breathe a sigh of relief, he ran a fingernail from her navel down to her pubic hair. Lightning chased over her skin there. Alarmed, she took a single backward step, then stopped. How could she move when she couldn't see?

"Ah, do you understand now how vital sight is?" He pressed against her mons with a single finger. At the same time, he gripped her hip, holding her in place. "I can and will touch you wherever and whenever I want, and you'll never know when, or if, it's going to happen."

Let me go, please! Don't do—

His hand was between her legs and pressing against her pussy before she could think how she might defend herself. She'd nearly stopped trembling, but now she started again. And lightning returned to energize her body.

"I won't force you to have sex with me. A Centrois warrior doesn't take a woman against her will, not even a sex-chattel." The pressure against her pussy increased. To her shock, heat radiated out from her belly and began flowing lower. "When you take my cock into you, it'll be because that's what you want."

Despite the risk of losing her balance, she whipped her head from side to side.

"Listen to me, Baasta female. Just because your people escaped doesn't mean the Centrois have been without sex-chattel. It's our way. It always has and always will be." His breath heated her forehead and cheeks. "You aren't the first female I've worked with. Just as you gentle wildings, I'll gentle you."

She shook her head again but not so vigorously. How could she concentrate on anything except his *promise* and the warrior hand claiming her sex?

"When a wilding has been tamed, he accepts a human, not just as his owner, but his master, right?"

Dread—and something else—gripped her.

"A wilding wants to please his master." The hand on her hip glided toward her buttocks, and he pulled her closer. "When I'm finished with you, when our relationship has been forged, you'll live to please me. And in the effort, you'll please yourself."

6

Did she have any idea how much her body was giving away? Touching her intimately, controlling everything about her let Tarek know that his captive had entered a place she'd never known existed. He'd come as close as he could to describing the journey he'd planned for her when he likened her to a wilding about to be tamed. What he didn't understand was why he'd told her anything.

Yes, he'd *trained* sex-chattel because the process taught him a great deal about what made humans think, which was something a warlord had to know. In addition, the training gave him a sense of power. He understood the delicate balance between breaking a female's spirit and turning her on to her body's needs, but he'd never before explained what he was doing.

In an effort to keep a hard but necessary hold on his self-control, he reluctantly dropped his hands to his sides. She turned her head in one direction and then the other. The tension in her shoulders and arms told him she was straining against her bonds. If he thought she might injure herself, he'd hug her to him and imprison her with his body, even if it meant subjecting himself to impossible frustration.

Cursing his weakness, he gripped his cock. The days and nights of frustration had kept his warrior's edge keen, but now—now he was asking so much of himself.

She was beautiful in a way he had no words for, like a wolf loping along the horizon, an eagle soaring, spring's new life. Since his father's murder, he'd hated flame-haired people, but hers put him in mind of a red waterfall—a waterfall framing healthy, tanned flesh.

"On your knees!"

She tensed, and he repeated his command. His cheeks were on fire and his cock all but screamed for release.

"On your knees, now!"

Despite her trembling, she managed to obey without losing her balance. How graceful she was, how wild even with his restraints on her. Despite her blindness, she stared up at him. If he ungagged her and placed his cock against her lips, would she take him in or bite?

Bite.

He walked behind her, a hand trailing over her shoulders as he did. "I'm going to untie your hands, but you are to do only what I allow you to. Do you understand?" Grabbing her hair, he pulled her head back. Despite the restriction, she managed to nod.

He held on to her hair a moment longer, then released the sleek length. In his mind he saw her standing in breast-deep water as she washed her hair, drawing out the task, making it sensual. Although he warned himself not to, he stroked the sides of her neck. When she relaxed a little, he aimed his cock at the top of her spine and guided it over her there. She twitched, briefly leaned against his cock, then tried to jerk away.

"No!" He pressed his hand against the side of her neck. "If

you want your hands free, you do only what I tell you. Move only when I command. Do you understand?"

A faint but harsh sob broke free.

Feeling the sound deep inside him, he again touched his cock to her soft skin. "Do you understand?"

She gave a short nod.

Good. Make this easy for both of us. "Feel my cock on you." With fingers that twitched and threatened to spasm, he guided his organ over the back of her neck as if painting her with it. She had to know how close he'd brought himself to the edge, how hard restraint was. By all that was holy, he should leave her like this while he jacked off. Then he could return to her satisfied, sexually at rest, and take her to that edge.

But he couldn't force himself to leave her that long.

When she stopped shivering at his every touch, he reluctantly released his cock and took hold of her forearms and forced her to lean forward. "Listen to me. I'm releasing your hands, briefly, for two reasons. One because I'm going to order you to do something. The other because your arms have been behind you long enough, and I don't want to risk injury. But if you disobey me in any way, you'll be punished."

Reading her response in her passivity, he untied her slender wrists. Her arms dropped to her sides, and she continued to lean forward.

"Stand."

Although she probably wondered why he wanted her on her feet so soon, she wasted no time obeying. She fingered the collar and leash, then dropped her arms back to her sides. No matter how firmly he ordered himself not to, his gaze locked on her body and the unspoken messages in her stance. She was far from beaten, wise in choosing her battles. She'd comply with his orders, for now. She might even submit her body to him, for now. But given the slightest chance, she'd try to escape, and if she could kill him before running, she'd gladly do that.

Good. He needed her to have fire, needed a woman who was his match.

At the thought of her standing at his side, self-anger lashed him. A sex-chattel had one function—to serve her master. And because Baasta blood ran through her, her total submission was vital. Once he *had* her, he'd turn his energy to doing the same to the rest of her breed.

"I will say this only once, captive. If you don't obey immediately, I'll whip you."

Her fingers clenched. She lifted her head even more.

"Take off your garment."

Not breathing, he waited and watched. To his surprise and admiration, she reached for the material he'd tucked under the rope around her waist. After briefly fingering it, she tugged. Bit by bit she drew it under the rope belt. Perhaps, he pondered, she found this part of the disrobing easy because he'd already exposed her from the waist down. And maybe she was testing her limits, pushing herself.

Her head sagged forward. Her breathing was labored. Finally, moving with a speed that said she wanted to be done with the chore, she pulled the dress over her head.

Naked. Exposed. Skin that reminded him of morning dew.

"Hand it to me."

She tossed it in his direction, her aim true. Knowing she was keenly aware of where he was should have heightened his sense of superiority. Instead, he hated himself. Hated what he was doing to this wild creature, longed to wrap his arms around her. After dropping the garment to the ground, he stepped back. "Turn around, slowly."

Only her still-ragged breathing gave her away as she turned her back to him. He had to grind his nails into his palms to keep his hands off her magnificent body. How was it possible for a woman to have such sleek, smooth skin? But maybe it wasn't her physical perfection. Maybe his too-long abstinence had destroyed his objectivity.

And maybe only this Baasta woman could make him feel this way?

His head was roaring, and his groin felt knotted by the time she was facing him again. She had a young maiden's breasts, full and ripe, high with dark centers. Noting her hardened nipples, he told himself their condition was proof that she wanted to fuck as much as he did. But surely she hated the man who'd blinded her, robbed her of speech, and placed a collar around her neck.

"Extend your arms toward me, wrists together."

Her slow obedience left no doubt that she knew what he intended, but she didn't make the mistake of trying to tear off the blindfold. She kept her head high, but he read the effort it took in the way her shoulders slumped.

When he tied her, he left enough space between her wrists that he could easily grip the leather holding them together. He didn't want to put undue strain on her shoulders, and he might need to see what her hands were capable of. For now, however, he wanted complete control, which was why he then secured her wrists to the rope around her waist.

Her head sagged a little as she accepted her condition. If he removed the blindfold, would he find tears? He didn't think so. Could he make her cry?

You don't want that; you know you don't.

True, but he did want to fuck her. He needed her sleek body against his, her femininity easing his harsh warrior lines, to think of nothing beyond release. To forget why he was doing this to her.

Digging her toes into the grass again, Nari cursed the man

who'd forced her to strip. And she waited, waited for him to touch her again. What remained of her senses as well as her nerve endings whispered that he didn't intend to hurt her, but what if she was wrong to trust her instinct?

He was studying her, looking at her naked body, seeing its strengths and weaknesses, reveling in his mastery, making plans for her. Planning her sexual slavery.

Warm fingers on the top of her breasts froze her thoughts. No matter that she would give everything to escape, she forced herself to stand in place and, maybe, send him the message that she didn't care what he did. His fingers lingered, pressing a little, saying without words that he'd taken possession of her breasts.

His. She was his.

Something began melting inside her. She'd always been bone and muscle, strength and intellect, but now she'd become nothing except a woman with a man's hands on her breasts. He was heat, her heat, smoothing away edges and angles and exposing flesh and nerves. She breathed, no longer for herself but for him. Her nipples tightened because he wanted them to.

His. Only his.

Slowly, unrelentingly, his fingers journeyed down her soft and swollen flesh to her nubs. For too many heartbeats, he lingered at the pebbled flesh. "What does it feel like, captive?" A fingertip kissed her nipple, kissed again, then stayed. Possessed. "Do you hate giving up ownership, or do you want it?"

Hate. Want.

"Think about this." He took her nipples between thumbs and forefingers. "I claim these for myself. You must always keep them accessible to me. When I tell you to place one in my mouth, you will."

Shiver upon shiver assaulted her as he rubbed her nubs. Heat and friction became one, coiling through her and stealing her breath. "If I want them sheltering my cock, you'll drop to your knees before me and close your breasts around what you pray will find its way into you."

No, never!

Now, please, now!

The unwanted chant distracted her from reality. Too late she realized he'd released her breasts and had left her alone and waiting, wanting. Her belly felt heavy, her crotch hot.

There. Another touch.

His hands were like water on her hips. They slid over her skin, grazed along her bones, lingered at the join of pelvis and legs. She thanked the gag because otherwise he'd hear her mewling.

Ah, fingers traveling down, gliding through curling hair. Lingering again, then moving again. Hating her bonds, she fought to free her hands, fought for the right to touch as she was being touched. And when the leather cut into her wrists, she forced herself to relax, to experience. Yes, his fingers on her core. Wise in the ways of women, he repeatedly stroked her clit, but each touch was quick and light, tease and not promise. Moaning, she widened her stance and pushed out her pelvis.

She hated herself. Loved his touch.

"You're wet there, chattel. Crying for me."

Am I?

Rocking from side to side did nothing to dampen the fires he'd set. Again and again his fingers claimed her clit. Again and again he dipped into her entrance and drank of her. Repeatedly, he took hold of her sex lips and drew on them. When he did, she became trapped by need.

Spreading herself even more, she stepped outside herself and watched the creature he'd turned her into. In her mind's eye, she saw his strong and dark fingers close over her loose and hungry flesh. He drew one cunt lip aside to give himself greater access to her core.

There! Finger invading. Plunging deeper than before, exploring, taking, claiming. Promising—but not enough.

Closing her teeth around her gag, she bit down. *Grind, chew. Think of nothing else.*

No good! No good because his finger was now all the way in her, warmed and bathed by her, pressing up so she was skewered by him, forcing her onto her toes, making her sob.

"Dance on me, chattel. Dance with my finger inside you."

She did, calves and thighs hard in contrast to the soft recesses he controlled in ways she'd never believed possible. Although she was in danger of losing her balance, she didn't care. Didn't care about anything except him drinking from her and her dancing with what she desperately wished was his cock.

Two fingers now, two spreading her even more and pressing against her weeping flesh.

She breathed the way she always did when nearing a climax, loud and hard and honest. Desperate and determined.

"Sing for me, chattel. Scream."

Behind her gag she did.

Again she floated out of herself, studied, saw. He no longer held a sex lip but was vigorously rubbing her flank. The heat he'd created flowed toward her too-hot core, her invaded center. She nearly laughed at the trembling, thrashing woman trying to free herself yet swallowing her captor's fingers at the same time. Her cheeks had turned bright red, and her hair whipped about in time with her jerking.

Then her calf cramped, and she started to fall.

7

Instinct pushed everything else from his mind. Pulling his fingers out of her, he caught her around the waist. For a length of time, she slumped in his embrace. Her dependence on him rolled through him, yet again changing their relationship. She needed his strength; he wanted to hand it to her.

Then she grunted and tried to twist free. Noting that she was shaking her left leg and that what he could see of her face was pain-contorted, he eased her to the warm grasses. Made wise by endless seasons of knowing that staying alive depended on a healthy body, he spotted the knotted muscle. Kneeling beside her, he began massaging the hard knot. She squirmed about but didn't try to get away, and memories of like pains kept him at his task. The knot started loosening under his fingers, and bit by bit she relaxed. Before long, only smooth muscle remained in his grip, but he kept at his task. And he looked at her legs, not her bound hands or silent, unseeing face.

He might have remained where he was, communicating with her in ways that didn't need words, if his knee didn't start hurting. Shifting position, he saw that he'd knelt on a rock.

Although he should return to her *taming*, he didn't trust himself. He told himself that the only thing she cared about was her response to what he'd been doing to her. It couldn't possibly matter to her that dealing with his needing-to-explode cock had become an all but impossible task.

Leaving her on the ground, he stood and stalked off. By the time he turned around, there was enough distance between them that he could no longer focus on her body's nuances, not that that made enough difference.

She had a body made for nudity. Lines and angles, curves and sleek flesh all spoke to him as he'd never been spoken to. Even the burnished thatch between her legs fascinated him. She'd sat up and was resting her weight on her right hip, her back and shoulders straight. No matter that he'd robbed her of freedom; he hadn't begun to break her—if that's what he truly wanted.

What was he thinking! He needed her on her knees before him, head drooping in submission, body crying out for him. Revenge lay in stripping first her and then the rest of her people.

But would revenge bring his father back to life?

The answer beat in the sounds his feet made as he stalked back to her. He was Centrois! His people attacked and were attacked, but they also claimed and owned. It was the order of things, what the Divine Eternal wanted. A man who didn't heed the creator's orders couldn't call himself Centrois.

Reaching down, he yanked her up beside him. Her flesh sliding against his sent his head to raging again. He should have killed her! Maybe he would, once he'd learned from her what he needed to know about today's Baasta.

He wants to kill me.

Nari couldn't say how she knew her captor had come close to slitting her throat. Yes, he'd handled her roughly before, but

there was something in his breathing and taut body that made
her fear him in a new way.

Fear? Hadn't she already been afraid?

His hands at the back of her head stopped her questions. For
a moment she didn't dare believe, but then there was no doubt.
He *was* removing her blindfold. After blinking to clear her
sight, she forced herself to look up at him. His features had taken
on a masklike quality, and she understood that he was deliberately keeping his emotions from her. Although she should take
in her surroundings and do what she could to anticipate him,
she simply studied his eyes. His body's strength was played out
in the dark depths so in contrast with his near-white hair, mark-
ing him as a man who thought of himself as a warrior above
everything else.

So did she think of him as such. A warrior and a man. Sexual
energy and undeniable knowledge of her body.

Draping her blindfold over his shoulder, he began working
on the knots holding her gag in place. When he pulled it out of
her mouth, she licked her lips but didn't speak.

"Tell me, how important are wildings to the Baasta?"

His question was so matter-of-fact that she nearly answered.
Why do you want to know? she asked with her eyes.

"I can make you tell me. But I don't want us to be adversaries."

We already are. "What will you do with the knowledge?"

"Nothing, for now. I'm a curious man; that's all. What use
do you make of wildings? Do they eat them?"

"No!" The thought made her shudder. "They're too valuable."

"For what?"

He was staring at her, his hand on her leash loose and still.
His tone made her think of acquaintances engaged in casual conversation. Tarek was a changeling himself, one moment ruled by

one mood, the next swept clean of that so another could take over. The changes kept her dangerously off balance.

"For what?" he repeated.

Praying she wasn't putting her people in even greater danger, she told him that they rode wildings when they traveled and used them for hunting. Other wildings helped in the gardens or hauled logs used for houses.

"They've become your muscles?"

"Yes."

"Hmm. Maybe the Centrois could. So the Baasta are still farmers, are they? They haven't forgotten the skills they learned at the hands of their old masters."

Much as she wanted to argue that the Baasta had always worked the land and that long before the Centrois had turned them into chattel they'd been nomads, she didn't.

"What are you thinking?" When he reached out as if to touch her breast, she stood her ground, but he'd left her standing at the edge of a fire, needing more heat.

"We . . . we'll never speak with the same mind."

"You believe we should?"

Surprised by the question, she stared.

"Tell me, do you wish we spoke the same language?"

They used the same words, but he was right. Being able to communicate didn't mean they saw the world in the same way. "No, never."

"Hmm." His fingers crept along the leash, drawing closer to her throat and sending unwanted heat there. "Why not?"

I'll never be what you want me to become. I'll die first. "Because the differences between us are too great."

"What differences?"

Tell him. Say it! "The Centrois are wrong to believe they have a right to control others."

"You know what the Divine Eternal intended for my people?"

"Yes. The Baasta would never want to make slaves of the Centrois."

He cocked his head to the side, fingers nearly on her skin; her sex was weeping. She struggled to make sense of his expression but couldn't. Finally, he blinked and shook his head as if trying to clear it. "Tell me more about wildings. Are they hard to capture?"

Capture. That's what he'd done to her.

"You don't need wildings. You have motos."

"Answer me!"

Don't fight him over this. It doesn't matter. "When we first found them, yes. Some fought so hard they killed themselves or injured themselves so badly that they had to be destroyed."

"And now?"

Because she'd become a vital part of caring for wildings, she found the telling easy. When the Baasta discovered the lush country they named Hevassen, they decided to make it their home. They'd been so intent on building shelters and hunting and gathering food that they hadn't known wildings existed until winter lost its grip. Then some hunters had spotted the swift-running creatures and seen their potential. Attempts to capture them using traps and ropes had been unsuccessful. Because she'd used the same technique to entice rabbits and other small creatures to her, she'd suggested tempting the grass-eaters with vegetables. It had worked.

"You were the first to slip a rope around a wilding's neck?" he asked. "You aren't strong enough to fight it into submission."

"I didn't have to."

Her leash had lain loose and perhaps forgotten in his hand, but now he again gathered up the slack. Perhaps he was imagining how she might have held that first young mare, but she couldn't make herself believe that. "Why not?"

"I know how to be gentle." She stared at what he was doing.

"I speak softly and sometimes sing. I tell a wilding that I am his friend, saying the words over and over again until he becomes used to my voice. And I keep handing him wonderful things to eat. By the time I touch him, he no longer sees me as the enemy."

"You're the only one who can do this?"

He didn't believe her, but why should he? "Yes."

"Why?"

"I don't know." Did he understand how honest she was being? Did he care? "Animals are all instinct. Perhaps wildings feel my touch and know I'd never hurt them. That once they've turned themselves over to me, they'll be cared for, safe."

"You aren't safe with me."

I know.

A cold, calculating smile changed him. "You're valuable. Because of your *gift* with wildings, your people need you."

Alarm slid through her at the thought of what he might do with her knowledge. "When we first found the wildings, yes." She hurried her words. "But now many have been tamed."

"So you're no longer any use to your people? Other than your role as a wife and mother, they don't care what happens to you?"

On the verge of telling him he knew better, she kept her mouth shut.

"What is it, Nari?" Tugging on her leash, he forced her to lean forward. "You're afraid to say anything? Don't bother. I know everything I need to."

Was that possible? she pondered as shadows stole the day. In the short time they'd been together, he'd dug deep inside her and pulled out her deepest secrets. Although she suspected he'd been simply trying to unnerve her, he'd exposed more than her body. And more was to come.

Not long after their conversation, if it could be called that, he'd released her hands and told her she could relieve herself.

He'd kept hold of her leash while she selected a broad leaf and then squatted and urinated. Hauling her over to his moto, he'd shared his water with her. Then he'd led her to a tall tree with thick branches and backed her against the trunk. After tying her hands behind her and connecting that rope to the trunk, he'd gagged her. When he'd gotten on his moto and taken off, she'd guessed that he wanted to take a look at his surroundings.

He'd left her in the shade. She supposed she should be grateful, but all she could think about was what would happen when he returned. As a small child, she'd been oblivious to her family's position as chattel. True, she'd known not to get close to the Centrois, but she'd had playmates and the freedom to do whatever she wanted. Hearing what the adults had been subjected to had filled her with hatred, but her knowledge of restraint and confinement had come from others' words, not personal experience.

The suns glided toward the horizon. Proclaiming the day's end with a show of reds and oranges, they seemed to be welcoming all living creatures to a time of peace and rest. But there wasn't any peace for her. Or rest. Or control.

He'd left enough slack in the rope tethering her to the tree so she could sit or stand, and she'd conserved her strength as best she could by sitting.

When he returned . . .

The energy and wanting he'd planted between her legs sprang back to life. And as her surroundings lost distinction, she lost the ability to kill the wanting.

No man had ever handled her pussy the way Tarek had; she would have taken a knife to anyone who tried.

But he knew how to fuel her fires. And once he'd ignited that first spark, he'd thrown branch after branch into the blaze. He'd created heat in her. And although he'd eventually stopped feeding the blaze, the coils remained hot.

How easily could he make the flames spark and reach for the heavens?

Admitting that she now thought of herself as existing for his pleasure filled her with self-loathing, but along with the loathing came something else; she wanted to burn for him.

Tears born of helplessness, fury, and expectation welled in her eyes. She blinked and shook her head, determined to be rid of them, but one tracked down her cheek. If only she could wipe it away!

Touch herself.

Satisfy herself.

Sound. That sound.

At first the moto's rumbling reminded her of a mother singing her baby to sleep. Then it grew in intensity, and she longed to shrink from it, but she couldn't do more than struggle to her feet. He'd left her as her people left wildings they intended to use—ready, accessible.

Only a little of the suns now remained above the horizon, but she had no trouble making out the moto—or the man riding it. He stopped a short distance away and, still straddling the moto like a warrior astride a wilding stallion, studied her.

Perhaps she should be used to his ability to keep his emotions to himself, but the straight line of his mouth unnerved her. His gaze slowly ran down her, touching face, neck, shoulders, breasts, belly, and then the place she tried to hide by keeping her legs close together. A new flame slid over her there.

Without him, you'd die tied to this tree.

"This is incredible land. Blessed with water and rich earth," he said. "Your people chose well."

A compliment?

"I saw no sign of the savages, but they come here, don't they?"

Although maybe she should have warned him, she didn't nod.

After giving her a look she couldn't interpret, he dismounted and walked toward her. She counted the steps, felt the growing closeness, and despite herself leaned toward him when he reached out to touch her shoulders. Thankfully, the gag swallowed her faint sigh.

"Think about this, chattel. I'm all that stands between you and death if the savages attack. You need me."

I wouldn't if you hadn't captured me.

Turning her away from him, he released her from the tree. With her back still to him, she absorbed the feel of his fingers gliding over her arms. Instinct said she should hate his confidence, his insistence that he could do what he wanted, when he wanted. But didn't wildings reach the point when they lowered their heads to accept halters and bridles?

Was she getting there?

The question faded. He'd moved from her arms to her fingers. Maybe he was only interested in finding out whether her circulation had been compromised, but if that was his goal, would he have slid his fingers between hers? Would he gently squeeze her hands as if reassuring her?

Releasing her hands, he turned her around and reached behind her. Another sigh rose in her to be swallowed by the gag. She became lost in the whispered touch of nails and knuckles brushing her ass cheeks. Goose bumps sprang to life. Sucking in a noisy breath, she widened her stance to keep from losing her balance.

Slowly, so impossibly slow that she was afraid she'd scream from the wanting, he claimed her buttocks. No matter that she stumbled back looking to place distance between them, he kept pace. He was teasing her, pushing her limits, teaching her lessons, and all she could do was try to keep her feet under her. She kept looking up at him but couldn't say what she was looking for—maybe a sign that he was about to take pity on her.

Just when she thought she couldn't take it anymore, he

stopped pressing against the base of her buttocks with the heels of his hands, wrapped his arms around her, and pulled her hard against him.

"Alive, are you?" His breath heated her ear. "Hungry for more than food."

She started to shake her head, then stopped because he'd spun her around and cupped his hands over her breasts. He used his new hold to cinch her against him, her captured hands on his cock.

"Touch me, chattel."

Her fingers must have taken on a life of their own because even with the distraction of his hands on her breasts, she cradled his cock in her palms. His erection had pushed his cockcloth to the side, giving her access to smooth, soft skin stretched over the rock-hard length.

A mist rose around her, and she walked into it. In this *world* she'd created, she was no longer tied or gagged. Instead, she'd come to this Centrois warrior because she wanted to. He felt the same way, wanted her, not master-to-chattel, but man-to-woman. No order had placed her hands around his penis. The hands on her breasts no longer spoke of mastery but shared lust, affection even.

Lust. Affection.

Although she tried to hold on to it, the mist faded. Back in the world she couldn't escape, he was drawing her breasts apart. Her nipples tingled. Her belly clenched. And hot juice ran down the insides of her thighs. Unnerved by how easily he brought her hunger to life, she tried to twist away.

"No." He pulled her against him, forcing her off balance. "No fighting, chattel. Touch me! Listen to your body." Drawing her flesh into his palms, he again caught her nipples between his fingers. "It wants one thing, to fuck."

What about you? Can I weaken you the way you're weakening me?

Desperate for the answer so she could use it to her advantage, she ran her palms up and down his length. If he backed away, she'd fall, but she couldn't think about that now. He either trusted her not to hurt him or had allowed her to fondle him as a kind of test. Injury to their cocks and balls brought men to their knees, made the strong weak. She could, maybe she could—

Warm. Strong. Huge. Filled with promise. In her, maybe, sometime, if she pleased him.

Just as he was now pleasing her.

Sucking in a breath, she smelled herself. More fluid leaked from her, pooled around her entrance, tracked down her legs, gave away everything.

Too late to try to fight, to keep her body for herself.

Surrender was so easy. All she had to do was rest the back of her head against his chest and trust, completely, that he'd support her. Her breasts belonged in his grip, and she thanked him by rocking in one direction and then the next. Her deepest gratitude played out in the way she handled his gift. Even with limited use of her hands, she stroked and finger-kissed. When she reached his tip, she painted it with her thumbs and forefingers.

The mist returned. In her mind, her hands became her womb. In her mind, she took him deep so his cock glided over her pussy walls, the wet and wonderful friction like new life. Desperate to reach the place of no holding back, she repeatedly clenched her sex muscles. Her throat and cheeks burned; her back ached, and her fingers grew tired from trying to simulate what she wished was the real thing.

His grasp tightened. So did hers. She twisted and rocked. He thrust against her, pushed and drew back, pushed again. As her hands fucked him, his moved relentlessly over her breasts, sometimes rough, sometimes so gentle she wasn't sure he was still touching her.

There was heat in the mist, and wetness. Communication despite the silence between them.

Her world took on a deep red cast as if someone had painted the mist, and she plunged into it. Here, in this place that couldn't and didn't exist, she became someone she'd never been, more animal than woman.

The greatest heat lived deep in her cunt, but it also flowed out to embrace the rest of her. No longer thinking herself as a captive, she reveled in her power. This stranger's cock was in her embrace. She controlled not just it but everything about him. At the same time, his control of her was complete, so perhaps they'd fallen into a single pit and fallen prey to a common hunger.

Pain sparked across her breasts. Before she could react, the sensation faded, became power—his power. Her breasts seemed to have swelled. Maybe they fed off his fingers and nails, the expert way he flattened and stretched them, constantly covering them, owning them.

Yes, let him own her! As long as he allowed her to live in the mist, she didn't care.

"Easy. Easy."

Although she hated concentrating on anything except her body, she forced herself to latch onto his warning. Had her grip become too strong? She stroked from base to tip, finger-bathing everything. His hands remained possessive but still; perhaps nothing mattered to him except what she was doing.

She'd bring him to climax. Please him. Make him grunt and maybe curse as he exploded. Then, please, he'd do the same to her.

But no matter how hard she tried, she couldn't ignore the strain in her shoulders, and her spine now burned. Gasping into the gag, she rolled away and faced him, freeing him and distancing herself from him. Sweat coated her. Either he'd understand or punish.

The day's dying light highlighted his glistening chest where a moment ago she'd rested her head and shoulders, and her body carried the memory of that embrace. She strained against her bonds, then slumped. As she did, her body hummed, waited. Risking her self-control, she studied his cock. Despite the strength and health that radiated throughout him, this one vulnerable organ said the most about what kind of man he was.

And what she needed from him.

"Do you want it?" He aimed his cock at her crotch.

Tell him no! Make him believe he hasn't broken you.

Broken, no. Alive was more like it, alive and animal in her need.

"Do you want me to fuck you?" he demanded. "Will you cry for it?"

8

Play with her. Make her beg. Take her deep into herself and feed her need. Bring her close to release, then stop so she understands what it means to be owned.

The word *owned* reverberated through Tarek, forcing him to spend precious energy fighting it into submission. It was now, when his body's demands were so powerful, that he wasn't sure whether he or the sex-chattel held the upper hand, but because he'd done this before, he knew what to expect. Tonight shouldn't be any different from the past.

Except that he'd spent years hating her breed and now she was his—she with her swollen pussy, hard nipples, sweet smell, and surprisingly soft voice.

Too late he wondered whether he should have kept her gagged, but he'd wanted to hear her beg and plead as he brought her tantalizingly, dangerously near climax only to deny her.

If he could control himself enough to know where her edges lay.

Fingers clenched around her neck rope, he sucked in the just-born night air and looked up at her from where he knelt on his sleep-pelt. The moon was working its way into the sky, silhouetting her in light blue and making him think of a soft rain.

Before removing her gag, he'd told her that her pleasure depended on what she did for him. To keep her from protesting, he'd ordered her to spread her legs so he could finger-fuck her. Not giving her time to consider the ramifications of her acceptance, he'd wasted no time entering her. When he'd rested his forefinger in her, she'd moved up and down on him, doing for herself what he refused to. When he'd withdrawn and slapped her exposed cunt, she'd stood frozen in place while grunting repeatedly. He'd been so close to her sex that her smell had nearly overwhelmed him. Fighting her small victory, he'd stood up.

Now she waited, helpless and wanting.

"You're ready to fuck, chattel. You might deny it, but I know the truth. Beg for it. If you don't, you'll spend the night alone and unable to satisfy yourself. And in the morning . . ."

"In the morning, what?" she demanded, her voice heavy.

"That's when I'll truly make you plead."

She took a backward step and might have taken another if he hadn't tightened his grip on the leash. She might be standing while he remained on the ground, but she couldn't possibly feel she held the upper hand with his ropes on her and the memory of his finger in her still speaking to her. "You've become my wilding, chattel. No matter how much you fight, you'll eventually surrender. And in the surrender you'll find joy."

"I hate you!"

"I know." Just staring at her indistinct form and listening to her breathy tones sent fresh blood to his cock. *And I hate you.* "Straddle me, now."

"No! I'm not—"

He slapped her cunt again, a wet and telling sound. Then, still gripping the leash, he leaned back and rested his elbows on the ground behind him with his legs outstretched. He lifted his pelvis toward her. "Yes, you are. Straddle me."

Head high, maybe so she didn't have to look at him, she obeyed. His cock, defying his attempts to control it, strained for her.

"Crouch over me, come down, slowly."

At the command, she looked down at him, her gaze sliding from his face to his cock, then quickly back to his eyes. "No," she whispered. "Please."

"Yes." He rubbed his knee against her calf. "Do it! Now."

Taut and trembling, she repositioned herself so her pussy was over his cock and began her descent. Dropping the rope, he gripped her thighs. Using his hold to guide her, he held his breath until her heat kissed his tip. That was all it took for him to acknowledge an undeniable fact. His explosion wouldn't take long.

Seemingly oblivious to his fingers on her thighs, she arched her back slightly, improving her position. A slow shudder ran through her.

"What is it?" he demanded.

Instead of answering, she bent her knees even more. His cock, smashed against her labia, strained to find entrance. She stood between him and the moon and became his everything. Unnerved, he grit his teeth. If she tried to escape, he'd grab her leash, but he didn't think she'd be so foolish as to run naked and without use of her hands into the night.

Still, the possibility stayed with him, making her elusive and thus an even rarer prize.

Yes, she was *his*.

Perhaps she sensed his thoughts because she shivered again, and despite the obvious tension in her legs, she didn't move.

"Now," he ordered. "Fill yourself with me."

Down she came, just enough for anticipation to gnaw at his sanity, not enough for his cock to begin its journey into her. Again, she paused. Slick moisture coated his tip.

"What are you afraid of?" he demanded.

"You."

"Me? Or yourself?"

"I hate you."

"Do it!" He squeezed a thigh, forcing out a yelp.

"No, please, no."

Releasing her thighs, he slid his hands between her legs. One went to his cock so he could direct it. The other sought and easily found her ready opening. How strong her legs were! How able to stand the strain! After gathering some of her fluid, he wiped his fingers on her belly. She trembled. "You're afraid of yourself, admit it!"

Yes, yes, yes. Determined not to cry out, Nari bit her lower lip. She couldn't stop shaking, her reaction having only a little to do with the tension in her legs. The more she tried to divorce herself from what was happening on this beautiful moonlit night, the sharper the images and her body's reactions became. She who loved to race the wind from a wilding's back now stood over her captor with her arms lashed behind her, naked, a collar around her neck and a rope dangling from that.

But instead of seeking a way to kill him, all she wanted out of life was to feel her enemy's cock fill her.

An inhuman growl escaped her when he parted her cunt lips and positioned his cock at her entrance. Something raw and feral took over, and she quickly, surely settled her body over Tarek until her knees touched the ground. His cock filled her, touched every part of her, tasted and explored, invaded. She growled again.

Closing his hands around her waist, Tarek held her in place, his fingers burning her skin. "Damn you," he spat.

A thought, a sense of power really, sparked in her but died before she could grab hold of it. This hot weight pressing against her pussy walls defined her life. No matter that she'd fucked before. No matter that his cock might not be that different from others who had come before.

Only his mattered.

Only his would satisfy.

Wise in what it took to feed this insatiable hunger, she began working her body. With each slide of cock against cunt, she came closer to her edge. Despite the impossibly long day, her empty belly, and tired muscles, her hopeless, helpless position, she gathered her strength and rode him.

Not content to let her sweat and strain, he repeatedly powered into her. The hair that had worked free from her braid obscured her vision and stuck to her sweating cheeks and throat. Her breasts shook, the sensation pushing her to increase her pace. There was no distinction between the various parts of her sex. Everything was on fire, demanding, crying, maybe laughing.

"Damn you, damn you." He seemed to be taking leave of the ground, pushing against the air in his determination to lock himself inside her.

For a heartbeat, his oath connected her with reality, but then it was gone because nothing mattered except silencing the tension he'd forced into her. She'd fuck and fuck, punish both of them, command her cunt to eat him.

Lightning licked everywhere. She didn't know whether her eyes were open or closed, whether his thrusts or hers were the most powerful, how close she was to climaxing.

Close. Nearly there.

"Damn you!" he bellowed, and sat up. His cock sucked out of her, and she screamed. Then, although she twisted and kicked, he too easily wrenched her off him and onto her back with her legs splayed, her pussy and inner thighs sopping wet.

Then he was kneeling beside her, holding his cock, grunting and growling. Every time he jerked, more cum landed on her breasts until she was bathed in it. Until the smell overwhelmed her.

"I use you, chattel. You don't use me."

* * *

Careful not to lie on the rope connecting her to Tarek, Nari turned away from him and curled up in a miserable ball. Every muscle ached. It would be a long time, if ever, before she could fall asleep because first she had to replay what had happened. Once he'd spilled himself on her, he'd gotten to his feet. Standing over her, he'd ordered her not to move. If she'd been able to use her hands, she would have satisfied herself somehow. But although her cunt's demands chewed on her nerves with sharp teeth, she'd lain on her arms while his cum dried on her breasts.

Caught tight in her body's frustration, she hadn't resisted when he sat her up and untied her arms. She'd had to fight to keep from attacking him when he calmly rubbed circulation back into her wrists and fingers and then given her several hunks of dried meat and some nuts. She'd thought he might have thrown his victory in her face, but all he'd done was eat while making sure her hands didn't stray to her crotch. Only when they'd eaten and drank and he'd watched her relieve herself did he order her onto her knees.

She'd tried not to think while he dribbled water over her breasts and washed away his seed. Although she'd shivered as his fingers roamed her flesh, she'd refused to look at him. She hadn't spoken because only one thing mattered. How long did he intend to punish her?

And why.

Granted, having a soft pelt under her and another tucked around her couldn't be called punishment. In addition, her belly was full, and she wasn't thirsty. But he'd again fastened her hands to her waist in such a way that she couldn't reach between her legs, and he'd tied her leash to his wrist to make sure she couldn't escape.

His soft snoring signaled sleep, but why shouldn't he? After all, he wasn't sexually frustrated.

After listening to the strangely comforting sound for a while, she realized her frustration had all but disappeared. Approaching unconsciousness herself undoubtedly had something to do with it, but the real difference came because he was no longer stimulating her, torturing and teasing her.

Good!

Maybe.

The moment the thought broke through, she shoved it away, but it returned, and this time she didn't bother with denial. She certainly didn't want to be handled like some possession, but there was no denying that he'd played her well. And that she'd loved the music.

He'll play me again.

Nostrils flaring, she turned and faced him. He'd become a shadowed lump, an inert mound. Helpless. Vulnerable. Human. Male.

Tarek woke to find his captive pressed against his arm. As he waited for his mind to clear, he took note of the dawn's cool air. Already he felt the promise of a day full of the kind of heat that could make him lethargic. For the first time since leaving home, he wasn't surrounded by his fellow warriors and didn't expect them to return for a while. Given the undeniable danger of a savage attack or even one from the Baasta, he didn't dare drop his guard. But he could imagine a languid afternoon made even more pleasurable by a sex-chattel giving him a massage.

Careful not to disturb Nari, he untied the leash from his wrist and slid out of bed. Although his bladder demanded attention, he was in no hurry to leave her. She'd undoubtedly spent much of the night cursing him, but although she might long to dig her nails into his chest, he doubted if, in her heart of hearts, she hated him. After all, he had given her a great deal of pleasure.

And I'll bring you even more, little one. All you need to do in exchange is surrender your freedom.

Unless freedom means more to you than fucking.

After relieving himself, he returned and pulled the covering off her. Muttering, she drew her small, smooth body into a ball. Although part of him wanted to leave her to her rest, he nudged her buttocks. She woke, the process as smooth and graceful as she'd proven herself to be.

"On your feet," he ordered.

Her obedience nearly stole his breath. He told himself it was because his cock was morning hard, because the collar and leash hanging between her breasts reinforced his ownership. She was graceful, muscles working in sweet harmony, a possession any man would be proud to own.

"You slept well?" he asked, studying her expression.

Shoulders back, she squared on him. "Well enough."

"Are you stiff? Sore?"

Head high and proud, she rotated her shoulders.

He repeated his question.

"Do you care?" she retorted. "Where are they?"

"Who?"

Her eyes darkened, brows pulling together, gaze becoming even more intense. "My cousin and the man who claimed her—where did he take her?"

"I don't know."

"Will they be back today?"

"Don't concern yourself with another Centrois's chattel." He emphasized his command by dragging her toward the bushes where she'd relieved herself last night. He waited until she'd finished and then turned her toward him. "You have much to learn, chattel. You have no right to ask questions of your owner beyond those concerned with his wants and desires. Do you understand?"

"Will he hurt her?"

In the past, he would have slapped defiance out of a chattel, but he couldn't ignore her deep concern. "J'ron is young, impulsive, full of himself. Courageous and willing to risk his life for his people. He's a lion, a night beast."

"That doesn't tell me enough."

"Enough!" He tugged on the leash, causing her to lock her knees to keep from being pulled off balance. He'd been concentrating on her words and the emotion behind them, but he no longer cared about those things because this creature who was as much wilding as woman was his. His to train and tease and enjoy. His to present to her breed so they'd understand what the Centrois were capable of. "I require servicing. There is much you need to learn about how to please me."

He waited for fear to settle in her eyes, but if that's what she felt, she hid the emotion well. Instead, he sensed her intellect, her determination to learn all she could, not about servicing him, but his strengths and weaknesses. She was indeed a worthy foe. Slight and beautiful, desirable.

Desirable? Frowning, he pulled her close and untied her hands. He allowed her a few seconds to work stiffness out of her arms, then spun her around and rebound her wrists behind her. After tossing the leash over her shoulder, he stepped back. Her hair had come loose during the night and lay tangled around her throat and down her back like a blanket. There was a crease along her cheek from the sleep pelt, and dried sweat had trapped dirt against her skin. As soon as he was done with the morning's lesson, he'd drag her into the pond and wash her.

The thought of scrubbing her clean jerked his cock to full attention. Nostrils slightly flared, she studied it. "I require sex in the morning," he said unnecessarily. "There's only one reason for a man's cock to become hard, because it demands satisfaction. You will learn to heed its commands."

Never.

A sudden gust of wind caught some of Nari's hair and threw it about her face. Although the sweet scented air spoke of freedom, she couldn't embrace it. Grounded, not just by her lack of wings but also by her helpless hands and the piercing gaze of the man who'd claimed her, she wondered at her willingness to stand naked and exposed before him. Even if her hands were free and a wilding stood nearby, would she leap onto the creature's back? Race for the hills? The thought of never seeing Tarek again or knowing his touch weakened her.

But why should she want *his* touch?

"Why are you shivering?" he asked.

"I'm cold."

Looking skeptical, he closed his hands over her sides. Then his thumbs slipped under her breasts, lifting them slightly. "You don't feel cold. Maybe you aren't telling me the truth."

"Maybe I'm not."

"What's that, defiance?"

"You love this, don't you?" she spat. "Treating me like some animal you've captured and not a human—"

"Have you ever had a cock in your mouth?"

Heat flamed her cheeks. She could barely breathe. "What?"

"Brought a man to climax that way? Swallowed his cum?"

A few seasons ago, she'd stayed awake one night when her aunt was visiting her mother. For a while the women had laughed and gossiped, but at length their conversation had turned to what life had been like when they belonged to the Centrois. She'd had to press her hand against her mouth to keep from gasping as they talked about some of the things the men required of their sex-chattel. What had shocked her the most wasn't learning that there was more than one way to have sex but that her aunt and mother hadn't sounded disgusted or ashamed. Quite the opposite, her aunt had admitted that she'd finally gotten up the courage to suggest what she called mouth sex to her husband and they'd both loved it.

"Did you hear me, chattel? Have you swallowed cum?"

"No. Never."

"Follow me."

Feeling like a wilding being led by its halter, she trailed behind Tarek as he walked over to a fallen log. She should have tried to run, but she didn't. And not because he'd only overtake her and haul her back.

He sat on the edge of the log and spread his legs. No matter how much she was risking by looking at his cock, she did. Sleek and hard at the same time, it had been designed to fit perfectly in her cunt.

But that wasn't the only place.

"Come closer." He indicated a spot in front of him.

No! No, no.

"Now!"

I'll kill you. Somehow I'll kill you for making me do this.

Although she again started to tremble, she managed to do as he commanded. She swore she felt heat rising from his cock.

Don't think. Go into the mist you found yesterday. Return home in your mind. Don't—

"On your knees."

Relieved to not have to support her suddenly great weight, she sank to the ground. Doing so placed her mouth level with his penis, but thankfully he was too far away to reach, yet.

Soon. Soon.

"Think about this, chattel. If you want pleasure, you must first please me. That's what it means to be a master, to be placed first." He cupped his hand around his cock and began stroking it, making her wish that she knew what it felt like to be a man.

"Spread your legs and lower your head."

Don't think. Do what you must, but hide in the mist.

What mist? There was nothing except reality.

Defeated and yet curious, she did as he commanded. Her forehead now rested on the ground, and she imagined what she looked like with her hair about her head, her ass in the air, bound hands resting at the top of her crack. Her breathing was somewhat constricted, and concentrating on getting enough air in her lungs put her even more in touch with her body. This had become her existence, her world. She existed to pleasure him, and if she was successful, he might do the same for her.

Whether she wanted it or not.

She'd sometimes wondered at a wilding's seeming willingness to allow a human to rule it, asking herself if no longer having to be responsible for safety and food gave it a sense of freedom. She might not know any more about a wilding than she had, but she now understood something about herself. Being his, obeying him, was liberating in a way she'd never expected. This morning she belonged to him. And if she pleased him, he might reward her subservence.

His sex-chattel?

Blood ran to her brain, causing a headache. At the same time, the breeze caressed her back, ass, and legs. Less than a day ago she'd been as wild and free as the wildest wilding, but now she was naked and on her knees, surrendering her body to a powerful man.

"What is it like, chattel? What are you thinking as you wait for my next order?"

Don't do this. I can't think when you—

"Answer me!"

"I . . . I wait."

"And anticipate?"

"Yes."

"Your pussy cries for me?"

No. "Yes."

"Good. Now lift your head."

When she did, her hair obstructed her vision. She shook her head, instantly becoming dizzy. Despite her effort to bring him into focus, he remained a dark naked blur just beyond the veil of her hair. She could make out his powerful calves and thighs and noted that he was leaning forward slightly, either because he was concentrating on what he was doing to his cock or because he wanted to get closer to her.

Yours. I'm yours to teach.

9

Nari had scooted closer, but until he told her to, she wouldn't bring her mouth any closer to his cock. She tried not to think about the unwanted heat bubbling in her crotch, but her hold on self-control was so tenuous.

What was it about him that called to her so fiercely? She should loathe this man and everything he stood for, abhor what he was putting her through, but something about this unknown journey touched her as she'd never been touched. Even having her hands locked behind her, his collar around her neck, and a rope resting between her breasts was exciting, even liberating.

Surely he knew what she was experiencing. A man experienced in the taming and training of those he called chattel.

"Tell me." His sharp tone cut into her thoughts. "If you had a knife, what would you do with it?"

"What? I don't know."

"Perhaps you'd slice this off me." He indicated his cock. "And then watch me bleed to death."

A shiver ran through her. "No."

Surprise turned his expression from wariness to something

vulnerable, and in that moment she understood something she never thought she would. This bold, strong fighting warlord was also mortal, needful in ways perhaps he didn't understand. What was it like to live one's life accepting that each day might be his last?

She knew enough about the Centrois to understand that warriors placed their breed's safety above their own. From early boyhood, men were taught to fight, to stand strong before each and every enemy. No true Centrois warrior ever turned and ran. Even if they'd been wounded, they stood their ground and fought as long as life remained in them. And he wasn't just a warrior. He was their warlord, leader of fighting men.

But in the middle of the night, alone with their human fears, did these fighters ponder the manner of their death? Did they ever want to till gardens instead of carry weapons?

Of course.

No wonder they sought to control others. Dominant, they could tell themselves they weren't prisoners of their fear. Maybe they even believed their own lies.

Feeling alive with new and powerful knowledge, she licked her lips. "I have no wish to kill you, Tarek. Your death should come at the hands of a worthy foe, not a naked woman."

Releasing his cock, he leaned forward, his hand reaching for her. When he lightly touched her temple, a quiet sob settled in her throat. Her vision blurred as she imagined closing her mouth around his fingers. He again brushed her hair out of her eyes, then caught its length and settled it behind her shoulders.

"I've never . . ." he started. Then, fingertips still on her pulse, he cocked his head. After a moment, she heard a sound she knew all too well. A number of Centrois were returning. Although he hadn't said she could, she scrambled to her feet. *Please let it be Reyna.*

The wheels were kicking up so much debris that at first she wasn't sure how many there were—at least ten. One moto carried two riders. When Tarek started toward them, she followed. And when he stopped, she stood a step behind him, wondering whether he regretted not having put his cock-cloth back on. Walking toward so many of the enemy, forcing herself to study the magical motos, filled her with dread. They looked so strong, so powerful, so alien—the enemy.

Maybe because she was standing naked before them.

Reyna and the man who'd claimed her brought up the rear. As soon as she saw Reyna, nothing else mattered. Her cousin's dirty, tangled hair was in her eyes. Her body slumped forward, and she was being supported by the man sitting behind her. Her hands were secured behind her.

"Reyna!" Nari sobbed. "What happened?"

At first she thought Reyna hadn't heard, but then her cousin lifted her head. One cheek was bruised. There was a cut on her chin, and dirty tear tracks rendered her nearly unrecognizable.

Before she could utter another sound, Tarek stalked toward Reyna and her captor. "What have you done to her?" he demanded.

"He raped her." Nari recognized the speaker as Tarek's brother. "We were hunting when we heard her crying. He'd staked her to the ground and—"

"Enough!" Tarek closed the remaining distance between himself and Reyna and almost gently drew her out of her captor's arms and off the moto. Reyna staggered and then collapsed.

"No!" Nari cried. Ignoring the others, she rushed forward and knelt beside her cousin, tugging in vain against her bonds. "Free me!" she ordered Tarek. "Damnation, free me!"

Two men, obviously disapproving of her outburst, told her to shut up, but she didn't care. And when Tarek deftly released her wrists, she gave him a grateful glance before helping Reyna sit up. Still not caring what anyone thought, she untied Reyna. To her relief, Reyna fiercely returned her hug. With Reyna's naked body pressed against hers, she glared up at the man who'd done this to her. "I will kill you," she said through clenched teeth. "For this you will die."

"Control your chattel," the man shot at Tarek. "Silence her."

"Dismount, J'ron," Tarek ordered. When J'ron did, Tarek stood toe-to-toe with him. "Is it true? You raped her."

"She's mine. I took my possession."

"Not this way. By all that's sacred—"

"Don't speak to me of what's sacred. Have you forgotten what the Baasta bastards did to my grandparents?"

"No worse than what was done to my father."

"Your father died while fighting, a warrior's death. He wasn't murdered in his sleep. And when she tried to cradle her husband's body, no Baasta slaughtered your mother as they did my grandmother."

Horrified, Nari stared at J'ron. The young man's eyes looked haunted, making her wonder if the small child he'd once been had seen his grandparents being killed. The idea that her people could be capable of such cruelty sickened her, but maybe whoever had been responsible had been so desperate, he'd—

No. Nothing justified murdering a sleeping man.

I'm sorry. If there's any way I could tell you how I feel—

"Put it behind you," Tarek was telling J'ron. "If you don't, hate will always twist you. Poison your heart."

"What about yours?" J'ron shot back. "Your need for vengeance is as strong as mine. Don't try to deny it."

When she'd first embraced Reyna, her cousin's strength had matched hers, but now Reyna started shaking. Although maybe she shouldn't have, Nari shut out what the men were saying and held Reyna at arms' length so she could study her. More bruises marked her belly and legs, and dried blood coated her pubic hair.

No matter what Tarek had put her through, he hadn't done this.

"Can you stand?" Nari whispered. After a moment, Reyna nodded. "Good. I have to take you to the lake and help you clean up. Until I do, I can't know how badly you're hurt." *And don't anyone try to stop me.*

"What is the chattel saying?" J'ron demanded. "Silence her, Tarek, or I will."

Not backing away from J'ron, Tarek looked over his shoulder at her. "What are you doing?" he asked, his tone gentler than she'd thought he was capable of.

"Taking care of her."

Tarek nodded, and she felt touched, not just by his silent approval, but by the compassion in his eyes—compassion and something else. Then he faced J'ron again. "I will not call you a warrior," he said sternly. "No one here will after what you've done."

"She's chattel. A wild animal in need of training."

"Not by ravaging her! That has never been the Centrois way. The Divine Eternal—"

"Is *our* creator. What does he care what happens to Baasta?"

"He created them too."

The hostility between the two men lay heavy in the air. J'ron wore an ornate cock-cloth and had a knife at his waist while Tarek was naked and unarmed, but if the difference concerned Tarek, he didn't show it. Quite the opposite—every line of Tarek's body proclaimed him the leader. If not for her concern for Reyna, Nari would have stayed and watched the courageous and determined man prove himself.

By the way Reyna shuffled, Nari had no doubt that soon she'd be so stiff she couldn't walk. She hated having to force Reyna into the cold water, but maybe it would numb her. Perhaps watching her footing gave her cousin something to concentrate on other than her injuries because by the time water lapped at their knees, she started talking. Nari would have given anything not to hear the details of the brutal attack, but she didn't try to silence Reyna, sensing that the words themselves were healing.

"I didn't know what he wanted," Reyna admitted as Nari repeatedly ran water over her shoulders and back. She seemed oblivious to the chill that had Nari shivering. "He kept ordering me to do things I didn't understand. It was as if . . . as if he was deliberately taunting me. And when I couldn't obey, he said I was being defiant."

"You, defiant?" Nari lightly pressed on her cousin's shoulders, indicating she wanted her to kneel so she could wash her hair and face. "You have always been the gentle one." *The one who wanted nothing more than love and acceptance from those around you.* "What did you say to him?"

"Nothing. He kept me gagged."

Nari thought she'd succeeded in burying her hatred of J'ron so she could concentrate on Reyna's needs. Now the threat she'd thrown at the so-called warrior echoed through her. Encouraged by her outburst, her imagination took over, and she laughed.

"What is it?" Reyna tilted her head back so her hair floated on the water. "You find something funny?"

"Not in what happened to you. Never. But, remember how when we were children, we'd threaten to bury boys headfirst in ant mounds if they didn't stop teasing us?"

"I could never do that, but how I longed to stick Storr and Lal's feet in the mounds."

"If only they hadn't been stronger than us. Why did the Divine Eternal make men stronger than women? Remember when we spread honey over their sleeping mats and ants—"

Reyna chuckled. "There were ants everywhere. Biting and crawling all over Storr and Lal."

"They told their parents that we were responsible. I thought we'd get in trouble, but their father only said they'd gotten what they'd deserved."

Reyna sighed and straightened, water streaming off her long hair. "How I wish I had some honey."

"And ants."

Smiling faintly, Reyna nodded agreement.

Determined to keep Reyna from sliding back into shock, Nari dug through her memory for other times when the two of them had bested their insufferable cousins. Storr and Lal had eventually turned into admirable men, and Storr had become a fine rider of wildings; but where other women called them handsome and desirable, to Nari and Reyna, they remained pests and teases, something the women still delighted in telling their cousins.

And now the time might come when Storr and Lal and other Baasta men would be forced to fight J'ron, Saka, and Tarek.

No, please.

Reyna still seemed divorced from her body, although perhaps she was deliberately trying to ignore it. Whichever it was, Nari guided her to a nearby grassy spot and sat her down so First Sun was on her back. "Please," she whispered. "I need to see between your legs. If you've been torn—"

"I . . . I don't think so," Reyna said as she spread her legs. "It's my bleeding time. That angered J'ron."

To Nari's great relief, Reyna was right. The blood came from her womb, and although her pussy was bruised, her skin hadn't been lacerated. Massaging Reyna's thighs and calves, she looked around. There were a number of hills nearby, most of them alive with sheltering trees. If it was just her, she'd run. What did cut feet matter as long as she was free? Once hidden, she'd find a sharp rock and try to cut through her collar. Even if she couldn't remove it, at least she could sever the leash that tangled around her legs with every step. Let Tarek look for her! She'd lived in Hevassen all her life and knew its secret places.

But she wasn't alone. Her bruised, aching, and traumatized cousin was with her.

"What is this?" Reyna asked as she fingered Nari's collar. "How does it open?"

"I don't know. I think only *he* can release it."

"What is he like?"

She should be grateful that her cousin was showing interest in more than what she'd endured, but Nari honestly didn't know how to answer. "He's their warlord. His hawk tattoos—I'm certain he's the man I saw that first day."

"What did he do with your dress? Did he . . . Nari, did he rape you?"

"No! No," she repeated more softly. "We'll speak of this later."

Reyna leaned back and looked into her cousin's eyes. "Later because you can't bring yourself to tell me what happened? Please, what did he do to you?"

Awaken my body. Make my sex weep. He walked into my world and life and took it over. "I don't have any bruises."

"Did he force you to sleep next to him?"

Yes, but his warmth seeped into me, and I wanted his arms around me. Earlier his cock nestled in my core; I wanted it there.

"Later, later. You need to rest."

"Are you afraid of him? Do you tremble when he's near the way J'ron makes me tremble?"

"Don't ask! I don't know what I feel."

Reyna had dozed off with her head in Nari's lap when Nari again heard the motos. Tense and frightened for Reyna's safety, she waited. How quickly her world had gone from centering around her breed and the work she was doing with wildings to these newcomers. Had everything changed? The Baasta would never again enjoy the peace they'd found in Hevassen?

Thank goodness J'ron wasn't on one of the two motos. She wasn't surprised to see Tarek but didn't know what to think when she spotted his younger brother Saka. After silencing the motos, the men approached on foot. Looking up at the two strong forms, she nudged Reyna awake. Gasping, Reyna snuggled close as if Nari could protect her.

"You didn't run." Tarek held his gaze on Nari. "I thought you might."

She'd carried this man's seed on her breasts and taken his cock into her body. No wonder he dominated her thoughts, her world. "I couldn't leave her." She hugged Reyna to her breast. "Where is he?" She couldn't bring herself to utter J'ron's name.

"With the others."

Taking a deep breath, she blurted what had been haunting her. "The things he said about his grandparents—was he there when it happened?"

"I don't know. Maybe he wasn't; he was so young. So much took place during the uprising. Everyone has their own memories, their own nightmares."

"Centrois and Baasta alike."

"Yes."

Was there something in the fact that Tarek hadn't called them chattel? She'd be a fool to believe that, and with Tarek's cock now hidden behind his only clothing and his knife within easy reach, she felt overwhelmed by him. Less than him. Why hadn't she fled?

"What . . . what's going to happen to me?" Reyna asked.

"He'll take you." Tarek nodded at his brother. "Can you stand?"

"No!" Nari blurted. "Please, don't make her—"

"Silence!" Tarek's features hardened. "Stand. Both of you."

Cowed and hating feeling that way, Nari helped her cousin to her feet, both because resistance was useless and because she hoped to gain a feeling of strength from facing her captor. If only she could cover her nakedness.

If only awareness of her body didn't make her so aware of his.

Saka started toward Reyna, tearing her attention off Tarek. If the younger man harmed her cousin in any way, would she jump to her defense? And if she did, what would the consequences be?

Perhaps Tarek sensed her turmoil because he indicated he expected her to come to him. Over the sound of her pounding heart, she heard birds singing. The sounds whispered of freedom. Why hadn't she found a way to take Reyna with her?

Where would I go? How far could I carry her? And if he caught us...

"It's no longer about you and me," he said.

Alerted by his somber tone, she waited—waited with him standing too close.

"I must know everything you can tell me about the two-legged creatures who share this area with us. They're human and yet—"

"The savages."

"Yes. My men found fresh signs of them."

"How do you know—"

"They attacked us. I know what they're capable of."

With his words, awareness of his body faded. She swore she could smell the savages, hear their incomprehensible shrieks and cries. "Where are the signs?"

"In the hills closer to where Second Sun rises. Is that where they live?"

"Only signs?"

Although she'd worked to keep her voice calm, maybe he sensed her tension because he cupped her chin in his hand and forced her to look up at him. "What are you afraid of?"

On the brink of explaining that the creatures were more animal than human, she reconsidered. If the savages attacked unsuspecting Centrois warriors, maybe they'd kill all of them. Make Hevassen safe for her people again.

"What?" he demanded.

Keeping her fantasy at bay, she studied not just his expression but the depths of his eyes. The man was like digging into the earth, layer after layer being revealed. His gaze made it clear that he wouldn't automatically believe anything she told him and was committed to getting to the truth. His determination came from much more than his position of power. As leader, he was responsible for the lives of all his men—and hers.

"I'm not a hunter or warrior, so I can only say what I've been told, but our men say the savages are like cougars. If they so wish, they show themselves so everyone will fear them and stay away. When they're like that, they laugh and make loud noises. They shake their clubs and point their knives."

"Not just clubs and knives. Their claws are powerful weapons."

Is that what happened to you? Awareness of his heat returned, and she felt more naked than she had just moments ago. If he'd been killed, they would have never met, and she wouldn't know such a man existed. "I think they must love killing because they do so even when they aren't provoked."

"Love killing? Maybe. Are there times when they don't attack, when they realize they're outnumbered?"

Why didn't she want to answer? It couldn't possibly be because she was loathe to add to his leadership burdens. "Cougars slip through the wilderness like the wind through grass. They're silent and sure-footed. Their eyesight and hearing—our warriors say the savages' senses are just as keen."

He nodded thoughtfully, and for a heartbeat she thought he was going to give her a comforting touch. Instead, he turned his attention to Saka and Reyna. Doing the same, she noted that her cousin wasn't leaning away from the young Centrois. Saka was saying something to her, but his words didn't carry.

"A cougar stalked me once," he said. "Although I didn't hear or see him, I sensed him."

"A cougar is all fangs and claws. He'll kill a newborn wilding or one that can't run and fill his belly. A savage is more. A savage hates in a way a cougar never would."

Running her words around in his mind, Tarek wondered at his chattel's wisdom. He'd already come to the same conclusion about the savages' capacity for rage because he'd spent his life fighting and defending. A female, especially a Baasta, shouldn't have such insight. Perhaps she was just repeating what she'd heard Baasta men say, but he couldn't quite convince himself of that.

"You haven't answered my question. Do you know where they live? And if you do, will you tell me?"

10

By the time his captive had explained that the savages lived in caves but were always on the move, Tarek believed on a gut level that she was telling the truth. Because there were countless caves throughout Hevassen and only a few savages stayed in a particular cave, only twice had attempts to trap them succeeded. Both times several savages had been killed and their weapons seized, but the Baasta were only able to guess at the total number of wild creatures..

"How many Baasta have the savages killed?" he asked

"I don't know. None for a number of seasons. Our chiefs believe that the savages have learned that attacking us is too dangerous. When I was a girl, they surprised a large number of women who were working in our gardens. I remember, every house had crow feathers scattered around it as mourning signs."

"Why do the Baasta stay in Hevassen? Surely there are other places they can—"

"Hevassen is our home, a gift from the Divine Eternal. The land nourishes us."

He was about to point out that the danger from savages outweighed nourishment, but he changed his mind. The savages could have learned to avoid the Baasta, just as he intended for them to learn the same thing about the Centrois, not that he'd tell her that because he'd never talked to a woman the way one warrior speaks to another. And she wasn't even a woman. She was his captive, soon to be his sex-chattel.

Damn it, that's what she was! Yes, he'd needed to learn everything she knew about the savages, but he couldn't possibly care what happened to the Baasta. In fact, shouldn't he want to see them slaughtered?

"I've seen the savages' weapons." He assumed a superior tone. "They're nothing compared to ours."

"When the savages attacked, did you win?"

His hand snaked out, catching her on the side of her jaw. She staggered back, then stood her ground. Seeing the red mark his palm had left, he struggled to remember why he'd hit her.

"Are you done?" she asked, her voice calm and quiet when she should have been terrified. "Or are you going to beat me?"

She was taunting and pushing him, maybe trying to learn all she could about his temper. He'd have to remember that she was willing to risk injury in order to search his depths. The limp rope resting between her full breasts reminded him that he'd given himself the same goal about her. When he reached for the leash, he drew out the gesture.

Although he wanted and expected her to cower, once more she stood her ground and kept her head high until he forced her to bend her neck. "I won't need to beat you. There are other ways of breaking you. Never doubt this; I *will* hear you beg."

Hearing a moto come to life, he looked toward the sound. His brother was already straddling his machine and was in the process of positioning his new *responsibility* in front of him. Saka hadn't wanted anything to do with the female J'ron had abused, but Tarek had stood firm. As warlord, he commanded, and not even his brother dared defy him.

But his order had nothing to do with exerting his power over his younger sibling and everything to do with trying to bring Saka back to life. Saka had only rarely fucked since the woman he'd loved had died. Now he'd have to spend days and nights next to a soft, feminine, and available body.

"Where is he taking her?" Nari asked.

"Have you learned nothing?" He released the leash but immediately snaked his arms around her and yanked her against him. "You have no right asking questions."

"I—"

"No! You don't speak unless I give you permission."

Tarek was full of himself. In some respects he wasn't any different from the savages who hunted wildings simply to see if they could kill something that ran that fast. Because Tarek was a man and pride ruled him, she doubted that he'd ever admit how much he needed her knowledge about the savages. Of course not! Instead, he'd demonstrate his superior strength, his conviction that he owned her.

Instead of placing her on his moto as his brother had done to Reyna, he'd secured her hands in front and had run a rope between her legs rather than immobilizing her arms as he'd done before. That rope was now tied to the waist restraint in back and to her wrists in front. Every time she tried to move her arms, the crotch rope tightened. Even more demeaning and unnerving, he'd attached a leash to her wrists and was using that to haul her behind him as he eased the moto over the leaf-coated ground.

Every time she stepped on a rock or twig, she cursed her inability to concentrate on where they were going. But how could she think of anything except the strands pressing against her pussy lips? The rope was soft enough that it didn't hurt, and the way it glided against her sensitive flesh nearly drove her insane.

By the spirits he knew what he was doing! Oh yes, he intended to keep her aroused. And he was succeeding! To make things even worse, they were returning to where they'd left the others so everyone would see her like this.

Tears scalded her eyes and cheeks. Furious at her weakness, she tried to wipe the tears onto her shoulders. At that moment, Tarek looked back at her.

"You're crying, chattel? Why? Because you're ashamed?"

How well he knew her! All she had left was silence. That and the determination to return his stare.

"Remember this moment," he said. "When I'm finished with you, you'll have learned to never glare at me. Instead, your eyes will plead and promise."

If he was closer, she'd spit at him. Or would she? Her sex juices had soaked the crotch rope, and as long as the relentless pressure and movement continued, she'd respond. Heat from the suns and her arousal combined to separate her from reality. Even the birds and wind seemed to be serenading her mood. She was floating, drifting in air or water as her body whispered of possibilities.

Sex had always been a matter of demand and release, both conditions experienced within a few moments. She'd sometimes wondered if it was different for mated couples who had entire nights to spend together, but it had never been like that for her. Either a man's touch spoke of need or she reached out. If both heard the same message, they'd hurry to the nearest shelter. Clothes were discarded, positions assumed, rutting begun, exploding, ending.

This afternoon with a teasing rope gliding over her labia, she dreamed of a long night with a cock in her—Tarek's cock—always moving, always caressing.

The frightening idea that she might really want to fuck him shattered her lethargy but not her hot need. Desperate to dispel the notion that she'd ever welcome him into her body, she stared at his back, but instead of loathing his tanned strength, her fingers tingled with the need to explore his suns-heated flesh. He might not be the largest man she'd ever seen, but something separated him from the rest. Breasts jiggling and nipples hard, she was helpless to fight the need for an answer, and when he once more glanced back at her, his features caught in shadow, she found the answer.

He was mystery and danger, a powerful unknown. A Centrois warlord. Energy from a building storm or the sight of wildings fucking had the same impact on her. Both winter's fury and sharp squeals from an impaled mare became part of her. She wanted lightning and thunder, craved a stallion's relentless thrusts. At times like that, she ceased to be a Baasta woman destined to sacrifice her youth and strength so her people would survive and flourish. Standing in a wind-whipped downpour, she *became* lightning and danced to thunder's song.

Blood rushed to her cheeks and throat, and even though she sought a breeze to cool them, that heat was nothing compared to what pulsed between her legs. With her own features suntouched, she had no doubt that he could see her flushed face and know why. Of course. He'd done this to her.

If he stopped and walked back to her right now, she'd force him onto his back on the ground and straddle him, settle herself on his cock.

But she couldn't! She was helpless—helpless to silence her hunger.

By the time they reached the encampment, Nari was exhausted. In the time she'd been gone, the Centrois had constructed a wooden platform high in a tree with a thick trunk and few but sturdy branches. Spotting a man armed with a sunstick on the platform, she concluded that they intended to stay here for a while and were making sure neither savages nor Baasta could surprise them.

The warriors had each claimed his own place within the

brushy area, and although they were all probably visible from the platform, there was enough distance between the sleep-mats that everyone was afforded a measure of privacy.

Reyna and Saka were already there, as was J'ron, who was deliberately ignoring her cousin and her new captor. Saka had placed a collar similar to hers around Reyna's neck, and a leash was fastened to a stake driven into the ground. He'd provided her with her own mat, and she was stretched out on her side on it. Although Reyna nodded at Nari, she looked about to fall asleep.

Thank you, she told Tarek with her eyes.

If he understood her message, he gave no indication. Instead, he silenced his moto and drew her close. She didn't know whether or not to be relieved when he removed the ropes around her waist and against her crotch. When he slid his fingers over her sopping folds and held them up for everyone to see, she cursed him and tried to shrink into herself. Why was he humiliating her like that? Or maybe the Centrois didn't care whether such treatment of a chattel embarrassed her. After untying her leash from the moto, he extended it toward her.

"Kiss it," he ordered.

Anger surged into her and stole her breath.

"Kiss it!" Grabbing her bound wrists, he jerked her toward him until her shoulder rested against his chest. His heated strength weakened her, and she obeyed. After a few moments, he helped her straighten. Then, to her horror, he drew the leash between her legs and tugged, forcing her hands against her mons.

When he stepped behind her, she remained in place, watching him over her shoulder. Another tug on the leash forced her to take a backward step followed by another. Any hope she'd had that her arousal might die faded, and if she didn't have to concentrate on not losing her balance as he hauled her behind him, she would have pressed her fingers into herself. Hot and alive as she felt, she would have come almost immediately.

The pressure let up, allowing her to concentrate on this man who knew so much about a woman's edges. He'd brought her to a tree with a thick branch slightly higher than her head. Tarek tossed the leash over the branch; then he pulled until pressure against her labia forced her onto her toes. Keeping her there, he tied off the rope.

No!

Yes.

So far the strain on her legs was bearable, and as long as she remained under the branch, the pressure against her cunt was pleasurable, not painful. The rope rested on her clit, but she couldn't move enough to create any of the wonderful but over-whelming friction she craved.

Caught within her body. Forced to the edge but not over.

For how long?

Nervous and excited in ways she wasn't sure she could keep to herself, she studied Tarek. To her shock, he indicated he wanted the others to gather around. They did, sitting cross-legged in front of him. Their presence overwhelmed her. Was this how her people had once felt? Outdone?

Some studied her, and she sensed their hunger for a female body. The others kept their attention on Tarek. He was so much like the tattoos adorning his chest, fierce and free.

I hate you!

And need you.

When everyone was settled, Tarek planted his hand on her flank. The touch was like fire, causing flames to lick her sex and steal her breath. "She knows a great deal about the savages. She told me some while we were alone. You weren't lying, were you?"

No! After your kindness to Reyna, I wanted to answer your questions. But that was before this.

"Listen to me, chattel." His fingertips pressed against her. "I've positioned you like this because I intend for you to remain in front of all of us until we're certain you've told us everything we need to know. Our survival—and yours—depends on your honesty."

About what?

"Your and my relationship is a complex one and will become even more so." Now he was stroking her thigh, the gentle touch both calming and yet exciting her even more. "You have every reason to hate us. You want us dead, and if you could make it happen at the savages' hands, I have no doubt that you would do so. I'm right, aren't I?"

Because she had no other weapons, she closed her eyes.

"It isn't going to work, Nari. Never forget that I know how to get to you."

I won't let you. I swear—

"Listen to me. You may have more knowledge about this new enemy, but I know your body. Its needs. Its weaknesses."

Because she was struggling to gather her thoughts, his fingers had reached her inner thigh before the greater intimacy registered. She should have tried to turn away, but she didn't, couldn't. Her legs started trembling; she couldn't attribute that to the strain he'd placed them under.

"Tell us about the savages' leaders, if they have them."

Desperate to place distance between her mind and body, she opened her eyes. J'ron was sitting in front of her, glaring hatefully up at her. When she returned his stare, he smiled. Superiority ruled him.

Pressure on her right breast tore her attention from Reyna's rapist. Tarek had clamped his fingers around her nipple while his other hand remained on her inner thigh, caressing in contrast to the firm grip.

"Speak, chattel. Tell us everything you know or have been told. And it must be the truth or you'll be punished. Remember, not everyone is here. The others are out there, observing, learning."

Unable to move, claimed by Tarek in ways that over-whelmed her, she struggled to concentrate—on anything. "I . . . I don't know what you want me to say. I told you—"

"Tell everyone. And remember, I'll know if your story changes."

Why are you doing this to me?

Even as she silently asked the question, she knew the an-swer. Hadn't Tarek already said it? He and the others' survival depended on knowledge of the enemy. And intimate knowl-edge could only be gleaned from another enemy—her.

As she spoke of older savages who wore claw and teeth neck-laces and appeared to be responsible for planning attacks, Tarek kept up his assault on her body by running his hands over her breasts, hips, thighs, and buttocks. Twitching and squirming, gasping sometimes, she dug deep in what remained of her mind for everything she'd been told or had observed about the filthy beasts who used animal leg bones as clubs. Sweat ran from her temples as she recalled that she'd never seen a woman warrior and that bearing and raising children seemed to be the females' primary activity. No Baasta had ever ventured into a cave while the savages were in it, but several times they'd entered right after the savages had fled.

From what they had left behind, it appeared that savages' diet consisted primarily of meat. Wildings were considered a prime source as evidenced by the abandoned carcasses and her own knowledge. Once, she told them, she'd been sneaking up to a small wilding herd when a number of savages attacked, killing with hurtled spears and clubs. She wept as she described seeing a savage beat a foal to death as its helpless mother watched.

Deep mutters made her wonder whether they were acknowl-edging her softheartedness or expressing their disgust. Maybe she could have sorted things out if Tarek wasn't now lightly running his fingers over her throat. Even when his thumbs pressed against her windpipe, she told herself that her emotions mattered to him. That he cared about her.

Moments later, he demanded she describe the weapons in minute detail, and she called herself a fool. He wanted her—his chattel—aroused and defenseless. Under his expert manipulation, how could she be anything but honest? She'd do anything to please him!

And he knew it.

11

How much she has to learn.

His and the others' questioning over, Tarek brought his chattel down and allowed her to sit while they discussed what she'd told them. He kept her nearby so he could study her expression, strengths, and weaknesses as options were addressed in minute detail. If she escaped and returned to her people, what she was learning would give the Baasta an advantage, but he had no intention of allowing that.

"I disagree," J'ron said in response to a comment about the savages' stupidity. "They survive and thrive because of their strength and the fear humans and animals have of them. They exploit their appearances, but only a fool would believe they aren't capable of thinking like humans."

Tarek nodded agreement. Although J'ron was like a grizzly, quick to charge and kill, his ability to place himself inside their enemies' minds had always impressed him. Maybe it came from learning at an early age how fragile life was.

"I agree," he said. "They use fire to force animals into the open, and they only steal from the Baasta's gardens when vegetables are ripe. We must face the savages as they haven't been faced before."

"How?" Saka asked.

As Tarek began outlining the beginnings of a plan of how they could draw the savages into a trap, he shot several glances at his chattel. If he hadn't looked beyond her half-open eyes and unmoving body, he might think she wasn't listening, but he could tell her eyes were following the conversation. And the muscles at the sides of her neck stood out, proof of her concentration. No. He could never allow her to leave; she knew too much.

She'd become his responsibility.

The discussion wound down and then stopped when A'tala announced that he was hungry. Immediately, men stood and headed toward the fire pit where wood had been stacked in preparation for cooking the evening meal of fresh venison and some of the dried vegetables they'd brought with them. The vegetable supply would soon run out, but it didn't matter thanks to the Baasta garden. And whether she wanted to or not, his captive would lead him to the garden.

And show Centrois warriors where her people lived.

"Please," Nari said when he reached her. "I need to talk to Reyna. I need to know if she's—"

"No!"

If she asked why he was refusing her, he wasn't sure he could explain. Fortunately, she only glared. Judging by the moisture he found on her cunt lips, he'd done an expert job of arousing her and keeping her there. His cock-cloth did a poor job of hiding his own arousal, and he wanted nothing more than to house his cock in her, but he didn't dare.

Not yet. Not until he'd brought her down even more.

A hungry chattel is unable to focus fully on her lessons. Still, because he wanted to give her something new to think about while the meat cooked, he brought her hands up and secured them to the tree but didn't force her onto her toes because all he cared about was that she couldn't reach her sex. Although he'd rather stay near her so he could possibly hear her body's whispers, he needed to speak in private to the others.

Joining them around the cooking fire, he used a stick to draw a crude map of what they knew of Hevassen's valleys and mountains. Because they'd come across the area not that long ago, much was still unknown. It might go on forever or end at the edge of a sea. And although so far they'd only seen signs of the savages and Baasta, others might have made the place home.

"Those who left to track the wildings haven't returned," he said, his voice low. "There's a chance they've been attacked by savages."

"Or by the Baasta," his brother added.

"Yes, or by the Baasta. They may have become wolves and bears since they escaped."

"My uncle is among those who rode after the wildings," a tall but short-legged man said. "I promised his daughters I'd keep him safe."

Tarek idly added circles and curves to his drawing. "Everyone's safety is vital."

"Then why did you send them on a dangerous mission?"

Because he was expecting J'ron to confront him, he wasn't surprised by the harsh question. Besides, it was a necessary one. "What would you have done? Kept everyone together, ignorant?"

Most of the men muttered agreement, which caused J'ron to mutter under his breath. "I was wrong to send men in separate directions," he acknowledged. "I shouldn't have allowed my concern about the savages and wanting to see where the wildings went make my decisions for me."

"You had other things on your mind, and cock," Helki of the knife-scarred cheek said. "You'd just lain claim to a Baasta, a female worthy of becoming a valuable and useful sex-chattel."

In other words, he was being forgiven because lust had gotten in the way of his role as a leader? No, he couldn't accept that, especially when the excuse came from Helki, whose disappointment at not having been named warlord was well known. If this was Helki's way of undermining his leadership . . .

"All of us here are equals. I want to propose something, but we must all agree. If the others aren't back by midday tomorrow, I say we should all go after them. Track them."

"Is tracking necessary?" Helki asked. "We could force the females to take us to their village. Why haven't we already done that?"

He wasn't surprised by Helki's question, only that it had taken so long for anyone to voice it. "Because I refuse to take the chance that they'll lead us into a trap."

Helki's nostrils flared. "Force them to tell the truth!"

"How? By torturing them? If you believe anything a tortured captive tells you, then you're a fool."

"You call me a fool?" Helki's scar stood out against his reddened cheek, and he looked at J'ron and A'tala as if asking them to support him. "No warlord would ever—"

"No warlord would ever risk his warriors' lives, Helki. That comes before anything else."

Dark weight surrounded her captor. True, it was now night and she couldn't see him, so she shouldn't know what was going on inside him. He was leading her into a thicket where light from the fire didn't reach. That alone was enough to add weight to her own heart, but hadn't she learned to judge his moods?

Something was bothering him.

"I allowed you to eat as much as the others," he said when they reached the close-growing young trees. The middle of the thicket was bare of trees with enough room for two people to lie down next to each other while the rich growth served as a

natural shelter. Being surrounded both by the living wall and
Tarek made her feel claustrophobic, and his grip on the leash
didn't help. Neither did the way the touch of leather around
her neck seemed to permeate her entire body.

Most of all, she couldn't get beyond *him*.

"Did you hear me?" he snapped. "You were free to eat.
Don't you have any gratitude?"

"Yes," she blurted. "Thank you."

"Hmm. Do you use food to reward wildings?"

"I don't withhold food. It's important for them to see me as
the giver of good things."

"Ah." He'd been standing off to the side and turned away
from her as if concerned with other things. Now he spun around
and swept his hand over her breasts. "And that's a vital part of
the training, isn't it? Letting a wilding know who rules their
world."

That's not what she'd said!

"You're learning restraint," he went on. "And a little about
how I can give you pleasure." His fingers again trailed over her
breasts, this time lingering over the upper swell. "There are levels and layers. And reasons for everything I do."

Back up. Don't let him think you like this. "Reasons?"

Snaking his fingers through her loose hair, he pulled her
head back. Releasing her leash, he closed that hand over her
throat. She started to lift her bound hands so she could grip his
wrists, then stopped. What good would it do—and did she really
want to be free of him?

"Ah, the word matters, does it? What is this?" He touched
the pulse at the side of her neck. "Your heart's racing. Are you
afraid?"

"I . . . I don't know."

"You're honest." He sounded surprised. Despite the collar,
his hand on her neck seemed to claim every bit of flesh there.
His hands were strong and rough while her skin was soft, frag-

ile. "Tonight is about levels and layers, chattel. Becoming what I need you to be."

Was he talking about more than his determination to turn her into his sexual object? Then he released her hair and allowed her to straighten, and the question faded.

"Bondage can be a simple thing." He started untying her wrists. "Sometimes it's complex with many ropes and knots, leather, even chains, but it doesn't always have to be. That's where we're starting tonight."

Starting? Where will the night end?

Once he'd freed her, he massaged her arms until weakness spun into her and killed any thoughts of trying to run. The possibility returned when he removed the leash, but he was so close. So strong and swift.

"Turn around."

Feeling like a well-trained wilding, she obeyed. She stood with her back to him while he crouched and rummaged through the pack he'd brought with him.

"Remember what I said about simple bondage? A single rope, hands still free, delivers its own message."

Why? she ached to ask, but maybe she already knew. He wanted her groveling before him. But that wasn't all.

She would, if his force overruled her will, lead the Centrois to her people. Doom them.

Well aware that she had no chance of breaking free right now, she made a vow to herself and those she loved. She'd do whatever he demanded of her—up to a point. She'd become what he wanted—up to a point.

And he wouldn't comprehend her strength and determination until he tried to force her to cross a certain line.

Maybe because she was caught in her promises, he'd drawn her arms behind her and looped a rope around her elbows before she could prepare. Not content with a single strand designed to pull her elbows together, he wrapped the rope around them several more times. Her shoulders felt the strain, but so far it wasn't painful. The pressure increased a little when he secured the tie by spinning her collar around so the ring was at the back. He then ran a rope from the ring to the strands between her elbows. When he was done, he took a step back.

"Your hands are free, chattel. And your legs."

By bending her elbows, she was able to bring her hands forward, but what was the point? She couldn't reach anything, couldn't hope to stop him from doing whatever he wanted.

"You have beautiful breasts." He indicated the thrust-forward mounds and tension-hardened nipples. "But I don't want them free tonight."

She jerked away when he reached for them, but of course he easily brought her back around. Sweat beaded on her throat and upper lip. A heated rush softened her pussy. If he touched her there—

More ropes! The first going around and around her just above her breasts and tight enough to press the swollen flesh down. He'd left both ends of the rope free, and they now hung between her breasts. Despite her fierce attempt at silence, she whimpered and backpedaled when he made it clear he intended more rope to go under her breasts.

"Is that what a wilding does?" he demanded. Forcing his fingers under the already-secured breast rope, he pulled her back to him. "Defy her master?"

"You aren't my master!"

"Oh yes, I am, chattel. You just haven't fully comprehended that yet. But don't worry. I'll show you. I have to."

Despite her shaking legs, she remained in place while he wound rope under her breasts. Hating the strange confinement yet being excited by it, she looked down at herself. Her breasts had been squeezed together, making them appear larger.

"Whose are these? Who changed them? I'm not done, but first I need to judge your reaction."

Why was she trying to clamp her legs together? Making a lie of her feeble attempt at protecting herself, he reached for her crotch. The moment he touched her clit, she sighed. Weak, so incredibly weak. And alive.

"Your sex is awake, chattel." His voice was low, husky. "Begging for more."

She should have denied his claim, would have if he hadn't brought his wet fingers up to her face and made her smell herself. When she couldn't take any more of his superiority, she stared upward. The moon was a few nights past full but still round and bright. Revealing.

This tall, strong man wanted as much as she did. The proof lay deep in his eyes, his widespread nostrils, his parted lips. She heard his quick breathing.

He wiped her arousal on her cheek, then stepped back and stared down at her. She answered his stare with one of her own.

This is about sex, his expression said. *About fucking. Becoming animals. Both of us. Nothing more.*

I know, she told him.

And because she believed that with every beat of her heart, she stood unmoving when he held a breast in his hand while winding a loose strand around and around it, trapping it and making it throb. He secured his work by tying the end to the rope over her chest, then imprisoned her other breast in the same way.

Again she looked at herself. Again she felt herself slip out of her control and become his. She wanted. By all that was holy, she wanted.

His hands closed around her arms, and he pushed her back until she was leaning against a tree. "Don't move."

I can't. Surely you understand that my body has turned into something it's never been before.

When he pressed the heels of his hands against her belly, she thought he intended to test her sexual response again, and although she shouldn't have, she thrust her pelvis toward him. But instead of accepting the gift, he slapped her breasts, making the captured flesh sting. "What did I tell you? Do not move."

"I . . . I didn't mean—"

He slapped her breasts again. She moaned, not in pain but because the sensation had snaked down, and she was flooding herself. What was happening to her? How had he so easily stolen her will, her self-respect?

But wasn't this a gift?

When he leaned over and drew a breast into his mouth, she no longer cared anything about self-respect. Everything was about the fire raging through her. He sucked and pulled, ran his teeth over her nipple, bathed her swollen flesh and then licked off the moisture.

When he did the same to her other breast, she thought she'd faint. Beyond anything except need, she spread her legs and reached for him with her useless hands. He allowed her fingers to scrape over his side.

Back and forth, back and forth. Manipulating one breast and then the other. Bathing her skin with his saliva, nibbling her painfully hard nipples before closing his lips around them and pulling.

"Hmm, hmm," she moaned, and leaned into the mouth embrace. Her fingers again reached for his cock but were stopped by the damnable restraints around her elbows. "Hmm. Oh please!"

Releasing her breast, he shoved her hard against the tree. The moon spun silver light over him as he tore off his cock-cloth, revealing his huge and angry rod. Gripping it, he glared down at her. His gaze said he hated her ability to do this to him, but she didn't care and would never apologize.

"Damn you!" He furiously rubbed himself.

"Put it in me! I'll—"

"No!"

She didn't know how he mustered the strength not to bury his cock in her; maybe she'd never comprehend his self-control. Breathing hard, he spun her around and pressed her cheek against the smooth tree trunk. He left her like that, left her to fight with her breathing and heartbeat. Then he was back with more rope. After tying her wrists together, he released her elbows. Blood rushed back into her shoulders. "Thank you," she muttered.

"Don't thank me, chattel. Save your voice for curses."

12

Fuck her now. Get it over with.

But he couldn't because there were still lessons to be gotten through.

Careful. Otherwise, the lessons will touch you as well.

At the moment, she was on her knees, looking up at him even though he'd blindfolded her. He'd also gagged her—not because he didn't want her to speak, but so he wouldn't be tempted to put his cock in her mouth. Although he'd removed the ropes from her breasts, the marks were still there, and he traced them as he tried to place himself inside her mind. Undoubtedly she was afraid, although perhaps her fear came more from her body's betrayal than of him. He'd turned her on, not that he had doubts of his ability to excite a woman. What he had to guard against was taking himself too far while doing exactly that to her.

Spilling himself on her last night hadn't been enough.

"On your back." He punctuated his command by guiding her until much of her weight rested on her hands with her legs outstretched. Then he released her so she could reposition herself on her side, freeing her arms somewhat. "Spread your legs."

Shaking her head, she tried to sit up. Wondering how deep her defiance ran, he pressed down on her midsection. Under his hand, her breathing was quick and uneasy. He had a job to do, a journey to complete. Maybe she believed he was only interested in building her sexual fires and keeping them high and unsatisfied, but his reasons for everything he did ran much deeper.

Everyone, he'd learned long ago, had a line of defense. Whether they were sex-chattels, hostages, or war captives, the unfortunate creatures who found themselves pitted against Centrois' might fought to retain their dignity, their independence such as it was. But someone who had lost control over his or her body stood at the edge of that line. Sometimes it took almost nothing to force them into the dark pit of surrender. For others the battle took days.

Whichever it was with this one, he'd keep after her; he didn't want to destroy her spirit, but that might be the only way he could get the truth about her people out of her. And he had to! His people's safety and even survival depended on her knowledge—knowledge she'd eventually reveal to him.

And in the aftermath, she'd hate both of them.

Nari sighed, the sound tearing him from his inner battle. Seeing her clamped legs gave him a new idea—one more dangerous for himself but perhaps more effective.

After making sure he had a rope within easy reach, he rolled her onto her stomach and straddled her, facing her legs. Careful not to rest his weight on her hands, he created a loop in the end of the rope and slipped it over one ankle. Then, although she resisted, he bent her leg toward him. He tested his handiwork by running a finger between the rope and her. Good. Secure but not too tight. Making her even more his.

His groin throbbed as he loosened his hold on the rope and

allowed her to lower her leg. Leaning over her buttocks, he fought her sex smell's power while encircling her other ankle.

Obviously knowing he intended to hobble her, she tried to kick. Both loving and dreading the battle, he settled his weight on her ass and thighs. Unable to do more than weakly and ineffectively bend her knees, she put up little resistance while he worked. He'd left enough room between her ankles that he could get his hand around the connecting rope, which he now did. Then he pulled until her heels rested against his belly.

His buttocks pressed against hers, and his aching cock searched for a home. Where did her power come from? No matter, he *had* to destroy it, somehow. "You disobeyed me. I ordered you to spread your legs, but you fought. Now you'll learn not to do that again."

Her muscles strained as she tried to turn onto her side. At first he refused to grant her any movement, but her heat, her smell, her quick breathing and pounding heart were more than he could handle. Getting off her, he debated bringing himself to climax before doing any more to her, but along with the pain of need and want came a primal decision. In exciting her, he'd further excite himself. Judging how close he was to climaxing would tell him how close she was.

If only he could keep her—and himself—from flying into the abyss.

He helped her to roll back onto her side. Her breasts now hung loose and tantalizing, the effort of keeping her head up distracting her from him. She'd bent her knees to help her balance, and he took advantage by running a hand between her legs. When she tried to scoot out from under him, he grabbed a nipple.

His nipple.

And his body screaming in frustration.

"You aren't going anywhere, chattel. Tonight, and you, belongs to me." *If I can survive.*

In response, she pressed her thighs together. Although her

strength impressed him, he still found the space between her pussy lips. Burying his finger in the scant space, he started rubbing her there. She froze, her body tense and waiting. Experiencing. When she began rocking her head from side to side, he understood she was trying to distract herself. Maybe movement allowed her loathing of him to grow.

No matter. He knew what he had to do.

"It's not going to happen, chattel. Tonight is all about lessons of control and mastery. My understanding of you. And your surrender. Complete and total."

No, no, no, Nari chanted. She struggled to make the words a scream in her head, anything to override the sensations taking place in and around her cunt. She'd been wrong to believe she'd recovered from his earlier manipulations, wrong to believe she wanted anything except release.

Only, he wasn't going to grant her that. Instead, he touched and probed, taunted and stroked.

"Hmm. Hmm." The gag caught some but not all of her moans. She listened to them, trying to judge how much she was giving away, but what did it matter with his hand on her heated tissue and her body helpless?

Sudden tension ran through her. By the time she'd fought it into submission, he'd released her nipple. That hand now gripped her flank. The other—by the spirits—probed and kissed, taunted and rewarded, played at her entrance, promised more.

Gave not enough.

As long as she didn't try to move, he seemed content to hold on to her flank while doing what he wanted. Those teasing fingers were too much! Too intense. Too wonderful. She couldn't hold still.

Only, each time she jerked, he slapped her buttocks. It stung but only briefly. And in the aftermath, she found herself even more aroused. But what threatened to drive her to relentless screaming was the way he taunted her. A cock knows nothing about subtlety. It demands and gives. It owns rather than being owned, and a man only wants the ever-building tension to reach the top. To clench and release.

At least she believed it was the same for a man as it was for her.

If she was right, then he knew what he was doing to her. Damn him, damn him for giving her the smallest sip of water when she needed to dive into a swollen river!

He was shifting position again. Although he kept his hand between her legs, it had stilled. And his other hand was no longer on her. Even though she couldn't see, she lifted her head and strained to hear. Somehow kept from begging.

Her pussy spasmed once, twice. Those involuntary movements had always preceded a climax, but he'd just granted her clit a measure of relief, and the rest of her had eased back. She was still in heat but not desperately so.

Why, then, were her muscles twitching?

There! The hand no longer on her sex but joining the one in rolling her onto her back again. She managed to position her hands at the small of her back, and arching kept pressure off them. She stared into nothing.

"Do you remember what I said, chattel? I ordered you to spread your legs, but you refused. The next time you won't, because I'm going to reward obedience."

Weakness rolled over her at the word reward. Even as she imagined what she looked like silent and voiceless, limbs imprisoned, she couldn't deny that she needed what he was offering. And, although she didn't understand why, she trusted him not to hurt her.

Why would he when her value lay in her heritage and knowledge of her people? He wouldn't harm a valuable possession.

Possession.

She made herself face the question of what she'd do and say once he was done with her, but before she could begin to answer, he pushed her knees apart, forcing her to bend her legs so her pussy was open and available. Hating the blindfold, she again tried to look at herself. At him.

Warm air skittled over her wet flesh. His breath! As a convulsion slammed into her, she struggled to make sense of what was happening. He was sitting or crouched beside her, an outstretched arm on either side of her, and was leaning over, breathing in her sex smell, expelling his spent breath on her.

She waited, trembled, waited.

Another breath. Warmer and closer.

Desperate to protect herself, she started to straighten her legs. A slapping sound registered almost before he struck her breast. The rippling sensation fascinated her. Her nipple hardened even more.

"Unspoken message," he said, and closed his mouth over her breast. Alarmed by his closeness, his moist heat, she shivered. But instead of trying to escape, she struggled to press herself against him. She *was* in heat, no tempering, no control.

Gripping her flesh with his lips, he drew her deeper into his mouth. Was this what a man experienced with his cock housed in moist, heated darkness?

She felt herself flowing outward, bone and muscle melting, oozing everywhere until her world centered around that single breast.

Leveraging herself off the ground, she gave herself to him, thrashing from side to side in her attempt to surrender even more. Her legs and buttocks became all nerves, and the last of her strength stripped away. She panted, drooled.

Sudden cold!

Confusion gave way as she realized he'd released her breast. Behind the hated gag she begged him to take her like that again.

Catching a sharp sound, she willed herself to be silent. When it repeated, she understood that she wasn't the only one gasping for breath. He might have proclaimed himself master, but that mastery wasn't complete.

What did it matter? She couldn't change the balance between them. And even if she could, she didn't want to. She was his tonight. All of her. Scared and desperate. Living for and through him. Starved for his touch, his mouth, his cock.

"Soon I'll demonstrate certain sun-powered objects we've designed for use on sex-chattels, but not tonight. Tonight is about proving your body belongs to me."

With that, he grabbed her hobble and forced her feet up toward her buttocks. With her cunt even more exposed and his fingers there once again, dark realization weighed on her. Was there no way she could keep from telling him whatever he wanted to know?

Maybe not.

Despite her self-loathing, she simply shook, simply experienced. He started slow, two fingers barely reaching past the barrier of her labia. Other fingers claimed a swollen lip and drew on it.

"Haah. Ah."

The tension on her pussy increased, and she fought her way to the surface. Still, the drawing sensation became even more intense. Then suddenly she was free, at least there. When he wiped his slick hand on her belly, she realized she was too wet for his grip to hold. The victory might be a little one, but she took it and wrapped it around herself just as she'd taken heart from his less-than-steady breathing.

If she could find a way to bring him to his knees!

She almost laughed at the absurdity of that, would have if the fullness in her cunt hadn't continued to grow. If any strength remained in her legs, she couldn't find it. No longer did she want to close her legs. Instead, she lay with her head thrown back and her teeth gnawing on leather while he finger-fucked her.

She needed not this slow and steady tease but hard and

heavy. Not fingers but his cock. Still, she took his cruel gift and drenched him with her gratitude. She dimly realized he only rarely touched her clit, proof of how well he understood a woman's body. His fleeting touches were sunshine on a winter day, food in an empty belly, music and dancing.

And yet she didn't exist beyond his fingers, had no comprehension beyond that hot inner power.

"Hah. Hah-hah!"

"You're moving again." He slapped her belly, and the fingers inside her dove yet deeper. "Stop it! You do only what I tell you to."

I can't help it!

She thought he might slap her again when she ground her hips against the ground. Instead, he abruptly sucked out of her, hauled her to her feet, and pulled her against him, flattening her breasts. The arm around her waist kept her in place while he stroked and lightly pinched her ass with the other. Feeling his breath against the side of her neck, she leaned toward him. Although her weakness continued to bother her, she couldn't stop herself from pressing her pelvis against him. His cock burned her flesh, and she cried into her gag.

What was that? Fighting her way through the hot mist she'd fallen into, she realized he was raking his teeth over the side of her neck, the touch not gentle but not painful either. Unnerved by thoughts of what he might do, she arched away, then stopped because she was losing her balance. His grip on her waist tightened, holding her upright, reminding her anew of her helplessness.

He waited until she'd straightened, then resumed pinching her buttocks. Senses overloaded, she again fought to put distance between them. That earned her another of his light but stinging slaps followed by a brisk rub, followed by more pinching.

Giving up on her insane thoughts about escaping, she once

again leaned into him, her belly pressed against his cock. If only it was in her!

The hand around her waist inched lower, moving relentlessly to her crack. Dreading and anticipating, she froze. There. Palm and fingers diving into the space between her buttocks, a thumb pressing against her anus.

"Being touched there weakens a woman," he told her. "She feels invaded, maybe abused, maybe dirty, yet she loves the sensation."

No! Never!

"Has a man ever done this to you?" He ran his thumbnail from her waist to her cunt, pausing only to apply fresh pressure to her anus.

Like a dumb and compliant animal, she struggled to spread her legs. Like a wild and unthinking creature, she cried and begged, hating the gag.

"You didn't answer me, chattel. Have you been entered here?"

The instant his finger slid past the tight barrier, her muscles contracted. Her head roared; flames licked at her belly. Instead of retreating, he remained inside her, still as if resting. She stopped moving, stopped breathing. Felt.

"What is this? Something else I've taught you about yourself?"

Still not breathing, she nodded.

"Do you like it?"

No! Make him believe you hate—

"Never mind. Your body has told me the truth. You're ready."

For what?

"Confused? Good. That's the way I want you."

No, no, no.

"Listen to me, chattel. I'm going to let go of you, step back. I command you to remain where you are."

13

The moon loved Tarek.

At the thought, a cooling breeze slid over Nari's skin. She still needed to fuck as maybe she'd never needed anything in her life, but need's claws no longer relentlessly raked her flesh.

Not only could she now see because he'd removed her blindfold, but she could also think.

If the Baasta ever learned she'd allowed one of the enemy to touch her the way Tarek had, they might ban her, and yet she wasn't ashamed because she'd become powerful in a way that made a lie of her restraints.

When she'd spotted her first wilding, she hadn't known what to think, whether to be afraid, but her uncertainty had evaporated as she'd gotten to know and understand them. The same thing was happening now. What did she have to fear from a man blessed by the moon?

She'd worked moisture back into her mouth when he removed the gag but made no attempt to speak. In truth, she wanted to wait, to anticipate, to have the moon reveal why it blessed this man with its silvered light.

"What would your people think if they saw you now?" he asked as if reading her mind.

"Does it matter?"

"Oh yes, chattel. Answer!"

Don't fight him over this. Choose your battles. "They'd understand that I was doing what I needed in order to learn the Centrois' secrets."

His mouth twitched. "And would it be the truth?"

"I have no choice in what happens tonight. Don't ever tell yourself I wanted this." *Lie to him. Dig beneath his layers.*

All hints of a smile died. In its place now lived an expression she couldn't fathom. Maybe her words had stung him, but what did she know of his thoughts, of anything about him? "What is this about, Tarek? You hate me because I'm Baasta and are determined to bring me to my knees? Or are you after something else? Something you aren't willing to admit, even to yourself."

Moving so fast that his arm was a blur, he clamped his hand around the back of her neck and forced her head against his chest. As he'd done before, he cupped a dangling breast. "I should have left you gagged."

"Do it, then! Maybe it'll make you feel like a man."

He tensed. "I *am* a man, a warrior, warlord."

I know. I feel it in my every nerve and muscle. "And this is what a Centrois man does? He forces his female captives to beg to be fucked? Becoming a warlord takes nothing more?"

She'd barely finished when he roughly shoved her away. A rock dug into her instep, but she ignored it. The battle to control his anger had hardened both his features and his body, but the change only seemed to make the moon love him more. Its light danced on his muscles and pale, beautiful hair and caressed his tattooed chest.

"You're a brave woman," he finally said. "Taking great risks but brave."

The unexpected compliment brought tears she couldn't hide to her eyes. "A woman? Not a chattel?"

Again his expression changed. For a length of time that seemed to both go on forever and end too soon, they stared at each other. She tried to comprehend what was behind his intensity but couldn't, had never known such a man existed. A mix of stallion-like energy and great depth, he spoke to her body, her mind, and now her heart.

No! I don't want this!

He lifted his arm and slowly, so slowly extended it toward her. Mouth parted and muscles weak, she waited. And when he lightly touched her cheek, she leaned into it. "No, not a chattel."

Thank you.

Desperate to let him know how much his words meant to her, she turned her head so she could draw his fingers into her mouth. Wondering what had happened to her, she sucked, dampened, sheltered. And he stood there, free and wild. Gentler than she'd ever imagined him to be. The need to wrap her arms around him was nearly more than she could stand, but they were still tied behind her. His doing. His message of command and domination.

Maybe it was better this way. Maybe they needed to take the change in their relationship one step at a time.

If change was going to happen.

A night hawk cried out. Glancing up, she spotted the small predator perched on a treetop. Tarek, too, followed the hawk's flight, and when he looked back down at her, the warrior was back again, the man hidden beneath what life had made him.

Of course. Didn't he wear hawk symbols on his chest?

Drawing his hand out of her mouth, he wiped it on her breast. "Are you a black spirit? A witch?"

"No," she told him, although she wished she was. "I'm your captive."

"Are you? Is it as simple as that?"

"I don't know."

"You should. It's dangerous if you don't."

Instead of asking what he meant, she begged the moon to find its way into his heart and touch it with its cool light. But what would she do if that happened? Did she truly want to get close to the heart of a man who represented everything her people feared and hated?

As if answering her question, he hooked a finger through her collar ring. "What weapons do the Baasta have? They're able to keep the savages at bay, right? How is that accomplished?"

"That's why you brought me here, to discuss weapons?" Not giving herself time to think, she stepped closer. Once again his cock prodded her. "What about that weapon of yours, Tarek? Is it the only thing you believe you need to control your chattel?"

"Enough!"

Do you think I want it like this between us? "Maybe the truth is your penis controls you."

"Silence!" He forced her to her knees. She couldn't say whether he intended for her to be so close to his erection, couldn't say whether she'd destroyed the fragile peace between them.

Back arched so she could meet his hard gaze, knees apart to help balance, hands pressing against her buttocks and the memory of his hands on her body, she understood, at least right now, why a woman would accept the life of a sex-chattel. From the moment he'd captured her, she'd felt alive in ways she hadn't known were possible. Even when concern for her cousin had consumed her, a quiet but deep hum had remained to remind her of his power.

This man, this enemy, ruled her world. Her life and body.

And she wanted it. Needed it!

"I make you a promise, Nari. The time will come when you'll tell me everything the Centrois need to know about the

Baasta just as you told me about the savages. And I'll believe what you say because the truth will come willingly, not because I've used force."

She'd never betray her people! Never. And yet look where he'd taken her. What he'd wrenched from her body.

Her head grew heavy, and she stopped looking up at him. As her gaze ran down him, something in him reached out to heat her in a way that was both familiar and new. Settling onto her haunches brought her mouth closer to his cock. Her lips parted. Her teeth ached. Her breasts caught fire.

Like some mindless animal, she opened her mouth. Eyes unfocused, she stretched toward him, and when his tip touched her lower lip, she sucked him in. His body jerked. So did hers. He gripped her hair but didn't try to free himself.

He tasted sweet, like salt.

Hunger charged through her, turning her brave and reckless in ways she'd never known possible. Bringing more of him into her mouth-womb was both easy and the most insane thing she'd ever done. Walking into a savage-filled cave couldn't take any more courage and yet this was as natural as breathing.

To her shock and delight, he pushed himself in deeper. He still gripped her hair, now pulling so she was forced to look up at him. He stared down at her, eyes like midnight, chest heaving. His mouth opened, but he didn't speak.

In her mind, his cock became his gift to her, proof of his trust in her. For these magical moments, she'd let him know how much this trust meant to her.

More. Fill your mouth with him. Fuck him as you've never fucked a man.

A wavelike movement ran down his length, and she pulled the sensation into herself. A connection had been made, fragile but real. The growling energy that had claimed her pussy for so long roared again.

With her mouth full of him and his fingers pressing against

her scalp, she lost the distinction between them. She owned his cock, controlled him in ways he couldn't want but had no control over. And yet, her ownership was flawed and fragile, tested by her fierce heat.

"Damn you, damn you." He pushed, retreated, pushed again.

Damn you, damn you. She accepted him, let him go, accepted again. Every time she did, her cunt clenched.

Mouth-fucking Tarek was like being astride a galloping wilding stallion, like running into a storm, like touching the suns. Flames licked her arms and legs. Her fingers clenched, and she drove her toes into the ground. Lips locked around his hard weight, she pulled back as if trying to rip his cock from his body. Then, driven by her flaming body, she opened herself even more until his tip touched the back of her throat. She gagged, the sound angry and proud.

"Damn you!"

Curse me. Make me hate you!

"Ahh!"

There! The Centrois warrior driving into her as if he believed he'd die otherwise. She gasped and gurgled and held on as if her life depended on it.

"Ahh! Harr! Oh, oh, arr!"

He became a spear, a rock. For an instant, only his pelvis moved as he powered against her. Then he jerked, shuddered, jerked again. "Harr!"

Cum flooded her throat, his cock trapping it in her. A thin river dribbled from the corners of her mouth. Trying to swallow. Feeling slick heat on the back of her tongue. Tears rolling down her cheeks.

His climax died slowly, accompanied by grunts and curses. Looming over her, he roughly rubbed away her tears, then lightly slapped her cheeks until she released him. His smell continued to permeate her, and although she thought she might gag, she swallowed everything she could of his gift.

Then she slumped, back bowed and shoulders hunched. She couldn't stop trembling.

Couldn't silence her screaming, starving body.

"You *are* a witch."

"No."

"You cast a spell over me. Claimed ownership of me."

"No."

"Don't lie! Where does your power come from?"

Fury fed by her shrieking heat claimed her. "Don't blame me because you're a mortal! You wanted what happened."

"You can't possibly know what I want, chattel!" He walked in a slow, proud circle around her, and she had no doubt he smelled and sensed her arousal. Maybe he could taste it just as she still tasted him.

"Yes," she whispered. "I do. A man's needs are simple. It takes no great wisdom for a woman to learn what they are and grant them."

"That's what you believe you did? You took pity and let me come in you?"

"Not pity. Never that."

"Then what?"

"I don't know!"

He was still circling, coming closer with each circuit, making her dizzy, letting her feel him. "What about me?" she whispered when he trailed his fingers across her back. "My needs."

Even as he wiped sweat off the side of her neck, Tarek cursed himself. Damnation! Everything in him screamed of the need for physical and emotional distance between them. Although he still felt weak in the aftermath of his explosive climax, desire for more already began to grow. He could tell himself that the instinct to fuck was a given considering how long he'd been without a female, but he'd known lengthy celibacy before, and he'd never believed that only one female could satisfy him.

Until now.

The air had cooled since the suns set, and he was starting to feel chilled. It couldn't be any different for her, and yet he didn't think that was why she was trembling. He'd forced tension out of himself and into her mouth while pent-up need still filled her.

He circled her again, touching with fingertips and palm, telling himself to walk away and knowing he wouldn't. Couldn't. She was staring at the ground now instead of at him, which should have made things easier. Maybe it would be if his body didn't know hers, if her emotions weren't so naked.

Deliberately not questioning what he was doing, he hauled her to her feet, threw her over his shoulder, and stalked to where he'd set up the sleeping mat. Her weight felt right to him, her ass small and round and smooth under his fingers. She didn't struggle, didn't ask what he intended to do. And when he stopped and sought answers between her legs, she didn't try to reject him.

He set her onto her feet. "Kneel."

On a ragged breath, she did.

"Head down. Ass up."

Once more she did as he commanded. Then she spread her legs without him having to tell her, head to the side with much of her weight on her right shoulder.

He could have freed her hands. She wouldn't have fought. But her helplessness fueled his sense of command, and this way she wouldn't have to assume responsibility for her actions, unlike when she'd taken his cock into her mouth. This way he'd be in charge, maybe.

Stepping behind her took no courage, and straddling her seemed as natural as breathing. He briefly stroked her arms, then spread her ass cheeks and slid first one hand and then the other over her sopping sex. Over and over again he touched and tested. Her lips were large, soft, hot, the whole of her there like simmering meat. Slipping his fingers past her fragile defenses, he caressed her clit.

"Please, please, please," she chanted.

"What do you want?"

"To be fucked."

Turning his wrist, he ran his thumb into her dark heat. Her muscles clenched around him. "Like this?" he demanded. "Is this what you mean by fucking?"

"No. Damn it, no!" She pushed back against him.

His cock was expanding, responding. Right now he should walk away from her. If sanity and self-control meant anything to him, he would. But even as he harshly rubbed and then lightly struck her gyrating buttocks, he knew he wouldn't. Against all reason and understanding, he wanted to give her what she desperately needed—what he'd forced on her. She wasn't simply a captive, a hostage, a chattel-in-training after all. Somehow she'd become precious to him.

Bending lower so his body blanketed hers, he lifted her breasts, and took responsibility for supporting their familiar weight. She was trying to look up at him, the night giving away nothing of what she was thinking. Hopefully the same was true for him.

Pressing her breasts against her rib cage, he kneaded them. She'd been breathing as if she'd been running, but his manipulation awakened a new sound, a moaning, mewling that said she was weak and small and trapped by her fires.

"Your body loves me." Heeding the strain in his back and legs, he straightened a little. Whimpering, she struggled to do the same, but by pressing the heel of his hand between her shoulder blades, he easily kept her in place. "Your mind and heart may hate me, but your body sings another song."

Deep in his cock, a new fire ignited, making it difficult to concentrate on what he believed he needed to say. How he wanted to let her know he'd never admired or wanted a woman as much as he did her! But he didn't dare.

"No wonder you can tame wildings. You understand surrender."

"No. No."

"Yes."

To his surprise, she stopped arguing. Maybe her silence was deliberate, not that he could concentrate on the reason—not with her sleek thighs within easy reach. He shifted slightly and sealed the connection. At the touch, she stopped trembling. Her breathing still raged, as did his.

In his mind, she became a swan, a butterfly, a small bird. And although he'd never thought he could hold or comfort a bird, he wanted to give her what tenderness he was capable of.

No longer caring about the ache in his legs, he crouched again so his cock rested on the base of her spine. She stirred, then went still. Rocking back and forth caused his organ to glide over her, lightly abrading both of them.

He'd never held back when it came to fucking. For him, sex was all about achieving immediate and complete pleasure. Sometimes the woman climaxed, but he didn't care. Often, his lightning release left the female frustrated.

Still, he knew how to turn frustration into explosion and how to judge whether a woman teetered on the edge. Because he'd already found release, he could and would concentrate on more than himself.

He tested her readiness by placing his tip at her entrance. Holding back forced him to fight to bring enough air in his lungs, but he remained in position, waited, sensed.

As if hearing his unspoken question, she widened her stance. Then, despite her precarious position, she pushed back toward him and managed to suck a little of him into her pussy. Her muscles clenched, barely held him.

"You welcome me?" He spread her cheeks.

"Please. Please."

Are you begging? But if he threw her captivity at her, something would be ruined between them. "Have you ever taken a man like this? Like animals?"

"No! No!"

Counting slowly, he held back, forced her to anticipate. Forced himself as well. Then he reached ten. Powered forward.

There. In her. All the way.

Night pressed around him, but it was more than that. By sealing himself in her cunt, he'd become part of her and part of the nothingness that was fucking's instinct. His cock became his master, and he obeyed its commands.

Finally! Finally!

With his every thrust, Nari was pushed forward until she wondered if he might flip her onto her back, but she didn't care. Even with firelight dancing over her entire body, she concentrated on one thing—the hot pounding drums in her cunt. His cock was so large that the invasion terrified her, and yet she fed off the invasion and her fear. He'd become part of her, trusting his most precious organ to her. As a consequence, her inner recesses now belonged to him.

Breathing awkwardly, she struggled to turn to the side, hoping to catch a glimpse of him. She'd never felt so helpless while fucking. Never before wanted to wrap captivity around her.

As she locked her legs to give him more to push against a part of her drifted away from her straining body. In her mind she saw herself as a small and helpless animal caught in a monster's grip. The monster was feeding off her, yet feeding her at the same time. She'd turned into what he wanted of her, and he was gifting her with his great strength.

Overwhelmed by his power and yet determined to drink from his fire, she pushed against him. Although it seemed impossible, even more of him now filled her. His scrotum pressed against her ass, seeming to caress and pummel unbelievably sensitive flesh at the same time.

There was no way out! No hope of freedom. Only being fucked. Fucking!

A hot and heavy river swept over her. It swirled around her, rushing faster and faster, throwing her against rocks, trapping her in its raging caress.

"Yes! Ahh, yes!"

"Bitch!"

"Fuck, fuck, fuck!"

Clamping his hands around her midsection, he pulled her up and back. Sealed against him, she fought to swallow all of him. To force him to live in her cunt.

"Yes! Ah, fuck!"

There! The river everywhere! Water boiling. Her entire being rushing toward the top of the waterfall. Flying into space, then falling, falling.

"Ahh!"

14

"They're ghosts. Spirits."

"Maybe they live with the Divine Eternal."

Groaning to himself, Tarek fought back a response. The whole time the Baasta had been with his people, no Centrois had ever said that the Baasta might be blessed in any way. And yet why hadn't any of these experienced trackers seen a sign of the enemy?

He'd taken Nari back to the others at dawn because he didn't want to be alone with her any longer—didn't trust himself not to get even closer to her. During the short walk, he'd fought her impact on his senses and suspected she was waging her own private battle because she'd kept as much distance between them as possible. Upon their return, he'd ordered her to cook for him and the others. Although he'd kept her within sight, he'd called his fellow warriors to him so they could discuss whether to go after the still-absent trackers or wait a little longer.

To his relief, they'd returned while everyone was eating. As they filled their bellies, they described where they'd been and what they'd seen. True, they'd lost sight of the wildings when they'd all scrambled through a creek and hadn't been able to pick up the tracks, but fortunately they hadn't been attacked by either savages or the Baasta.

"At times we were certain we were being watched," Zareb, the eldest of the scouts, explained around the venison he was eating. "But whether by Baasta or savages we can't say."

"You saw no one?" J'ron asked sharply.

"No," Zareb shot back. "Remember, we were where we'd never been before. There was so much to look at, so much to be aware of. But we didn't imagine what we felt. Many men don't have the same feelings at the same time."

Nearly everyone nodded agreement. Out of the corner of his eye, Tarek noted that Nari was listening intently, as was her cousin, who'd helped with the meal preparation.

"If it was savages, they would have attacked," J'ron announced. "I defy anyone to say different."

J'ron would probably always be like a wolf, quick to attack, but because he shared a wolf's awareness of his surroundings and could easily determine whether other creatures were weaker or stronger than him, Tarek allowed him to continue.

"I say the Baasta know we're here." J'ron flung the thigh bone he'd been gnawing on at the women, just missing them. "While we sit and talk and our leader fucks his captive"—he glared at Tarek—"the Baasta plan our deaths."

Tarek sprang to his feet. Anger was like a storm raging through him, but although he stepped toward J'ron, that anger wasn't directed toward the younger warrior. How could he hate someone who spoke the truth?

"What would you have us do? Ride out in all directions? Spread out, we are weak and vulnerable. Or do we ride as one, making it easier for the Baasta to ambush us? What about the savages? Maybe it's them the scouts sensed."

"It doesn't matter. The Centrois need a leader of action, not one caught between a chattel's legs."

J'ron's attempt to ignore the hard questions Tarek had thrown at him only fueled Tarek's anger. That and hearing the truth repeated.

"J'ron's right," A'tala said. "This isn't the same as when we're home and training a new sex-chattel can entertain a man for many days. Tarek, force her to tell us what we need to know."

Force? Torture? No. Never that.

Before he could gather his thoughts, J'ron strode to where Nari and her cousin were. Grabbing Reyna, he wrapped his arm around her neck. His arm tightened, forcing a gasp out of her. Nari leapt at him, burying her claws in his arm.

"By the spirits!" J'ron bellowed. "I'll kill the bitch!"

Tarek sprang forward. Although Nari dodged, he easily clamped his hands around her wrists. Wrenching her off J'ron, he threw her to the ground and planted his foot in the middle of her back.

Breathing hard, he looked into the eyes of men who were like brothers to him. Only one set said he hadn't done the right thing—Saka's.

"Beat her."

"Tie her so tight that her bones break."

"Give her nothing to eat or drink."

"No!" As one, everyone fell silent. Never before had he defied his fellow warriors. He might be their leader, but survival depended on unity, and now men he considered part of his heart were determined to wrench the truth out of his hostage. Because that truth might be essential to their survival, he should want the same thing, but they hadn't spent nights alone with her, hadn't blended their flesh with hers. He had.

Only, it didn't matter. Only being a Centrois did. "There is another way to get the truth out of her."

Despite her frantic struggles, two men had easily secured Nari. She now stood with her arms and legs widespread, ankles secured via stakes that had been driven into the ground. They'd positioned her between two trees so they could tie her wrists to their branches. Other men had done the same to Reyna, but it seemed as if everyone's attention was on Nari.

Most of the Centrois were sitting, although several stood so close that she could hear them breathing. Tarek had ordered this, but she couldn't see him.

Don't abandon me, please! I need you.

What was she thinking? Hadn't Tarek said he knew how to force the information they needed out of her?

Fighting terror, she locked eyes with her cousin. Reyna looked equally frightened, but her gaze also carried a warning. No matter what was done to them, their people's survival depended on their silence.

I know, she silently agreed.

Even with the distraction of her public display and fear of the unknown, she had no doubt when Tarek returned. Conversations ceased, and men who'd been moving about stilled. All eyes turned in one direction. Tarek seemed even larger than before, darker and more intimidating.

He was looking at her and yet not.

He held something resembling a club that fit in his palm.

"Perfect choice," one of the young men said, pointing at the club.

"Gag her. Otherwise, every living creature will hear her scream."

"Take off the gag once she's exhausted. Otherwise, she won't be able to tell us what we need to know."

The words and horrid images all but wrenched a cry out of her. If she'd thought he'd take pity on her, she would have begged Tarek for mercy, but she barely recognized the man slowly moving toward her. This male was a stalker, a predator, more animal than human.

What was he carrying?

"No!" Reyna screamed. "Don't!"

"Gag her."

J'ron started toward Reyna, but Tarek's brother pushed him aside. "She's my responsibility," Saka insisted.

Reyna fought Saka's gag, not that it did her any good. Now wide-eyed, she could only make garbled noises beneath the thick leather strip.

A rough hand between her legs tore Nari's attention off her silenced cousin. She knew that hand, and yet it had never been this rough, this uncaring. "What are you going to do?" she demanded. "Please, what are you doing?"

His palm pressed against her trapped flesh. "This"—he held up the clublike object—"is proof of what the Centrois are capable of." He placed it against the side of her breast. "Proof of how we control our sex-chattel."

No matter how hard she tried not to, she couldn't stop shaking. Neither could she force her mouth to close.

"The suns power more than our motos, captive." The pressure on her breast increased. "We've discovered how to use Punta's suns to run a great many things, including this."

The *club* suddenly started vibrating. Was it filled with bees?

"Feel it on your breast, chattel. Experience. Know that it will continue to move as long as I want it to. And that this is only the beginning of its strength."

The vibration increased, creating a rippling sensation throughout her breast. She couldn't be sure but thought she now felt it in her other breast.

"Pleasant, is it?" Features impassive, he ground his palm against her pussy. "The kind of feeling that makes a woman moan while fucking."

He was right! The sensation was indeed pleasurable. Frightening but, what, desirable?

"Do you want to moan? Beg for more?"

No!

"Whether you do or not doesn't matter because in the end you will. Feel. Experience."

Feel what? Before she could form the question, the assault increased.

"Moan, chattel. Let everyone know how much you're enjoying this."

Even with the vibrations sending hot energy through her, she refused to utter a sound. What she couldn't do was stop herself from leaning into the object. *Careful. Careful. Don't let—*

"She likes it."

"I say she'll climax before the count of fifty."

"Fifty, ha! Increase it, Tarek. Bring her in forty."

"And then?"

Concentrate on what they're saying. Think. Never stop thinking.

She didn't believe the vibrations were getting any more powerful, and although she couldn't ignore their impact, she no longer felt overwhelmed. In truth, his hand against her crotch commanded more of her attention. If she could—

"Force it out of her, Tarek!"

J'ron's voice! The young, fierce warrior stood behind Tarek, and the look he gave her spoke of hatred, clear and clean.

"We're enemies, Nari," Tarek said in a low, unemotional tone. "Our having fucked changes nothing. I want one thing—my people's safety and victory. You want another—your people's survival."

Yes!

"Only one of us will succeed. Me."

Stronger. Insistent. Unbelievably fast movement relentlessly shook her breast, and the sensation flowed riverlike throughout her. Backing as far as her leg tethers allowed and leaning away from him, she fought her world.

"Ha, the chattel is already learning."

"Give up, captive. Enjoy, at least now."

"Listen to me!" Tarek leaned closer. "You will hear only one voice—mine. Earlier when I said I owned your body, you said I was lying, but before this is over, you'll have been silenced. You'll want only one thing in life, the pleasure I give you." Rough fingers brushed her hair off her cheeks. "But it'll go on and on until you can't take it anymore. You'll beg me to stop. I will, eventually. When you've told me everything I order you to."

This wasn't the man she'd spent the night with. She didn't know this stranger's voice and feared the determination behind it.

"Watch. Learn."

He removed the club from her breast and settled it in the valley between her breasts. As he ran it up and down, the pressure on her cunt let up, letting her know that he was no longer touching her there. Then, as the vibration became even more intense, he suddenly slid a finger inside her.

"Wet. Do you understand what's happening? Your pussy wants. It has begun to demand, to scream."

He was right. Even as she silently cried no, the part of her she had no control over demanded more stimulation.

"You're too easy on her. Take her down, now."

If she'd been able to concentrate, she would have cursed J'ron, but how could she speak when the only thing that mattered was what Tarek was doing—leaning close with his mouth near hers. Hating herself, she turned her head toward him and reached for him. Surprised registered in his eyes, and then his features blurred. His lips were waiting for her. She drank from them, took courage.

"Look at that! The chattel already crawls to her master."

"Be careful, Tarek! She's trying to cast a spell over you."

Something was flowing from Tarek to her, the sensations

soft, warm, real. Then, before she could return the message, he pulled back.

"Slap her! Show her her place."

"Silence!" Tarek roared. "Otherwise I'll do what I have to in private."

Have, not want? Could she believe that?

But she couldn't think with the ever-moving object branding every inch of her breasts. Not content with fueling fires there, he ran the club over her neck and arms, then down her sides before painting her belly with energy. He kept his finger in her sopping entrance. Desperate to deepen the contact, she sank lower. She closed her muscles around him. A moment later, they clenched and held.

"What's she doing? Damn it, Tarek! All we can see is you."

"Listen to her. What more do you need to know?"

At the comment, she forced her mind onto the sounds she was making. There was nothing human about them, nothing quiet or calm or in control.

Gone! Empty.

How foolish she'd been to believe he'd finger-fuck her until she climaxed! She should have been ready for this cruel desertion.

"Gag her, Saka," Tarek commanded. "I don't want the mountains to hear."

"No!" She looked wildly around for Tarek's brother. His approach was slow and deliberate. She saw no anticipation in the younger man's eyes, only the look of a man doing what he had to.

Seeing the length of leather coming closer, she started shaking her head. Suddenly her right leg quivered. Distracted, she looked down to see that Tarek was running the club up and down her thigh. "Feel the magic, chattel," he told her. "Think of nothing else."

He was right. She barely noticed the leather pressing her mouth open, barely reacted as Saka snugged it into place. Only then did she comprehend what had been done to her, and why. She'd been silenced again, her voice trapped just as the ropes trapped her limbs.

And her flesh belonged to the object in Tarek's hand.

"Does she climax easily?" someone asked.

"Easily enough." Moving the club to her left leg, he started running it up and down the inside of her thigh.

Shaking, she tried to draw away.

"Give up, chattel. You can't move. Don't try."

Despite the tension it caused to her wrists, she leaned forward so she could watch Tarek. The object wasn't as firm as a stick, and the hide covering was so smooth that it glided over her. She couldn't tell about the handle, but the knob where the energy was concentrated had been designed for pleasure, not punishment.

Taking his time, Tarek trailed the club from her thighs down to her foot, then up the outside. When he was done, he pressed the knob against her buttocks.

"Concentrate. And ask yourself if there's a limit to its power." He lessened the contact so it fairly shimmered over her skin. The sensation raced up to her armpits, then to her throat, making breathing difficult. "Concentrate."

The vibrations were becoming even more powerful, endless rippling seeking her core once more. She struggled to separate herself from it. At the same time, she longed to embrace the hot movements.

"Fight it. Fighting makes the surrender even more complete."

With his head bent forward, she couldn't concentrate on his features. If only she could! That way, maybe, she'd think of something other than her body.

No more pressure on her buttocks. Instead, the club now repeatedly tapped her side, and the finger in her core swirled. She gurgled into the gag.

"Scream, chattel!" J'ron hissed. "Scream over and over again."

15

Sweat was making her hair stick to her neck, but even worse, she was losing feeling in her arms. If she didn't take the tension off them . . .

The act of straightening shouldn't have been that all-consuming, but by the time the ropes were no longer digging into her wrists, Tarek had removed the club. He'd also withdrawn his finger from her pussy and was holding it under her nose. "Smell yourself, Nari."

Nari? He hadn't called her a chattel.

Before she could ponder the reasons, he positioned the club so she had a clear look at it. It was still vibrating but not as intensely as it had been a few moments ago. "The truth lies in this." His tone was flat. "There's no need for us to torture captives or hostages, no need to force sex-chattel to submit. Without causing pain, this simple object turns enemies into our pets. Experience."

His features tense, he ran the club down her torso. Then, as she shook and sobbed, he slid it between her legs. Movement quickened. Her cunt tightened, heated.

"Hmm." She couldn't stop her head from thrashing. "Hmm."

"Experience. Love and hate."

The vibrations were increasing, increasing, reaching the level she'd experienced before and then passing it. The club pulsed against her cunt like some concentrated earthquake.

"Hmm. Hmm!"

"Feel this, Nari. Understand helpless pleasure."

Although she rocked forward and back as rapidly as her splintered muscles were capable of, the club settled against her clit. Wailing, she cursed the warrior strength that made it so easy for him to trap her like this. And she cursed the waves of pleasure he'd trapped her in.

"Do you want to come?"

"Hmm. Hmmm."

"Answer me, Nari. Do you want to come?"

She wasn't there yet. The sensations were too new, still building, confusion reigning. But the vibrations were never-ending. Driving her further and further into herself. By turn she fought for freedom and embraced this assault on not just her sex, but also everything. Heat and cold attacked her at the same time.

And his voice. Always his voice.

"Thank me for what I'm doing. Thank and curse. Love what I'm doing to you. Love and hate."

Her throat was becoming raw. She *had* to stop sobbing into the gag, but how?

"What's happening, Nari?"

Nerves snapping, eyes burning, needing, *needing!*

"Can you hear me? Maybe there isn't enough of you left."

Even as she struggled to hold on to what was left of her resistance, it flowed out of her. Died. Replaced by, what? No matter how desperately she tried to concentrate on her bonds and the enemy all around her, most of all the man doing this thing to her, pleasure held her in its grasp. She wanted freedom! She craved this imprisonment.

Most of all, she was rushing toward a violent climax.

Nearly too late, she remembered how sensitive her clit became after climax. If he kept the club against her, how could she stand it?

Fight. Fight! Deny your body.

"You have no secrets, Nari." Tarek slid the club from her clit to the puckered skin over her anus. "We know everything you're feeling."

You can't! You're men.

"Go on, fight this."

Leaving her ass. Returning to the entrance to her womb. Gifting, relentlessly gifting. Making her sob in helpless frustration.

"Fight, Nari. It's the only weapon you have."

She should ask what he meant, but how could she with her entire body moving in time with the club's rhythm? She lost herself in sweet agony. Felt water rush around her as if she was being hurtled toward the edge of a waterfall.

"Gaah! Gaah."

"Surrender now. Surrender!"

"No!" The gag swallowed most of her cry.

Fighting herself was exhausting, and yet she shook and shivered, trying to break free of the instrument she loved and feared.

Despite the film that had settled over her eyes, Tarek's face came into focus. She couldn't say what she was looking for, if anything. She found not victory but compassion and regret. Unless he was lying to her.

"Do it!" someone insisted. "Stop playing with her."

Tarek cursed, then leaned close. "I won't hurt you. If nothing else, I won't do that."

Confused, she tried to look at him again, but he'd crouched down in front of her, and the moment he spread his hand over her mons, she lost touch with her world. Colors swirled and blended, and the air was full of birds singing in tune with a faint but deep drumbeat. Weightless, maybe formless, she moved to the beat. In her mind's eye, the colors glided over her naked and miraculously free body. Yellows, reds, and oranges blessed her with warmth while blues and grays brought a cool breeze. Arms spread wide to embrace everything, she began singing with the birds. The where and how of her existence didn't matter, only the experience.

Only one man's touch.

As quickly as her dream world had appeared, it died like mist under the summer suns. Once more her legs and arms were restrained, her voice silenced. The instrument of torture and pleasure pressed against her cunt, and Tarek's hand embraced her mons. Claimed her body.

What?

No, not that! Not the club pushing on her labia, lashing them with the promise and threat of a climax.

Not just one but endless explosions.

Until she'd lost her mind.

Even before the tip slid past her fragile defenses, she knew it was going to happen. With no barriers left, the fast-paced humming invaded not just her pussy but also her entire being.

"Haah. Haah!"

"Listen to her. Sounds like cougars fucking."

"A cougar's scream puts her pitiful cries to shame."

"But she's there, isn't she, Tarek? Helpless and hopeless, right?"

If Tarek answered, she didn't hear. Her body was clenching, tightening until she thought her bones might splinter. A climax slammed into her, burning like lava, shattering her mind and muscles. "Haaa! Ahh! Haaa!"

"Look at her. Damnation, what I wouldn't give to feel that."

The tidal wave slowly subsided, jerking and erratic. But instead of the deep drifting into nothing she'd always experienced before, waves continued to slam into her. She dimly understood that the constantly buzzing club housed in her was responsible.

"Ahhh! Ahhh!" Her head fell forward, then snapped back. She lifted herself higher onto her toes, reached for the ropes securing her arms to the branches so she could possibly leverage herself up. And as she struggled, her climax continued. "Ahhh!"

"Got her! Feel it, Baasta whore! Feel and fight."

Cunt muscles jerking, flames melting her down, waves rolling through her, rolling, rolling.

Exhaustion ate at her and buckled her knees. She sagged in her bonds, twitching in time with something beyond pleasure.

Take it away. Please, please, please! I can't take—

Before she could think how she might give voice to her plea, the assault abruptly ceased. A small measure of strength returned to her wrecked muscles, and she blinked until things came back into focus. Tarek was standing beside her, his neck tendons so taut she thought they might snap.

"What are you doing?" J'ron demanded. "You can't stop now."

Others voiced their agreement, but Tarek ignored them. No matter how intently she stared, his eyes told her nothing of what was going on inside him. Then he touched the vein at the base of her throat, and at the contact, her spent pussy convulsed one more time.

"Go after her." J'ron stepped closer. "Break her down. It's the only way we'll learn the truth."

With his finger still on her vein, Tarek spun toward J'ron. "Silence!"

"What is it?" someone else asked. "J'ron is right. You can't stop now."

"Yes, I can. And I have." He again brushed hair back from

her sweat-coated forehead. "This isn't a warrior's way. And I'm a warrior, a warlord."

J'ron reached for the club, but Tarek knocked his hand away. The two men squared off at each other, making Nari think of grizzly about to do battle. J'ron was slightly taller than Tarek, but the younger man lacked Tarek's deeply defined muscles and mature features. J'ron's shoulders weren't as broad, and his hands were smaller. Most telling, Tarek's determination coated his entire being.

She wanted to believe he'd come to her rescue, but he was her captor. The man who ruled her body as she'd never guessed possible.

"Enough." Saka stepped between the two. "I speak with my brother's voice. How can we call ourselves warriors if we treat our prisoners like animals?"

"They *are* animals!" J'ron insisted. "Not human."

What was she? Surely no self-respecting woman would willingly surrender her soul for more of the sexual stimulation Tarek had subjected her to. But although its intensity still frightened her, now that the storm no longer gripped her, she faced the truth. She'd never experienced such intense pleasure. Never known a man could take ownership of her the way Tarek had.

"Think about what our *leader* just said." J'ron directed his comment to the assembled Centrois. "He believes we should risk our lives because he places his whore above us."

Tarek started toward J'ron, then stopped. Silence tightened the air, and although she desperately needed to be let down, Nari didn't try to get Tarek's attention.

In the distance, a moto hummed. As the sound increased, all eyes turned in that direction, all except for Tarek. When he looked at her, she believed he wished he'd never seen her.

"It's Helki," someone said. "Traveling as if the savages are after him."

* * *

Helki's announcement was simple, and yet not. He'd been following fresh turkey signs when he spotted a trio of savages fishing at a nearby creek. Because he'd been on foot at the time, he didn't believe the savages had heard him. From what he could tell, they hadn't posted a lookout and were intent on spearing as many fish as they could.

Although too much of his mind remained on Nari, Tarek forced himself to concentrate. He'd released his chattel—if that's what she was—from her spread-eagle position and after removing her gag had secured her near her cousin. The two females were out of earshot, for the moment no longer his fellow warriors' concern.

But they were still his. As J'ron had demanded to know, who came first with him—his people or a woman he hadn't known existed until a short time ago?

Icy fury filled his veins. Standing, he clenched his fist to his chest. "Maybe the savages are like feeding wolves. Right now they're thinking of nothing except filling their bellies, and that makes them vulnerable. *And* when they're done fishing, they'll return to their caves."

"With us trailing them."

Tarek nodded. "On foot."

He thought someone, most likely Helki, would disagree, but no one did. Even as he acknowledged their nods, a weight settled over him. When he'd been with Nari, his responsibility as warlord hadn't mattered. Even with knots of sexual tension deep in his belly, he'd felt free. A man with a woman.

But that had been fantasy. Planning an attack against the savages was reality, as was finding the Baasta.

Nari waited until the Centrois had taken off before giving her cousin a tentative smile. Tarek and Saka had connected new leashes to their collars and the stakes that had earlier immobilized her legs. These leashes had hard fastenings that locked around the collar rings, and similar ones were attached to the stakes. Although all she wanted to do was continue to sit, the leashes allowed for considerable freedom of movement, but a thorough examination had confirmed what she'd suspected. Only the Centrois could free them.

"I have plenty of water left." Reyna held up the water bladder she'd been given. "Drink all you want."

"I have." She patted her stomach, only vaguely aware that she was naked while Reyna wore her dress.

"Are you all right?"

"Fine," she answered without thinking. Then she reconsidered. She had to tell someone about what she'd experienced, and if not Reyna, who? "I am now, but back then I thought I might die. Maybe, if he hadn't stopped, I would have."

"You looked as if you were being struck by lightning. The way you thrashed around . . . I hate him!"

"Don't!" Shocked by her outburst, she uncrossed and recrossed her legs, stalling. Her pussy was still red and swollen and she didn't dare touch herself there. "I'm sorry. I didn't mean to yell at you."

"I know." Reyna sighed. "What was that thing? No Baasta has ever thought of trying to capture the suns' energy, and yet the Centrois—"

"Yes."

"I've been thinking about what our aunt and other women told us about when they were sex-chattel," Reyna said after a brief silence.

"About there being as much good as bad in their lives?"

"I was dying to know what they were talking about, but I didn't dare ask. The way they'd look at each other and giggle—"

"And the way their faces turned red."

"Your cheeks are inflamed."

Nari pressed her hand against her cheek, not surprised by the heat there.

"And not just there." Reyna indicated her crotch.

Careful to keep the touch light, she ran a finger over her clit. A pleasure wave rolled through her.

"What was it like? Agony?"

"No! No. As if I was being fucked by a suns-powered cock."

"Ah." A wistful smile transformed Reyna's somber features. "I wish—"

"No, you don't."

"Certainly not with so many men watching."

That's right. She had had an audience made up of men who hated her. "I kept coming. No matter how hard I fought, my cunt continued to scream."

Wide-eyed, Reyna reached out. Although they'd been positioned so they couldn't touch each other, Nari felt the contact. "If he hadn't stopped, pleasure would have become pain, and pain would have turned into something worse."

"Yes."

"And to make it stop, you would have told him anything, wouldn't you?"

Would she have betrayed her people? Could she have stopped herself? "I can't bear to think about what the Centrois are capable of. I fear they're like we are to the savages."

"Don't say that! Were you terrified?"

"I'm not sure I was capable of thinking. He . . . he whispered something to me. He said he wouldn't hurt me."

"He's a monster! He raped you."

"No, he didn't."

"What?"

"Don't look at me like that. Despite what he called me, I haven't become his sex-chattel, and when we fucked, it was because we both wanted it." She took a deep breath. "Do you think I want to admit that? But I have to. You deserve . . . he knew how to excite me and used his skill well, but I wanted it. Every time he touched me—"

"The Centrois are our enemy. How can you say you wanted anything from him?"

Suddenly exhausted, Nari rested her head in her hands. "When I'm with him, I see a man, not the enemy."

She expected Reyna to call her insane or even a traitor, but when her cousin didn't, she looked up. "What?"

"It . . . was like that when I was with Saka."

16

If it hadn't been for the trees, the suns would have burned them before Reyna finished. At the beginning, Saka had given every indication that he'd wanted nothing to do with her and had reluctantly accepted responsibility for her only because otherwise she might have been subjected to more of J'ron's hatred.

Still shaken by her rape, she hadn't tried to break past Saka's silence, but when morning came without him having forced himself on her, she'd thanked him. He'd barely acknowledged her gratitude. Instead, he'd asked if she had children. When she'd told him no, he'd looked relieved. She couldn't say why she'd told him about her older sister and the newborn niece she'd helped bring into the world and how much she wanted her own baby.

"I cried when I told him that. I tried not to let him see, but he did. That's when he said he has a son."

"A son?"

"And a woman he wanted to make his wife. Maybe he would have succeeded if the man she'd been sold to hadn't beaten her so badly. She died in childbirth, and he hasn't spoken her name since because it hurts too much."

"Sold? She was a chattel?"

According to what Saka had told Reyna, the woman he'd given his heart to had been captured along with others from a tribe unwise enough to step onto Centrois land. As a young and beautiful female, she'd been entrusted to an older Centrois man to train in the ways of sex-chattel. Saka's uncle had pressed Saka to learn from the older man's skills, and the longer he'd spent with the woman, the more he came to care about her.

"I kept asking questions because he seemed to need to talk," Reyna explained. "He spoke of the music in the woman's voice. According to him, when she sang, children stopped crying, and those weighed down by grief found peace."

"He told you that?"

Blushing a little, Reyna nodded. "Neither of us slept more than a few moments last night. Instead, we talked—even while we were having sex."

"I was so afraid for you."

"As I was for you. Saka is so different from Tarek. He doesn't want to ever be a warlord. He admitted he's only rarely had sex since her death. He chooses sex-chattel he knows nothing about. His climax comes quickly; then he walks away." She sighed. "It wasn't that way between us."

"Because he *has* to keep you with him. Reyna, it's his duty."

"He didn't have to put his arms around me and comfort me when I had a nightmare, but he did. And when I cried and begged him to let me go, he wiped away my tears."

Even with what Reyna had told her, the thought of quiet, remote Saka showing such tenderness still shocked her. "What did he say then?"

"That he couldn't free me but wished he could."

"What? He could have followed you home."

"We talked about that."

"You did? What else?"

"Nari, promise you won't tell anyone this."

"Who do you—"

"Promise!"

"All right. I promise."

Looking relieved, Reyna explained that after having sex for the first time, they'd lain together resting and getting to know each other. She'd told him a few things about Baasta life, such as how much having wildings had changed things, but she had deliberately avoided any mention of the village's well-hidden location. "He's sick of fighting and deaths. He'd hate himself if he had any hand in shedding Baasta blood."

"And yet he's here."

"Because he's Centrois." Her cousin's tone was soft and melancholy, nearly heartbroken.

"You can't be falling in love with him!"

Eyes downcast, Reyna shook her head. "Love? No. I barely know him. But something happened between us last night that went beyond fucking. While we were together, it didn't matter who we were, just that we were getting to know each other. I want to lighten his heart, to help him look forward instead of mourning what he lost."

"A Centrois heart shouldn't matter to you."

"Don't tell me what to think or feel!" Reyna's youthful features hardened. "And don't try to tell me you don't feel anything for Tarek. I know better."

"He did this to me." She indicated her still-tender pussy. "Forced that incredible object on and in me until I couldn't stop coming. Locked this around my neck." She tugged at her collar. "Made me his prisoner." *I hate him.*

Don't I?

* * *

"There."

Although he'd already spotted the distant trio of savages, Tarek nodded in response to Helki's extended finger. Because he and the other Centrois warriors had been crawling on their bellies, he was fairly certain the savages hadn't spotted them, and they'd been careful not to be make any sound, but he was still uneasy. Even with what Nari had told him, the ways of the savages were largely unknown. Yes, killing the three as Helki wanted to would send a message to the rest of the savages that the Centrois were a powerful enemy, but that wasn't enough.

"We must take one alive," he whispered. "Force him to take us to the others."

"And then I'll slit his throat." That came from J'ron.

Tarek acknowledged J'ron's bragging with a long stare. Because they'd discussed their plan earlier, he had no need to direct the others' actions now. Most would remain where they were while no more than six would advance. As one, those he'd chosen to accompany him started crawling again, the distance between them close enough so they could keep each other in sight. Everyone's sun-stick was at the ready. He would have preferred to insist that Helki, J'ron, and A'tala remain behind, but if he had, they might accuse him of excluding them because they questioned his leadership. He didn't mind the questioning since it forced him to keep his fighting skills sharp. He just didn't want to be distracted from today's goal.

As he made his way on his hands and knees, the familiar rhythm of warfare settled over him. For as long as this took, he existed only as a warrior, a fighter, a predator. He lived to protect his fellow human predators. They had a common goal and had made a common commitment to risk their lives. At times like this, he felt more animal than human. Everything condensed down to primitive emotion. Fight. Kill. And when the killing was over, fuck.

Nari. Alone and helpless. Waiting for his return. Her life depending on his.

Unnerved because a female had never distracted him like this, he forced her image out of his mind. What he couldn't close himself off from was the feel of her, her and smell and warmth.

By the time he'd covered half the distance separating him from the savages, the creatures had stopped fishing and were cleaning their catch. Their voices carried, proof that they believed they were safe. He couldn't understand what they were saying, and the harsh tones of their occasional laughter grated on his nerves. Although they were using their knives, their spears lay nearby.

Despite the risk, he stood, sun-stick held in front of him. Quickly looking around, he saw that the others were in position, waiting for his command.

"Now!" He fired.

The blasts from his and the other sun-sticks hurt his ears. Well-trained in handling his weapon, he hadn't closed his eyes. One of the kneeling savages flopped backward, his legs trapped under him. The creature jerked once and then went still. Another grabbed his bleeding arm and started screaming. More blood gushed from a thigh wound. The third savage started to stand; then the strength went out of him, and he sank back onto his knees, his hair turning red.

In the past, he would have been shouting with excitement, but now all Tarek felt was a sense of a task having been completed. His ears were still ringing, and his fellow fighters were either shaking their heads or pressing their hands against their ears. He couldn't remember that many sun-sticks going off at the same time before.

At another signal from him, they approached the savages. The savage with his legs under him still hadn't so much as twitched. The one with the head wound remained on his knees and appeared oblivious to his surroundings, but despite the blood flowing from his arm and thigh, the third stood on wide-spread legs.

Tarek answered the savage's look of disbelief by nodding. Maybe the creature didn't know he was bleeding to death, and perhaps it was better that way. Leaving him, he stood over the one who was on his knees.

Kicking him in the belly, Tarek ordered him to stand.

The savage lifted his head. His eyes were unfocused, mouth open, nostrils flared.

"Stand up." Tarek kicked again.

If the savage felt the impact, he gave no sign. Instead, he sank toward the ground, folding inward. His head drooped.

"He's dying," Tarek announced.

"So is this one." J'ron indicated the bleeding stander.

The length of time it took the savages to die didn't concern Tarek. What did was accepting that there'd be no hostages, although since communication with them was impossible, maybe it didn't matter. He gained a measure of satisfaction from taking possession of the fish and crude weapons, which he intended to show to the others once they returned to them.

"We can't stay," he said. "The noise—"

"You want us to leave? Run like jackals?"

He'd expected J'ron to argue, but that didn't make him any less weary, especially not with Helki and A'tala backing him up. "No, not like jackals. Like seasoned warriors who know how to avoid being ambushed."

"Ha." J'ron's interest in the spear he'd picked up was far from casual. "You want to return to your chattel. Don't deny it!"

All weariness at having a handful of others question his decisions evaporated. "I'm a Centrois warrior, J'ron. That comes before anything else, as it should with you. Look around. We're in the open with ridges all around. As long as he has two ears, even an old savage with only one eye could find us."

If J'ron was chagrin, the young warrior gave no indication, but at least he didn't argue. And unless he was mistaken, Helki was paying close attention. "I speak from long experience as a warrior and warlord," Tarek continued. "We're going to return to camp. At first light, we'll come back here. If savages have concern for their dead, if they need to bury them, they won't leave these for animals to devour. They'll take them back to their caves and in doing so, they'll leave tracks." He didn't bother adding that he intended to follow those tracks.

As the others muttered agreement, J'ron concentrated on the spear he'd claimed. Would the headstrong warrior ever learn to think and observe before speaking? If not, a brave fighter would never become wise, and that lack of wisdom could kill him.

Despite his gnawing unease at the possibility that the sun-sticks's noise had carried, Tarek took off at a brisk walk toward where the rest of the warriors waited. From here, he couldn't see them, proof of how far the six had traveled.

The others matched his pace, their attention frequently going to the high ground around them. They'd spread out as defense against presenting a small target, and he relaxed a little as they began climbing. Only once did he look back at the dead savages who'd indeed struck him as less than human because of their long body hair and rank smell. Their thin penises extended nearly to their knees, further disgusting him. The idea of being forced into hand-to-hand combat made him shudder.

"I'd like to fish here sometime," Saka admitted in a low voice. "And hunt. Did you see all those prints?"

"Yes. Some could belong to wildings."

"Maybe you should capture one and get your *chattel* to gentle it for you."

His brother's emphasis on the word *chattel* caught his attention. Not slowing his pace, he glanced at him.

"That's not how you see her, is it?" Saka asked. "If she was nothing but a possession or hostage valuable for her knowledge, you would have driven her crazy from climaxing, maybe forced her into unconsciousness. But you haven't stripped her of her will."

And I won't. I can't. "Do you believe I should?"

A quick shake of Saka's head gave Tarek the answer he'd expected. "When I first took control of her," Saka said, "Reyna was terrified of me, but she refused to beg. That surprised me, and I wanted to learn more about her. She didn't say much until I asked her what brings her the most pleasure." He shook his head again. "She told me she loves summer's warmth on her hair and butterflies on her fingers. Cradling a humming bird is like holding a baby."

"She said that?"

A wistful smile eased Saka's usually somber features. "I told her about Dio."

Dio, the son who'd been born as the chattel Saka had loved with all his heart, was dying. To have opened up his heart to a captive—

"Attack!"

As Tarek spun around, his brother did the same. The gentle rise to their left and slightly behind them boiled with life as savage after savage burst into view. "Down!" he yelled as he sprinted for a nearby boulder. "Don't fire until you have a target."

As the screaming savages rushed toward them, he crouched behind the boulder, which was large enough to shelter both him and Saka. His heart hammered, and his world took on the familiar red hue it did when his life was in danger. The savages didn't seem to care that they were in full view, but they zigzagged as they ran. Despite his erratic heartbeat, his grip on his sun-stick remained steady. It took the weapons time to recharge after they'd been fired; hopefully it had been long enough.

A shot, followed almost immediately by another. Shrieking, one savage fell forward. The others stopped and stared open-mouthed at their fallen companion.

"Shoot!" Tarek yelled.

Looking over the top of the boulder, he aimed and fired. The savage he'd targeted slumped to his knees, hands slapping at his bleeding belly. Tarek's ears rang as from nearby hills and depressions his fellow Centrois discharged their weapons.

Almost as one, the savages dropped to the ground, making it impossible for him to tell how many had been hit. With his sun-stick now useless, he shoved it back into its carrying bag and grabbed his spear.

Careful to keep all but his head behind the boulder, he studied the enemy, becoming calm, focused, and determined. At times like this when his life was in danger, he became one with the Divine Eternal and placed everything in the hands of the being responsible for Punta and everything on it.

Some of the savages had reached rocks while others found shelter behind bushes. Although a total count eluded him, he knew one thing: the savages outnumbered him and his five companions. Where were the rest of the Centrois?

Silence had followed in the wake of the explosions, but now the savages started jabbering, their voices making him think of angry crows. Unlike the fishermen who'd worn only cock-cloths, these had on bear or cougar capes and necklaces made from animal teeth.

One of the savages screamed and jumped to his feet, clutching a long, thick knife decorated to look like lightning strikes. His cheeks had been painted with the same symbols. When he screamed again, the others stood. As one, they charged.

Tension built around and in him. He became more than a

single warrior, part of a proud and brave people, raised like all Centrois men to fight, protect, defend, and die if necessary.

But he didn't want to die today, not just because the sky was blue and the sun warm, not simply so he could continue to protect and defend.

There was a woman waiting for him. Needing him if she was to continue living.

Despite their hairy bodies, the savages had no eyebrows or lashes. He'd noticed that unimportant detail because he waited until the last instant before hurtling his spear at the nearest attacker. Because he'd aimed at the unprotected gut, rather than at the chest with its barrier of breastbone, his spear penetrated so deeply that when the savage spun around, Tarek saw the tip protruding from his back. Any thought he had of retrieving his weapon died, and he grabbed his knife.

A quick appraisal of his surroundings told him all he needed to know, and more. There were more savages than spears. And not every Centrois spear had found its target.

"We fight!" Saka yelled, and vaulted over the boulder.

Instead of following him, Tarek raced around the rock. Out of the corner of his eye, he saw the savage he'd struck clawing weakly at his weapon.

Movement to his right spun him in that direction. Two savages. Their heavy necklaces bouncing. Small eyes like fire.

Strength filled him. Nothing of the world existed except for the duo. Bellowing, he charged the creature to his left. Instead of trying to stand chest-to-chest with him, he came in low, his knife driving upward. It hit resistance, and the savage screamed. Before he could stab again, the savage threw himself at him.

They went down together, Tarek under the stinking creature at first but scrambling out from under and desperate to plant his legs under him. He'd nearly succeeded when something struck him in the side.

Not daring to take time to look at himself, he fought to regain his balance. A shape loomed over him, and he looked up at filthy, hairy legs.

"Die!" Propelled by his voice, he slashed.

This savage screamed, the sound seeming to come from the pit of his being. Then he took a deep and ragged breath, then screamed again. Blood from the deep stab to his groin ran down both legs.

Something was coming at him! By dropping to his belly and rolling, Tarek managed to evade what might have been a stone knife. He thought it belonged to the savage he'd wounded earlier, not that it mattered because he *had* to regain his feet.

But as he planted his free hand against the ground in preparation for leveraging himself upward, pain bit into his side. Sudden movement pulled him off thoughts of his body. The stone knife!

He managed to turn so the weapon couldn't reach his face or throat, but a sharp burning along his shoulder told him the only thing he needed to know. He smelled his own blood.

"Spawn of a vulture's whore!"

The stone-knife-wielding savage whirled toward the curse. He was still turning when Saka barreled into him, his knife clutched in both hands. As Saka grunted, the knife disappeared into the savage's middle. Looking as if they were mating, Saka and the savage fell together, the savage hitting the ground first. For a moment, the savage's feet furiously pounded the earth, then they stopped. His arms fell away from his body.

Saka pushed back from the creature but kept his hands on the knife hilt. "You're bleeding."

Tarek concentrated on standing because a sharp-toothed animal had hold of his side. It wasn't painful so much as a deep and heavy dragging sensation. In contrast, his shoulder felt as if he'd been stung by countless bees.

"Are you all right?"

I don't know. "The others?"

As Saka pointed, Tarek took note of the sounds. He knew this wave of cursing and crying as well as he knew the nearly inaudible thump his feet made as he tracked deer. Battle. War. If only his vision would clear.

Someone cried out. Although he couldn't make out what the crier was saying, instinct told him it was a Centrois. After a quick and concerned look at him, Saka took off at a run. He tried to keep pace, but his legs now belonged to a toddler. Still, as long as he had his knife and the strength to stand, he'd fight.

From the way the savages were grunting and clicking their teeth, Tarek knew they were communicating with each other. They might be planning a change in their attack, but when he saw first one and then another start back the way they'd come, he changed his mind. Before he could send thanks to the Divine Eternal, he heard his name being called—too softly, barely more than a whisper.

Willing his legs to support him, he faced the whisper. A Centrois—he couldn't tell who—lay on the ground a short distance away; a savage stood over him holding a spear. The man who'd called to him was barely moving, and the savage was obviously relishing his superiority, drawing out the killing.

Teeth exposed in a horrid grin, the savage drew the spear upward, forearms and shoulder muscles hardening. Not thinking, Tarek launched himself. He couldn't reach the enemy in a single leap, and his legs trembled as he forced another step, but at least the savage had turned from his victim.

"Tarek!"

J'ron.

The spear was swinging toward him, reaching out as if to meet him in midstride, but at the last moment, he wrenched himself to the side. Whatever had been gnawing on his ribs bit down with all its strength, and his body became drenched in sweat; his head filled with pain.

Still, he straightened. Clenched his knife handle with his remaining strength. Propelled himself forward.

The spear slid along the top of his shoulder, pressing against but not opening any more flesh, and as his knife met resistance, his arms gave way. Sucking in air, he locked his elbows and pushed more than thrust. Despite the red waterfall filming his eyes, he knew he'd struck the savage's arm. Shrieking, the savage took a backward step, and as he did, the knife slipped out of him.

Gripping his wound, the savage continued backpedaling. Then he turned and ran.

"Tarek?"

"J'ron." The waterfall became thicker, darker, and his legs felt like melting ice. Although he vaguely comprehended that the others had arrived, it didn't matter.

17

Warned by his grim expression, Nari kept her eyes downcast. Tarek had approached her slowly, then stopped and stood on widely splayed legs, staring at her. There was a bandage on his shoulder and another fastened to his side, both soaked with blood. She'd barely managed to stifle a cry as he covered the last of the distance separating them like some old and exhausted man. His expression had spoken of pride and grim determination while he went about releasing her and then Reyna. He told Reyna to find Saka, and although she hated seeing her cousin leave, Nari wanted to be alone with Tarek.

"You found my people?" She forced the question.

"Savages."

Thank the spirits. "Were . . . were any Centrois killed?"

"No. The savages have a great deal to learn about fighting."

But they wounded you. "Then how many savages died?"

"I didn't count."

They were standing face-to-face, and although he was exhausted, she sensed his inherent strength. She'd seen Baasta men right after they'd returned from battle and had absorbed their excitement as they planned hunting trips, so she understood that despite the danger, men thrived on proving themselves in ways women didn't understand. Tarek might be asking himself how he could have prevented being injured, but he still thought of himself as his people's leader.

Still, he'd come to her first, freed her.

"Did you find where they're staying?"

"No. They found us."

She opened her mouth to ask how they'd been surprised, then reconsidered. "What are you going to do?"

"Rest. And in the morning, return to the battlefield."

He looked over to where the others were gathering around the cooking fire but made no attempt to join them. *I won't try to escape,* she wanted to tell him. *Let me care for you, please.*

Slowly turning back to her, he touched her cheek. "You're all right?"

Don't, please! I can't think when you do that. "Yes," she told him, even though it took all she had not to press herself against him, to wrap her legs around him and offer her cunt to him.

"What I did to you—it'll never happen again."

"The others—"

"You belong to me, not them."

You belong to me. Yes, of course, she reminded herself. After all, the only thing she wore was the collar he'd put on her. "You're bleeding."

"Hmm."

"Those bandages, there must be something better."

"Hmm."

Her prayer that he'd order someone to provide him with decent protection for his wounds faded as he continued to stand there. He swayed slightly, and she wasn't sure he could still lift his arms. If whatever had cut his shoulder had struck a muscle . . . "You must have brought supplies with you. Where are they? I'll get them."

"Why should you—"

"Tarek?" someone called. "J'ron wants to talk to you."

"J'ron?" she prompted when Tarek didn't respond. "He should come to you."

"He can't."

The barely audible words served as a warning that he was reaching the end of his strength. Not caring about the consequences, she reached for him, hoping to encourage him to sit. Just then, he slumped toward her. Locking her knees in place, she accepted his weight, and they sank more than knelt together. His harsh gasp tore at her. Once on the ground, he leaned against her.

"Tarek! Tarek."

When he didn't answer, she lifted his head. His eyes were unfocused, teeth clenched in pain.

"Damn him!"

Looking up, she recognized Saka.

"I told him I'd tend to you," Saka explained as he crouched beside her and put his arms around Tarek. "Damnation, I told him to take care of himself. Get his sleep-pelt, now."

Leaving Saka to support Tarek, Nari scrambled to her feet and sprinted for Tarek's sleeping place. As she ran, with her breasts bouncing and hair flying behind her, she took note of the eyes on her, but the only thing that mattered was that they didn't try to stop her.

"I don't need it," Tarek muttered as she spread out the pelt beside him.

"Yes, you do," Saka insisted. "Why did we make such a stubborn man our leader?"

"I'm . . . all right."

"No, you aren't. Your wounds must be deeper than we thought. Until we know, what I say, you do."

To her relief, Tarek didn't argue. Once they had him settled with a folded blanket under his head and another over his legs, she told Saka she'd stay with Tarek while he gathered what they'd need to tend to his wounds.

Tarek had no appetite, but at least he drank as much water as she gave him. To her relief, she learned that, like the Baasta, the Centrois treated wounds with a mix of yabey, alasa, and hemiphen herbs. She'd had to stifle a cry when she removed the bandages. After collecting herself, she'd asked Saka to entrust his brother to her. Saka had looked skeptical, but he needed to join the others.

Now it was just her and Tarek, and everything had changed between them. No longer was he the domineering warrior and she his captive. He watched through half-open lids as she washed his wounds in preparation for placing the herbs on them. She didn't tell him how much the swelling worried her.

"What are you thinking?" he asked.

"That I want you well."

"If you ran, I wouldn't be able to stop you."

"It shouldn't be like that. You're strong, healthy, brave, and self-confident."

"I'm neither strong nor healthy now."

Surprised by his truthfulness, she concentrated on making sure his torn flesh was clean. Her father's mother, who'd served as a healer until her death last winter, had believed that infection was caused by dirt and other things that stayed in wounds. She'd made sure that Nari, Reyna, and everyone else she could get to listen learned her techniques. But Tarek's wounds already looked infected, while it took dirt a while to do its damage.

"Growing old and losing one's strength is the way of things." She spoke in part to keep Tarek's mind off the pain she knew she was causing him. "My grandmother said the old must die to make way for the young. But everyone prays for healthy babies and for those babies to remain healthy as they grow. When we become men and women, we become the caregivers. Women give birth and raise the next generation while men provide food and safety." She lightly blew on his shoulder to dry it. "Everyone suffers when the caregivers can't fulfill their roles."

A whisper of a smile eased his tense features. "You're wise."

Touched, she ducked her head. "Not wise. I try to listen to the rhythm of life and learn from it. Maybe wildings understand that."

"How do you find the rhythm?"

The suns were setting, the sunset richly red—like blood. She was where she'd never been before, talking to a man she'd never believed she'd hear a quiet word from. Something warm and soft slid over her body, easing her. The sensation held hints of the sexual tension and need that had been part of her since Tarek had grabbed her, but this was gentler, deeper even.

Taking his hand, she placed it on her thighs. "I clean my mind of all worries and concerns. I try not to think of what I've been doing or need to do, who I've talked to and what we said."

"Is that possible?"

"Sometimes." Earlier, his hand would have claimed the space between her legs. Either he no longer had any interest in her cunt or hearing what she had to say meant more. She hoped it was the latter. "I watch the clouds until it feels as if I'm drifting with them. And I let the birds and wind sing to me."

His sigh held a wistful quality. "I've never done that."

"I'll show you."

Rolling his head toward her, he stared into her eyes. His cheeks took on the sky's red hues. "Thank you."

Not breathing, she waited for him to say more. Instead, dark intensity faded from his eyes, and his lids slid closed. "I'm tired."

"Sleep, then." *I'll keep you safe.*

If he'd felt her applying the herbs and securing new bandages in place, he gave no indication. As soon as she was done treating him, she pulled the blanket up over his shoulders and brushed his pale hair off him as he'd done to her. She left long enough to get a blanket for herself, then curled up next to him so she could keep him warm. Her stomach growled, but at least she wasn't thirsty. And despite the caress of his side against her and her arm draped over his chest, she soon became drowsy. Not far away, the Centrois continued talking. Twice she heard J'ron's name mentioned, and wasn't that Reyna's voice among the deeper tones?

She was sinking, seeping into something dark and warm. Whatever it was slowly wrapped itself around her, making her wonder if she was turning into a baby back in her mother's arms.

The question faded to be replaced by the acknowledgment that she was still a woman and not a child, and her awareness of her body grew. She was proud of her breasts and soft belly, her sleek yet strong legs.

In her mind, she stood on a riverbank looking at the constantly moving water. Despite the rough current, she was positive she could make her way to the other side. If she had a reason to, she'd dive into the cool depth and effortlessly propel herself forward.

But she wouldn't because what she needed was here, only a few feet away, walking toward her.

The approaching man was taller than any she'd ever seen, with shoulders capable of doing battle with a bear. He was as naked as her, his skin darker, muscles sharply defined, long moonlit hair blowing behind him.

Her attention drifted to the hard male organ presenting itself to her. The moment she focused on it, everything else about him slipped into a strange mist. His cock was whispering to her, enticing her to take it into her body.

I want, she told the cock and the man it belonged to.

Careful, the man warned. *If you embrace it, you'll never forget.*

It's already too late.

She was moving without moving, gliding even closer despite not having taken a stride. Excited and scared, she reached out. Touched powerful heat. Held.

This is more than a cock. It, and I, are one and the same. Allow it in you and you'll have taken me into your life.

I know. I have.

Had she ever touched anything softer than his foreskin? In contrast, the weight now cradled in her palms pressed down around her. The heat of his scrotum seeped through her fingertips, found her veins, and flowed to her heart.

I trust you, he said.

Yes, it took trust and courage for a man to offer himself up this way.

Eager to show her gratitude, she sank to her knees, her free hand trailing over his thigh as she went. She opened her mouth.

He gripped her shoulders. *No, not like that.*

What, then?

Like a woman who trusts.

A moment ago she'd been shaking, but now calm overtook her. Leaning forward, she reached between her legs and extracted some of the sweet fluid pooled around her labia. Then she rubbed it on her nipples. *Kiss me there. Kiss and drink of me.*

Suddenly he was on his knees in front of her, lifting her head with one hand while the other did the same with a breast. He leaned close and exhaled a quick, hot breath on the mound before lapping at her offering. When he'd taken all she had to offer, he licked the other one clean.

More. I have more.

Spinning away, she lowered her head to the ground, then scooted back until her ass found him. Feeling calmer and more sure than she ever had, she spread her legs. She reached for her crack, thinking to open herself even more, but he brushed her hand away.

You're sure?

Yes. Yes!

At a touch of thumb to labia, she gasped and struggled to look back at him but night had claimed him. Now he pressed the flat of his hand over her ass, a finger tickling where his thumb had been, and something broke loose inside her and floated away, perhaps remnants of the proud and respectful Baasta she'd always been.

My cunt belongs to you. Please, please, take me!

Although he didn't speak, she found his reply in the sure and certain way he worked her. In her mind, his finger became a soft new leaf, a feathery wing. Sensation shivered over her, faded, built again. When she reached the edge, she forced herself back and pulled air deep into her lungs. She floated on a river of heat, drifting with gentle currents, seeing the rapids ahead.

Painting her sex with her own fluids, rubbing and lightly slapping by turn, dragging his nails over the insides of her thighs, diving deep and true over and over again.

The river built, changed from calm movement to raging power. The rapids! Here. Now. Rushing over her.

Coming! I'm coming.

Timing her climax perfectly, he pressed on her clit and held the explosion inside her. No matter how she fought to free it, he trapped the necessary release beneath the surface, causing it to build and grow.

Not yet! he ordered. *I need to know everything you're capable of.*

Once more her forehead rested against the ground. Panting

did nothing to master her frustration, yet she reveled in her knotted muscles. Her body boiled.

Too late she realized he'd removed his hand and was replacing it with his mouth. With his cheeks pressed against hers, he flicked his tongue over her sex, his movements so rapid she couldn't begin to comprehend where he might touch her next.

By the spirits! Please, please, please!

The ground trapped and muffled her voice. Not caring, she whimpered like some frightened wild animal. His tongue, everywhere! Tasting her juices and taking the taste into him and his breath damp and hot on skin that felt as if it had been rubbed with sand.

Do you trust me, Nari? Do you? His unspoken question echoed in her brain.

No. No. No. But I need this. Need this!

He might have chuckled, but maybe he'd groaned. If she'd been saner, she would have asked what it was, but how could she think with his tongue pressing against her entrance and her pussy opening to him?

He worked her over and over again, tongue and teeth and lips hurtling her toward space, then abruptly stopping until she was tumbling back to earth. Then he pushed her to the brink again and again.

She sobbed, begged, whimpered, howled. But he denied her. Even as she cried, she worshipped his mastery. She knew nothing except for his mouth owning her, her muscles twitching, writhing, legs like water and blood pooling in her head.

Now, Nari. Now!

Where was he? Night air chilled her wet pussy and yanked her, fighting to stay where she was, toward sanity. Trembling with the effort, she sat up.

There! Surrounded by midnight with his eyes burning, on his knees, his arms folded. *Show me your trust.*

Trust? The word threatened to drown her, so she shook it

off, then became still so her body could whisper its secrets to her.

She still didn't have the all-important answer as she lowered herself onto her back, pressed her hands over her breasts, and spread her legs wide, but she had heard a single word: *Fuck!*

Despite her blatant offering, he didn't immediately take advantage of it, making her wonder if he was waiting for more from her. But she couldn't offer her heart, only her cunt.

A groaning growl rolled out of him. His eyes again lost in the night, he crawled toward her. Gripping her ankles, he lifted her legs. She rolled her crotch upward, then gasped as the head of his cock found her opening. He held himself there for a moment, perhaps giving her a final chance to change her mind, but she wouldn't. Couldn't. *Fuck me.*

Sliding in, in and deep, deep and strong. Her passage expanded, filled nearly to bursting with him. And yet despite his hard bulk, she could have taken more. Maybe all of him. Her nipples tightened under her own hands, and her throat threatened to catch fire. Panting didn't bring enough air into her starving lungs, so she took deep and rapid breaths. Her nostrils and throat filled with his scent.

Releasing her legs, he ran his hands under her buttocks and brought her up and even closer to him. She wrapped her legs around him, her heels pressing into his spine, her hands still grinding into her breasts. He started pushing, the moves measured and yet edged with urgency. Twitching and thrusting herself, she wondered at his self-control. Knew it wouldn't last. Didn't want it to.

His cock powered even deeper. Found a part of her she didn't know existed. Then he pulled back, taking that newborn part with him. In a strange and wonderful way, she knew he was pounding into more than her pussy. He was reaching her soul. Calling on every bit of strength in her body, she sucked him deep. Caressed and attacked and tasted. He'd become part of her, had intruded on what she'd always protected and kept safe.

Surrendering everything, she climaxed.

Screamed.

Screamed again.

18

Nari woke frequently during the night. Each time she had to work at remembering where she was and who was beside her, and when it came together, she told herself that her disconnect from reality was a result of her exhaustion. She repeatedly fought her way back to unconsciousness, not because she didn't care about the feverish man beside her but because she needed to sleep if she was going to have the strength to get through the next few days.

After what felt like a lifetime, the suns began their assault on the night. Careful not to disturb Tarek, she slid her arm out from under him and sat up. Her weary body slumped forward. Then she straightened and pressed the back of her hand against his cheek. She hadn't dreamed it; he *was* running a fever.

"Tarek?" she whispered. "Tarek, can you hear me?"

He muttered something and reached for her, but much as she longed to nestle next to him again, she scooted away and forced herself onto her knees. Overnight, she'd become an ancient woman filled with unwanted wisdom. His wounds had become infected, and unless he had enough strength to fight his fever, he'd die. And she'd been so careful to remove every bit of dirt.

Much as she wanted to talk to his brother, she first put on her dress. Being covered made her feel more confident, and when she walked over to the others, she held her head high. Instead of asking about Tarek, most simply studied her as she looked for Saka and Reyna, but A'tala pointed at a nearby thicket.

Not sure what she'd find, she headed for it. Morning cooking smells made her stomach clench—either that or she was reacting to having to get close to J'ron. If her cousin was being forced to treat him—

The moment Reyna looked up at her from where she knelt beside J'ron, Nari knew that force had nothing to do with what her cousin was doing. Reyna was leaning toward Saka who knelt on J'ron's other side.

"What is it?" Saka demanded before she could speak. "My brother—"

"Has developed a fever." After that, there didn't seem to be anything to say.

"So has he." Reyna indicated J'ron. J'ron's eyes were open, but he was staring at the sky, not those around him.

"Both of them and so fast?" Saka clenched his fist. "Why aren't you with Tarek?"

"I had to talk to you." Steeling herself, she slipped closer. The young warrior no longer reminded her of a fierce wolverine. Instead, he'd become both as limp as a sleeping child and an old man. Reyna had her hand on J'ron's chest. How could she touch the man who'd raped her? "I've never seen a fever come on so fast."

Reyna's eyes suddenly widened. "Never? Nari, remember when we were little? We were so afraid when Ochin became covered with sores after a savage attacked him."

Although Saka demanded to know what Reyna was talking about, Reyna simply rolled J'ron onto his side. Nari joined her, both women's hands going to J'ron's spinal column. A multitude of small, angry welts covered the skin there.

"Poison," Nari whispered, and eased J'ron back down again. "Why didn't I think of that?"

"No!" Saka exclaimed. "No. They cannot die."

"They don't have to because we know how to treat the poison, if we start in time." Reyna took Saka's hand. "The savages rub sap from a plant that grows only in rocky, shaded soil onto their weapons. If the sap gets into someone, it can kill them."

Although she could have told Saka the same thing, hearing the words turned Nari cold. Without proper treatment, Tarek would die. And Reyna was right because the herbs the healers had developed to counter the poison had to be administered as quickly as possible.

"Saka," she blurted, "Reyna and I know which herbs they are and where to find them. You have to let us—"

"No." Saka's grip on Reyna's hand tightened. "Not both of you. The others wouldn't allow that. Besides, I want you to stay with my brother and *him*."

"Me? But—"

"Reyna, you and I will go."

Although she had to force herself to touch J'ron, Nari now admitted that Saka's decision made sense. He and Reyna had taken off shortly after moving J'ron near to Tarek so she could care for both men at the same time. Now that the others understood how gravely ill the two were, talk of seeking revenge against the savages dominated their conversation. They seemed to take it for granted that she'd do everything possible for Tarek and J'ron, maybe because they were accustomed to chattels doing what they were ordered to, but maybe because Centrois warriors deliberately distanced themselves from injured warriors so as not to weaken their courage.

Tarek had led them to Hevassen! He'd risked his life protecting J'ron. Instead of praising his courage, his men had abandoned him!

By the time she'd eaten and gotten a little broth into Tarek and J'ron, her anger had faded. She couldn't imagine ever understanding the Centrois, but it did no good to judge them according to her standards. Besides, going by how one or another of them occasionally walked over and stared at the two semiconscious men, obviously they did care. They just didn't want to admit that the same could happen to them.

"There is so much to being a Centrois warrior," she told Tarek, even though he focused on her only when she shook him. "It's so hard to be brave, to allow no weakness."

J'ron stirred. When he relaxed, she focused on Tarek again but couldn't think of anything more to say. A moment later, J'ron tried to sit up. She easily pushed him back down and kept a hand on his chest because he seemed to relax a little when she did. She didn't think he was quite as hot as Tarek, although maybe that was because she was more concerned about Tarek. J'ron had a thin face with prominent cheekbones and a long, bony nose. If it wasn't for the lack of wrinkles, she would have taken him for an old man. Studying him, she concluded that he had the skeletal structure of a tall, long-limbed man but barely enough skin and muscle to cover the underlying bones. Did he ever feel inferior to Tarek whose well-developed muscles spoke of a warrior, a leader? Was there still something of a boy in J'ron?

Strange. She'd always believed that the Centrois were cruel beasts, a heartless breed. But after only a few days of being with them, she'd learned that every Centrois was different.

When she returned home, she'd tell her people that, make them understand that beneath the surface, the Centrois and Baasta had a great deal in common.

"If I told you that," she asked her unresponsive patients, "would you believe me?"

* * *

The day seemed endless. Because she and the two men were at a distance from the warriors, she couldn't occupy herself by watching them. They were working with their weapons and otherwise getting ready for battle, but if it was imminent, they hadn't said anything to her. She wondered if they didn't want to do anything until they knew whether Tarek and J'ron were going to live.

They were accustomed to having Tarek at their lead. Were they prepared for fighting without him?

And more than just fight, she reluctantly acknowledged. Tarek, and J'ron as well, were part of the rhythm of their lives. If the two died—

"Reyna, Saka! Hurry, please."

Tarek opened his eyes and focused on her. "What are you . . ."

"Do you remember what happened?" she asked, hoping to judge his level of consciousness.

"Attack. Savages."

"That's right. You were wounded, twice. Do you remember how it happened?"

"Twice?" His features contorted. "A warrior does not . . ."

"Doesn't what? Let himself be injured?" It took all her self-restraint not to shake him. "Only a man who hides escapes that risk. Saka told me you saved *his* life." She indicated J'ron.

"Is he . . ."

Because Tarek's eyes had closed again, she wasn't sure he was listening, but he deserved an answer. "He's alive. And like yours, his wounds aren't that serious. It's the poison."

"Poison?"

"It's all right." She stroked his shoulder. "My cousin and your brother will soon be back with what you need."

Opening his eyes again seemed to tax him. "And if they don't?"

"Don't say that!"

His lips thin, he nodded. And in his gaze, she read the truth. He knew how close he was to death.

I won't let you die! I'll fight your fever for as long as it takes, make you eat and drink, sleep beside you and give you my strength. And by tomorrow, you'll take my body, a strong warrior claiming what belongs to him.

But much as she wanted to, she didn't say any of those things because she refused to lie to either of them.

The suns had passed their height and were sliding toward the horizon when one of the men called out. Afraid it might be savages—or even her people—Nari jumped to her feet, but neither of her patients reacted.

To her great relief, she soon recognized Saka and close to him, Reyna. Their smiles said everything she needed to know.

She'd already located a bowl-shaped rock perfect for grinding, and she pointed it out to Saka and Reyna. Once he'd deposited what he had on the rock, Saka headed for his brother.

"You found everything?" she asked Reyna, whose attention was still on Saka. "And no sign of the savages?"

"None. Knowing how close they are, I thought I'd be afraid, but I feel safe with *him* protecting me."

"He didn't treat you like a chattel?" Picking up one of the two smaller, smooth rocks she'd placed near the large bowl-shaped one, she started grinding the herbs.

Taking the other smooth stone, Reyna did the same. "He hasn't almost from the beginning. Nari, he loved his child's mother so much. When she died, it nearly killed him. He said— he told me that for a long time, he wanted to die. I wonder if he would have taken his life if it wasn't for his son."

"He told you all that?"

Eyes glistening, she nodded. "Maybe I remind him of her."

Struck by her cousin's wistful tone, she shook her head.

"Reyna, in his heart, she was everything to him except for his wife while you're . . . you're a captive."

"Not to him."

"You believe that?"

"When it's just the two of us, I feel like his equal. This time he asked more about my family and whether I'd chosen who I wanted to marry and what I wanted from life. No one has ever done that."

Believing she needed to caution Reyna against falling in love, she opened her mouth, but she couldn't speak. No one had ever asked her what she hoped for her future. If someone—Tarek—did, what would she answer? And why would he care?

After pulverizing the dry leaves and seed pods, Reyna and Nari boiled everything in a small amount of water. When the water turned gray-green, they let it cool until they could place their fingers in the syrup it had become.

"Are you sure?" Reyna asked as they carried the cooking pot over to Tarek and J'ron. "We've included everything we need to?"

"I pray we have." She kept her voice low because most if not all of the Centrois were watching. "If we haven't . . ."

Only Saka was with Tarek and J'ron. If he believed his strength and courage would be jeopardized by staying around injured warriors, his concern for his brother overrode that. Just the same, his tension was a living thing.

"We can't make promises," Nari told him. "It might . . . it might be too late."

Saka didn't say anything, which was good because she wasn't sure she could concentrate enough to reply. Tarek didn't appear to be any hotter than the last time she'd touched him, but his skin was so dry. He shivered, yet when she tried to tuck his blanket back over his shoulders, he tore it off. She barely glanced at J'ron and was surprised when Reyna knelt beside him.

"We might have to hold them down," she told Saka. "The medicine burns."

He stared at the pot, then locked eyes with her. "Helki asked if you're trying to kill Tarek and J'ron, but I trust you. Both of you."

No compliment had ever meant more. If only she was confident that the medicine would save Tarek's life.

And if it doesn't?

Positioning herself near Tarek's head, she scooped out a little of the syrup with a stiff leaf. After taking a calming breath, she deposited it on his exposed shoulder wound. For a moment he barely reacted. Then, cursing, he surged upright. Saka threw his lighter body against his brother's chest as she and Reyna grabbed his arms. If he'd been stronger, he might have fought them all off, but they managed to get him on his back again.

She leaned close to his ear. "It won't hurt long. Once it has burned through the poison, you'll find peace." *Divine Eternal, please let that happen.*

Although she couldn't be sure, she told herself he'd heard and that's why he stopped struggling.

"Good," Saka said in a tone he might have used to soothe his infant son. "Good. Let the salve do its work. Rest while your fever dies." He stared at Reyna. "The fever will leave him, won't it?"

"If we've treated him in time, if this is the right mixture."

And if we haven't, this incredible Centrois warrior will die.

At length Tarek's body relaxed, and he seemed to be sleeping. They treated J'ron in the same way with Saka angrily ordering J'ron to stop fighting and cursing. To Reyna's credit, she added her gentle voice. At one point, J'ron's eyes opened, and he glared at her like some angry but helpless wild animal. Seeing his helpless fear, whatever hatred she'd had for him faded. He was who he was, a man ruled by instinct and the Centrois who said he had every right to treat chattels, captives, or hostages as he wanted. He'd been stripped of strength and weapons. Even his courage had caved under the reality of his wounds and the poison.

"I never thought I'd see him in that light," she later told an unresponsive Tarek. "I didn't want to think of J'ron as anything except a beast. A rapist. But there's a small boy beneath the surface."

Although she hadn't said much today, talking wore her out. After shifting position so the tree her back was propped against stopped digging into her shoulder blades, she stroked Tarek's hair. His head rested in her lap. The Centrois must have taken note, but she was beyond caring. Besides, she needed to track his temperature, to be ready in case he needed something; at least that's what she told herself.

"You're going to live," she whispered, because she couldn't remain silent after all. "You *have* to."

Why?

She tried to reply that the savages couldn't possibly bring down a well-trained warrior and that was why she sounded so confident, but that wasn't why she'd sounded so intense. Far from it.

She needed him alive and strong so he could help her fathom why he mattered so much to her. True, she'd never fucked in a way that came close to what she'd experienced with him. Yes, she wanted her dream of his licking her cunt to become reality. Yes, she needed to bathe his cock with her tongue, to close her mouth around his balls, to scrape her teeth over his belly.

But it went beyond that.

J'ron groaned and whipped his head from side to side. Although the unexpected sound and movement startled her, wasn't that better than having him lie like the dead?

When he stopped, she turned her attention back to Tarek. "When you took me, I never thought I'd willingly touch you. I wanted you dead. Because you hate the Baasta, I should still want you dead, but I don't."

Was she imagining it, or had he tensed? If he was listening to her . . .

Feeling both foolish and exposed, she slid out from under him and stood. The only restraint remaining on her was the collar. Perhaps she could have asked Saka to remove it, but what if he refused? Besides, the presence around her neck reminded her of Tarek's touch.

How complex things had become! How unsettling and yet, what?

Although she'd intended to walk away so she could relieve herself, she remained where she was, staring down at him. The fresh dressings hid the damage done to that perfect body. This way she could tell herself that he was simply sleeping.

And when he woke up . . .

19

The cave walls had been so hot that he'd been afraid to touch them. At times he'd been in water so thick he couldn't move his limbs. Frequently the water had threatened to suck him under and drown him. Each time that possibility threatened, he'd managed to fight his way back to the surface, but the effort had taken so much energy that he'd barely had the strength to breathe.

If his mother hadn't been there . . .

No. Whoever was sitting nearby didn't smell as his mother had. And not once had her touch been that of a woman soothing an infant.

Not sure where he was or even who he was, Tarek opened his eyes. It was night, stars like millions of bright sparks from a campfire.

She was still there, no longer sitting but stretched out with her breasts and belly against his side. Her arm lay across his groin with her fingers near his cock. His skin was so dry that he wondered if he'd been in a desert, but that couldn't be because dampness was seeping up from the ground onto his sleep-pelt. He shivered.

Perhaps she felt his tremor because she stirred, fingers inching closer to his limp and useless cock.

Limp? How could that be when he always woke with a swollen member, and it should have been more responsive with a female beside him.

No. Not just a female. *Her. Nari.*

Fighting the throbbing in his head, he worked at putting things together. Making sense of where he was and why it took longer than he wanted it to, but at length he remembered enough to satisfy himself, for now. Recalling the fierce burning that had gripped him when Nari put whatever she'd used on his wounds made him shudder again. He'd long known not to show pain, but he'd never felt this helpless.

Someone was snoring. Certain it wasn't Nari, he concentrated. J'ron. Yes, he knew that sound. As his awareness of the small hand near his groin grew, so did his desire to put distance between himself and J'ron, to be alone with Nari.

Rolling onto his side so he could sit up irritated his wounds, and for a moment he couldn't breathe. By the time he'd gotten things under control, she was awake.

"What is it?" she whispered.

Answering took too much effort when he needed to concentrate on getting his legs under him. Springing to her feet, she helped him accomplish the exhausting task of standing. When he was finally upright, he cursed his foolishness.

"It's all right," she muttered, her tone telling him that she understood how hard this was for him. "You're going to be all right."

He believed her, fully and completely.

"Your fever's gone." She draped his arm over her shoulder, indicating he could lean against her, and although he might knock her off her feet, he did. "What do you want to do?"

Sit down again, before I fall. But because he was a warrior, he didn't tell her that. "Walk. A little."

"J'ron's fever, too, has broken. His sleep isn't deep."

So her wisdom extended to knowing why he wanted to take those hard steps. Still leaning on her, he willed his left leg to move. Once that was accomplished, he had to command his right to follow suit, but with each step, a little strength seeped back into him. He was still weak, but at least he no longer feared he'd fall.

The surrounding trees and bushes swallowed them, and soon he could no longer see the embers from the night fire, could no longer hear J'ron's breathing. Instead, he felt Nari's warmth and strength and the short dress sliding over her, her loose hair under his arm. Now he was the naked one, naked and with a useless cock.

After walking a short distance, his legs started to tremble, and she asked if he wanted to sit again. Although he would have given a great deal to say no, he knew better. In fact, he might have pitched forward if she hadn't been there to ease him down.

After resting briefly, he changed from supporting his weight on his hands and knees to sitting with his legs tucked close to his body and his weight on his right hip. She sat nearby, her warmth a soft contrast to the cool night air.

"I should have brought your blanket," she said.

"It's all right." *For now.* "Tell me everything."

As the quiet words rolled out of her, he admitted that his memory was more flawed than he'd originally thought. One thing stood out. If not for her and her cousin's knowledge, he'd be dead.

"You didn't have to do that. If you'd remained silent, I'd be dead by now."

"I couldn't."

"Why not?" His sharp tone surprised him.

Leaning forward, she wrapped her arms around her legs.

For the first time since coming to, he truly noted her dress and the collar he'd put on her.

"You're no longer just a Centrois to me," she said. "Not simply my captor. So much has changed between us. Last night I dreamed . . ."

"What?"

"I . . . this is hard to say."

"Please finish."

"I dreamed that you made me come by licking my cunt."

He'd never done something so intimate to any woman let alone a sex-chattel, and yet the image spoke to his cock. "Is that what the Baasta do?"

"No! I . . . I didn't know such a thing was possible."

"It made you come?"

"In my dream, yes." She released her knees but continued to study the ground. "I didn't ask for it, but . . ."

He didn't ask for a further explanation, but maybe he didn't need to. Some part of her, maybe a part she hadn't acknowledged or believed in trusted him that much.

"I remember, when the fever had me, did you place my head in your lap?"

"Yes."

"I, ah, I felt safe. In my mind I became Dio."

"Who?"

"Saka's son."

Her head came up.

"I often held him when he was a newborn. He cried more than most, maybe because he knew his mother was dead. I'd cradle him in one arm and lightly rub his forehead with my finger. And I'd sing to him until he fell asleep."

She still didn't speak, and yet he knew she'd absorbed everything he'd said. What he couldn't comprehend was why he'd been so open and honest when only Saka and the woman who'd taken

Dio to her breast knew how fully he'd given his heart to his little nephew. And maybe his weakness was responsible. Maybe
he couldn't hold back in the wake of what she'd told him about
her dream.

An owl hooted, followed soon after by a night hawk's cry.
Although he was certain the sounds came from birds and not
one human signaling to another, he remained tense. The Baasta
and savages lived here, but other breeds might also be in the
area. Since boyhood he'd accepted that he'd been given life so
he could protect his people. When he was learning to be a man,
he could hardly wait to participate in battles. He'd wanted
weapons and war cries. Even the idea of bearing fighting scars
had appealed to him, but now he felt only weary.

"Saka should marry," she said. "That way his son could live
with him."

"My brother isn't ready to turn his heart over to another
woman, and he doesn't want to take a wife simply so Dio will
have a mother. He wants his son to be surrounded by love."

"Dio means everything to him, doesn't he?"

"Because Dio's mother was his everything."

"Tarek?"

"What?"

"Saka told Reyna that your father sold Dio's mother to keep
them apart and that her owner beat her when he learned she
was pregnant with Saka's child."

Going back to that time was the last thing he wanted to do.
"Not just our father. The elders had spoken. They wanted to
separate them because love between a warrior and a sex-chattel
cannot be. After she was sold, I thought he might die, so I insisted he come along as we tracked some Gailes."

"Gailes?"

"A breed known for stealing, cowards. I was certain the
Gailes would run instead of standing and fighting. Saka couldn't

keep his mind on what we were doing, but at least his days were full and his nights spent far from the chattel he couldn't have. We followed the Gailes for a long time, finally tracking them to where they lived. When we attacked, they ran, leaving behind what they'd stolen from us. We spent days at their village going through their belongings and choosing what we wanted to take back with us." His long speech had worn him out, but that wasn't the only reason he paused. "By the time we returned home and heard that Farih had been mistreating her, it was too late."

"She was dead?"

"Dying. She'd just given birth when Saka and I found her among some rocks. Farih had taken her there and beaten her, then abandoned her." His mind filled with unwanted memories. "I don't know how long she'd been there. Her leg was broken, so she couldn't leave. She'd tried to feed herself by digging for roots."

"Tarek, I'm so sorry."

"I was the one who came across her. We'd split up so we could cover more land, and I heard the baby crying." His voice sounded hollow. "I tried to keep Saka from seeing, but I couldn't."

"It . . . it was just you and Saka?"

"Yes. We hadn't told anyone what we were doing."

"She was all alone," Nari whispered. "To give birth alone and know she was dying . . ."

She understands. She knows what I felt. "She, ah, she was curled around Dio. Saka screamed. I've never heard a sound like that. Then he cried." *So did I.*

Tarek was quiet for so long that Nari thought he might have fallen asleep. He could have passed out, but she didn't think so because his temperature was back to normal. Being so close to him, even if he was in no condition for sex, should have been an assault on her nerves, but all she could think about was what he'd told her. He hadn't given her all the details of that horrific day, but she'd never ask him to because certain things were beyond words.

One thing she'd learned from what little he'd said, and the way he'd said it, was that Saka wasn't the only one who'd shed tears. This Centrois warlord was capable of tears. He held his brother's baby in his arms, singing to him and stroking his forehead.

He understood the meaning of love.

Love? Why are you thinking—

He shivered, distracting her from unwanted questions. She asked if he wanted to return to his bed, but he shook his head; then he shivered again.

"I'll get your bed," she said, and stood up. "It won't take long."

Before she could take a step, he wrapped his hand around her ankle, touching and not restraining. "You won't run away?"

"No."

His fingers relaxed, once more signaling that things had changed between them. They hadn't had sex; the possibility hadn't even come up. Instead, they'd shared words and thoughts adversaries never would. Morning might bring an end to this closeness, but she'd embrace it for as long as it lasted.

She found J'ron curled on his side and snoring loudly. His forehead was cool to the touch, and although she didn't linger beside him, she was left with the thought that he resembled a child, not her cousin's rapist.

Was Reyna with Saka? For his sake, and hers, she hoped so.

When she returned to Tarek, he was sitting up and gingerly examining his wounds. She couldn't make out his expression and didn't ask whether he was in pain. With each passing moment, he was becoming less someone on the brink of death and more a warrior ready to pick up his weapons again.

To attack her people.

"J'ron?" he asked.

"Snoring. And I think everyone else is asleep."

"Except for the guards."

Of course.

Pulling courage around her, she spread the sleep-pelt out next to him and dropped the two blankets on it. She was vaguely aware of her tired body, but the idea of falling back asleep was foreign since even with his cock limp and his muscles weak, she wanted him.

"What is it like where you live?" she asked once he'd moved over to his pelt. "I was so young when we left that I don't remember."

"Like?"

"Hevassen's weather is wonderful. It's never too hot or cold, and every season brings rain but not too much."

"Most of our rain comes in spring, so much that almost every year there's flooding and for days we're forced to stay inside. Winter, too, is wet, which brings a great deal of snow to the mountains, making hunting there impossible. Summers are hot with little rain, and the rivers become creeks. We've lived there too long. It's time for us to find a new home, a place like this."

"Hevassen? The Centrois might move here?"

"I don't know." He patted his sleep-pelt. "Join me."

It wasn't quite a command, and yet his words reminded her of when he'd controlled her every move. Unless she ran, it could go back to that. Torn between the need to stay and the need to leave, she sat down and draped her blanket around her shoulders. "I remember the rain and shivering in winter."

"I don't remember you."

Why should he? He'd been a boy concerned with learning a warrior's skills while she'd been told that she'd spent her days with other young children overseen by elderly women while their parents worked.

"What are you thinking?" His hand closed over her thigh, trapping and embracing at the same time.

"That we can't change the past. And that the present and future don't have to follow that path."

"You and I are who we are, Nari. That won't change."

Although she didn't agree, she didn't want to argue with him. In truth, she wasn't sure what she wanted the night to become. It would be easier if he'd go to sleep, but did she want him to?

She stretched out on her side, taking up as little of the sleep-pelt as possible while he remained sitting, a large dark shape looming over her. Unable to think of anything to say, she looked beyond him to the stars, which represented coolness and heat, two halves of the same thing. Like him.

"I hated you," she whispered. "Yes, I feared this man who'd captured me, but it was more than that because of what you represented. Things started to change after . . . When you were wounded, I told myself I loathed you."

"Was it still the truth?"

No. "I don't know."

"Is it now?" He trailed his fingertips over her hip, somehow reaching her skin despite her dress.

"Tarek, what we are to each other is unlike anything I've ever known. I don't understand what's happening."

His fingers stilled, then pressed deeper. "While you were gone, I asked myself what it would mean to me if I never saw you again. I don't want that."

I don't either.

20

Tears ran from the corners of Nari's eyes, dampening the hair at her temples, and if Tarek had asked, she couldn't have explained why she was crying.

Thankfully, he was asleep, on his back so he wouldn't put pressure on his injuries. Shortly after telling her that he didn't want their time together to end, he'd lain down with his arm on her hip. After a brief silence, he'd guided her hand to his flaccid cock. "I'm still sick," was all he'd said. Then his breathing had slowed.

She'd wanted to be with a man like this, not just having sex, but holding on to him and sharing their thoughts, their hearts. But even now she couldn't forget that Tarek was her enemy. Her people's enemy. Her captor.

Run away, then.

I can't.

Why not?

Because I want to learn more about him—and have him learn more about me.

Why?

How she hated the part of her that demanded answers! Wasn't it enough that she had to spend the night next to the Centrois warlord, just next to him and not fucking? Why couldn't she at least silence her mind?

Before the demanding part of her could raise yet another question, she lifted herself onto her elbow so she could study what the moon and stars revealed of Tarek. The blanket had slid down from his neck, exposing his shoulders and upper chest. Remembering what his shoulder wound had looked like before she'd bandaged it, she shuddered.

It needs a kiss.

Not just his wounds, his tattoos and muscles.

After making sure she was well braced, she lifted the bandage, then leaned forward and touched her lips to his ragged and still-raw flesh. She tasted sweat and dried blood and remnants of the salve she'd applied. And beneath those things, she tasted the man himself.

He moved, a slight stirring. When he'd stilled, she turned her attention to the two hawk heads that proclaimed his rights and responsibilities as a warlord. Had he ever wanted to wipe them away and be something other than a fighter? Maybe he envied boat and canoe builders or the elderly who'd passed responsibility onto the young.

Without warning, his arm circled her neck, and he pulled her against him, barely giving her time to avoid his wound.

"Why did you do that?" he demanded.

Although she wanted to struggle, she didn't, and after a moment, the impulse faded beneath the pounding of his heart. "I don't know."

"I want to fuck you. Maybe I've never wanted more. But I don't think I can make it happen tonight."

"I . . . I know."

"And I won't give you what I can't have for myself."

His hold on her slackened, but she still didn't try to lift herself off him. Not long ago, concern for his well-being combined with the desire to concentrate on what they'd been sharing had made it possible for her to keep her body's messages quiet. With her breasts pressed against his chest, she could no longer silence those signals. Still, she vowed not to let him know. "Go back to sleep, Tarek. We have tomorrow." *Maybe.*

They didn't because Saka and Reyna found them as it was getting light. "Wake up!" Saka nudged Tarek with his foot. "J'ron is calling everyone together. He's talking about revenge."

Despite his stiffness, Tarek got to his feet without having to accept his brother's offered hand. Standing on thankfully strong legs, he didn't look down at or acknowledge Nari. "Against who?"

"The savages, of course. He's saying you'll feel the same way."

Did he? Maybe his current lethargy was a result of his injuries, but maybe it had more to do with what he'd said and heard during the night. "J'ron should concentrate on getting well."

Saka smiled. "Calling for revenge is easier than admitting he lost a battle."

"It is, for J'ron." He took a step, then looked back over his shoulder. "Come," he told Nari. "Now." Instead of trying to read her expression, he noted how close Reyna stood to Saka and the way his brother was leaning toward her. Longing slammed into him.

Nari walked slightly behind him on the way back. Their slow pace was dictated somewhat by his wounds, but he had no doubt that she was reluctant to return. Her mood might be no more complex than not wanting her relative freedom to end but it could run deeper.

As the camp came into view, Saka touched Tarek's shoulder. After telling the women to go on ahead, Saka took a deep breath. "I'm falling in love with her."

"Does she know?"

"I think, yes. I haven't told her, but I can't hide what I feel."

Fierce protectiveness seized him. If Reyna ever did anything to bring Saka more grief, he'd kill her. As soon as the thought struck, it faded because the potential for heartbreak didn't come from the Baasta captive. Instead, it was inherent in what it meant to be a Centrois.

"You think I shouldn't have opened my heart?" Saka pressed. "That I should know how to keep ropes around it?"

Was it possible to contain one's heart? Not that long ago, he hadn't thought of the heart as a wild thing. Now, owing his life to Nari, he wasn't sure. "I don't want you to have to go through what you did before. Losing one woman is enough."

"You believe I'll lose Reyna?"

Yes. "I can't see into the future. But nothing changes the fact that the Centrois and Baasta are enemies. Baasta killed our father."

"Reyna hasn't killed anyone." Saka's gaze intensified. "Neither has Nari."

The closer she came to the waiting Centrois warriors, the louder Nari's heart beat, but she had no choice except to keep walking. Reyna obviously wanted to talk to her, but she hadn't done any more than give her cousin a tentative smile. Later, when they could be sure they wouldn't be overheard, she'd encourage Reyna to open up, even though she knew what she'd say.

Don't give your heart to a Centrois. Please, don't!

J'ron was sitting slightly apart from the others. He wasn't wearing a bandage, which gave her a clear view of his deep wound. How long would it be before he was strong enough to fight, and did fighting really still matter so much to him? Until yesterday, she wouldn't have the courage or desire to talk to him, but without her intervention, he would have died, and he had to know it.

"Do you feel as if you still have a fever?" she asked. "If so, I'll make more of the salve."

"You will *not* touch me!"

"I did earlier, J'ron."

"You had no right!"

"Would you rather be dead?" Given the heightened emotions she'd had to deal with around Tarek, her outburst didn't surprise her. "Do you remember your fever? Your body was burning itself up." She paused. "I hope you never forget that I and the woman you raped saved your life."

J'ron jumped to his feet, then staggered, and his face paled. "No! My warrior strength kept me alive, not you. The potion burned like a thousand fires. You were trying to kill me."

Maybe I should have when I had the chance. "If you believe that, you're a fool."

"How dare you call me—"

"I'm trying to reach you, J'ron. Don't you understand? You might have spent your entire life hating the Baasta, but I'm asking you to hold your hatred in front of you and examine it, decide whether it's time for you to change, for your heart to speak the truth."

Still looking so pale that she was afraid he might collapse, J'ron stared at her. His eyes were lighter in color than Tarek's and lacked the depth that made Tarek's eyes unforgettable, but for the first time something other than youthful courage and self-confidence lived in them. "What's your truth, chattel?" J'ron demanded. "How can you both hate and fuck a Centrois?"

Gripped by sudden ice, she nevertheless continued to meet his gaze. He was right, at least in one respect. "I don't hate you and your people, J'ron, not anymore. Instead, I thank every warrior here for showing me the real Centrois. And I want you to do the same thing."

"You want me to be something other than a warrior? It isn't going to happen, chattel."

Not trusting what might come out of her mouth next, she spun away and nearly bumped into Tarek, who clamped his hand around the back of her neck.

"What are you doing?" he demanded.

I don't know.

"Don't confront a Centrois warrior, ever!"

"I didn't confront!" She tried to jerk free, but he easily kept her in place. "How can he still hate me?" She glanced back at J'ron, who was swaying and looking for a place to sit. "Why?"

"He told you. He believes you tried to kill him."

Think. Think! But how could she with Tarek so close, so warm, so hard?

"Nari," Tarek said, "don't believe that everything has changed. You're still a captive."

His hold had relaxed, making it possible for her to fully concentrate on the words. Unlike J'ron, he hadn't called her a chattel. "I didn't want you, or him, to die," she whispered. "Doesn't he understand that?"

"I won't speak for him. I can't."

Her world had become a churning river, a winter storm. From the moment she'd realized Tarek had been injured, she'd forced away all thoughts of him as the man she'd fucked and who had fucked her and had done everything she could to keep him alive. He'd survived and was strong again.

A man.

The man she desperately needed to mate with.

Her captor.

Still feeling both numb and on fire, Nari stood near Reyna. She'd been afraid they wouldn't be allowed to listen to what the warriors said, but they *belonged* to Tarek and Saka, and the brothers had indicated they were to remain nearby. And silent. Tarek and Saka sat side by side, not looking at each other but with an ease no one could ignore. Saka lacked Tarek's muscularity, and someone who didn't know him might take him for an untested youth, but his eyes carried a wary wisdom. The same guarded intelligence was in Tarek's eyes.

Had she truly noticed Tarek's intellect before? Maybe she'd been so consumed by his body's impact on hers at first that she'd been blind to other things. Now she studied, not just the way he carried himself, but what he might reveal of his mood.

Tarek had put his injuries behind him. It was almost as if his walk with near death hadn't happened, and he was ready to resume the weight and responsibility of leadership. He might not want it, but he knew what he had to do.

And he wouldn't allow his emotions to get in the way.

She could love a man like that—him. She might fear and even loathe his decisions, but she couldn't imagine not respecting his ability to make those decisions, and him.

Dizziness seeped through her, forcing her to fight her way back to clearheadedness. Even as her thoughts and vision cleared, she understood that her soul had embraced the Centrois known as Tarek. And if she could, if she dared, her body would tell him.

J'ron waited until everyone was gathered in a circle before stepping into the middle of it. He still appeared weak but held his head high. "I'll speak first because no one has more right," he started. "There has been a lot of talk about what we should do. The savages are dangerous; they've proven what they're capable of. If we're to be safe, we have to defeat them."

Helki, who'd been crouching near the center of the circle, got to his feet. "The savages are animals! And a Centrois warrior should be able to defend himself from animals."

"What are you saying?" J'ron demanded. "That we were careless?"

Helki didn't immediately answer, but his confrontational stance held everyone's attention. "You're young, J'ron. The young rely on their leaders for safety and guidance." With that, he turned his attention to Tarek.

"Does he hate Tarek?" Reyna whispered. "Is that why he said that?"

"I don't know," Nari said. "I think he wants to be warlord."

Looking angry, Helki stepped toward Tarek. "I thought you would be the one to call this gathering. Instead, you remained with *her*." He locked eyes with one warrior after another, the act reinforcing the group's size and strength. He even stared at her and Reyna. "We need leadership. Decisions made. What are we going to do, go after creatures who bear little resemblance to humans and attack and retreat like jackals or, finally, right an old wrong? Proclaim throughout Punta that we're the Divine Eternal's chosen ones?"

Most of the others muttered agreement. Several held up their sun-sticks or knives. The sight of so many warriors ready to do battle made her stomach clench. Why did men always think of fighting?

"Is that what *you* want?" Tarek asked J'ron.

"No," J'ron said. "Twice the savages have attacked us. I say they're our greatest danger and that revenge—"

"Not just revenge," Helki interrupted. "We *must* honor our fathers' memories, must prove ourselves worthy of the Divine Eternal." Fist clenched against his thick chest, he looked skyward. "Hear me, Divine Eternal. I make this vow to you and my brothers in battle. For every drop of blood my elders shed at Baasta hands, I will take a drop."

Reyna grabbed Nari's wrist. "He hates us."

Nodding, Nari laced her fingers through her cousin's. Then, as had happened so many times, her attention went to Tarek.

Helki now stood over Tarek and was staring down at him as if challenging him to a fight.

"Say it," Tarek said after a heavy silence. "Hold nothing back."

A look of surprise passed over Helki's features. Then he turned his back on Tarek and walked over to Nari and Reyna. His stare screamed of distrust and hatred. "They tried to blind us to the truth to make us believe that what they put on Tarek and J'ron's wounds saved their lives, but the Divine Eternal was responsible. Nothing has changed between the Centrois and Baasta. An old wrong *must* be righted. Now! Before anything else."

Ignoring Reyna's attempt to keep her sitting, Nari stood up. Helki was taller and much stronger, but it didn't matter. "We saved their lives—we, not the Divine Eternal," she said, loud enough for everyone to hear.

"You lie!" For an instant, she was certain Helki was going to hit her. Instead, with lips curled in a cold smile, he addressed his fellow warriors. "You all heard her, heard a lowly chattel put herself above the Divine Eternal. This creature has cast a spell over our warlord and must be silenced! I live to take up my weapons and attack her breed, stop the evil. Can any of you say differently? Can you, Tarek?"

21

What are we going to do?

Although Tarek had led her away from Reyna, her cousin's desperate question continued to haunt Nari. Between struggling for a reply and trying to deal with Tarek's silence in the wake of Helki's challenge, she could hardly think. She hadn't tried to shake off Tarek's grip as he forced her to accompany him to his sleeping place. Neither had she asked why he hadn't answered Helki because it didn't matter.

Only somehow warning her people did.

"You're to stay here." He indicated the sleep-pelt. Grabbing her hair, he pulled her against him; his heat scraped her skin. "Decisions made by the Centrois aren't for their captives' ears."

"I'm *not* your captive. I'm—"

"Enough! Don't you know what you did by confronting Helki?"

"I don't care. He was wrong when he said Reyna and I had nothing to do with you and J'ron living. He's trying—"

"I know what he's trying to do."

"Then why didn't you say—"

"I couldn't with you there."

Confused, she fell silent. When he tied her hands behind her and secured her to a tree, she nearly screamed, but what good would it do? He'd probably gag her.

After checking the bonds, he took her face in his hands. "This is larger than you and me, Nari. We aren't just a man and a woman but part of two breeds at war with each other. You saved my life, and I'll always be grateful, but that was yesterday. This is today. And I'm still warlord."

No matter how she tried to put her mind on other things during the endless day, she couldn't shake his words. Maybe she should feel proud because he now considered the Baasta to be warriors and no longer escaped chattel, but did it really matter?

Because he'd given her no choice, she could only wait for his return, wait and agonize over how she could possibly warn her people.

From where she was, she couldn't see or hear Reyna. Occasionally, the murmur of deep voices reached her, but she couldn't make out what they were saying. Of course, Tarek didn't want to take the chance that she'd anger Helki further. He also didn't want her be there while they made their decision, and she suspected his main concern was making sure she didn't hear him.

But was not knowing any better than learning that he was turning his back on what they'd briefly been to each other?

Mother, Father. I know you're looking for me, afraid something has happened to me. Maybe you fear the savages have killed or captured me. Maybe you're thinking a wilding injured me. Please, can you hear my thoughts? The Centrois are here! Hide! Protect yourselves.

Dark fear spread through her. Pulling on her bonds, she

shook her head as if doing so would dislodge the hated collar. How could she possibly have put Tarek's raw sexuality ahead of her family?

No longer! She should have killed him when she'd had the chance.

When, finally, she saw him coming her way, she vowed to keep her emotions to herself. Whatever it took, she'd find a way to get Tarek to tell her what the Centrois intended to do. And, somehow, she'd get him to release her.

And then what?

Not looking at her, he freed her from the tree and secured her hands in front of her. Then he indicated the steaming bowls he'd brought with him. "Eat."

Trying to hold on to the bowl and spoon out the contents with her wrists nearly touching was difficult. It might have been less awkward if she sat down, but as long as he stood, she'd do the same. And she wouldn't be the first to speak.

How many days and nights had she been with him? Today's setting suns were painting in bright colors his features that were both new and familiar. So was her awareness of his tanned chest and the scrap of covering over his penis.

The flesh around his wounds showed no sign of infection. However, he might still be experiencing some pain, might be weaker than usual and in need of more sleep.

If his sleep was deep enough, could she escape?

"You'll come with me when we leave in the morning," he announced when he was done eating. "And Reyna will be with my brother."

"I see."

"Do you?" He put his bowl down.

"Yes," she said, and looked him in the eye for the first time since his return. "You and the others are going to try to find my people."

"Yes."

"Even though you and I—"

"I already said this; we're part of something that's bigger than the two of us. I'm warlord, but every Centrois warrior has a voice. Almost to a man, they want to finish what our fathers and grandfathers vowed."

Almost? What about you?

Placing her bowl on the ground, she straightened. "I won't help you find them. No matter what you do, I won't. Neither will Reyna."

"There'll be no force, no beating."

Who had made that decision? Him? And why should she care?

When he stepped toward her, she shrank away, but he easily grabbed her forearm and closed his fingers around the ropes binding her wrists together. At first, he forced her arms down in front of her, her body slightly off balance, but then he pulled her against him. She should fight! Should scratch and kick and maybe bite. Instead, her cheek rested against his chest while he stroked the back of her neck.

"I wish I'd never met you," he muttered. "And that we'd never fucked."

"I wish the same thing."

It didn't take Tarek long to prepare for an early morning departure. Only his brother could possibly know how difficult this was, and like him, Saka was keeping his emotions to himself. He couldn't say how many times he'd traced the hawk heads that proclaimed his rights and responsibilities as warlord, how many times he asked the Divine Eternal to lighten his heart, but if the Divine Eternal had spoken, it was only to hand him yet another image of his dying father.

He'd retied Nari to the tree before leaving her, and although he had no doubt that her mind was crowded with questions and fears, she hadn't said anything after insisting that she wanted nothing to do with him.

Hopefully she still felt the way, he thought as he reluctantly walked back to where he had no choice but to spend the night. If he was home, he'd order a sex-chattel to service him so he could concentrate on the journey and what might happen at its end, but he wasn't going to fuck Nari. He wasn't!

She was sitting cross-legged near the tree, turned so she could see him approach. Despite the weariness caused by his injuries, he squared his shoulders and didn't look down at her.

"You will *not* resist when I place you on my moto in the morning," he informed her. "Because if you do, I'll tie you to it as if you were a deer carcass."

"And if you find my people, what then? Will you force me to watch the attack?"

"Enough! I swear I'll gag you."

"Do it! Otherwise, I'll curse you."

After what he'd suffered at the hands of the savages, curses should have no impact, but if they came from her . . ."Do it quickly, then, because I'm going to sleep." Hoping to turn his words into reality, he hauled her behind him to a thicket where they relieved themselves. Walking back, he found himself concentrating on the barely audible sounds her feet made. He couldn't hear her breathe, and maybe because he wasn't looking at her, he wasn't sure whether she was real or an image born of his imagination.

This mix of captive and sexual woman had touched him in ways that couldn't and shouldn't be. Although certainly the same was true for her, he didn't bring it up.

He should bind her to the tree again and lay down as far away as possible from her. Instead, he ran a rope from her tied wrists to his and made room for her on his sleep-pelt. At his silent command, she knelt on it. Taking a steadying breath, he did the same, careful not to touch her.

Tucking her hands between her breasts, she rocked forward. "I hate . . ." Tears clogged her voice.

"What? Me?"

"No." She drew out the word. "It isn't that simple."

Night was upon them. Much as he wanted to study her expression, he was even more grateful for the dark because maybe this way he wouldn't reveal anything of what he was feeling. "No," he agreed. "It isn't."

"I want to leave my body behind. Even more, I don't want to feel what I am, to be so confused."

Why was she telling him these things? Surely she didn't expect him to make the same admissions.

"The first time I put a rope around a wilding's neck and rubbed between its eyes, I was so proud because I'd done something no Baasta ever had and knew our lives would become better as a result. But then my father piled branches onto a wilding's back and forced it to carry the wood for most of the day, and I cried because I'd taken something from the wilding. It's freedom."

Just as I've taken yours. "It's too late to go back to what was before that first time."

"I know." She sniffed. "Just as it is for us."

"Us?"

"Not just you and me but the Baasta and Centrois."

Sex-chattel weren't supposed to care about anything except giving and receiving pleasure, and he'd never before concerned himself with what one might think about when she wasn't fucking. Now, although Nari wasn't a sex-chattel, he believed he knew a great deal more about them.

"Certain things were set in place long before you and I were aware of them," she continued. "We're part of something beyond our control, and it doesn't matter whether we want it or not."

"I am what I am," he insisted. If he didn't say that, he'd risk telling her that he'd nearly turned his back on his leadership role tonight. "Just like you are."

"I know." Picking up her blanket, she awkwardly wrapped it around her. Then she lay down on her side facing him. Much as he wanted her naked, her dress was better. Safer.

Staring at the stars kept him from looking at her, but the distraction did nothing to quiet his awareness. Finding the Baasta stronghold might take days, days and nights during which he'd have to battle her impact on him. He could bring her down by forcing her to the edge of climax and leaving her there, stripping her of the ability to think of anything except her cunt's needs, but that would bring him to his own edge. And he wouldn't survive.

Where were the Baasta? Undoubtedly a number of them were looking for her and Reyna. Those searchers might have come across Centrois signs. It was possible they'd set a trap and were waiting for him and his warriors to ride into it.

Putting his mind on that question was easier than thinking about her trying to fall asleep next to him. The Baasta might have found where the Centrois and savages had fought, including proof of his and J'ron's injuries. The Centrois guards were skilled in watching for the enemy, but they might have been so concerned with whether he and J'ron would live that their eyes had strayed from their surroundings.

Was that why Nari wasn't resisting? She knew her people were out there?

A dark and ill-formed image of countless eyes staring out from behind countless rocks and trees briefly captured his attention, but there weren't that many Baasta or rocks and trees. There was . . . was what?

A familiar warm mist slipped over him. He embraced it, wrapped it around himself, sent its warmth to his crotch so it could ease the tension there. Sleep now. Think and plan and defend and fight tomorrow.

Look into *her* eyes tomorrow.

* * *

Nari repeatedly drifted off. Just as frequently, something snatched her back. Her mind was full of disconnected images: Baasta sitting around a campfire while a storyteller told of their beginning when spirits mated and gave birth to humans, the moment of her niece's birth, Tarek holding Dio in his big and capable hands.

The final image expanded and became clearer. It was as if she was standing beside him while he pulled in the sweet new baby smell and a tiny fist captured his finger. When that happened, Tarek's eyes grew softer, shining with unshed tears. When he started humming, the sound reminded her of a mother cougar's loving hum as her cubs nursed. In her mind, she touched his shoulder and he turned toward her, careful not to wake Dio.

"He's beautiful," she whispered.

"Not beautiful." Tarek smiled. "Handsome and strong."

"Not strong yet but soon with his uncle and father showing him the way."

Tarek's smile started to fade, then rose again, open and free. "I'll teach him how to ride a moto. You can show him how to handle a wilding."

"Together?"

Not only did his smile disappear, but so did he. Mist started claiming his edges, and a woman's hands reached out to take Dio. What was left of Tarek floated on the mist.

More hands reached for him, hers.

As consciousness returned, Nari realized that she had indeed touched Tarek's chest, but instead of jerking back, she increased the contact. She'd fallen asleep telling herself that she hated him, but it had been a lie; her fingers on him were proof. It didn't matter that he'd roped her hands together and tethered her to him. Neither did it matter tonight that he'd kill or be killed if he found her people.

Only the two of them did.

"Nari."

His voice saying her name carried on the night air. And now his hand covered hers.

"I want you," she whispered.

Groaning, he rolled toward her, his hand sliding from her wrists to her arms, shoulders, and now to her back, pulling her closer so her breasts caressed him. "Why?"

"I don't know! By the Divine Eternal, I don't know."

Wrapping his arm fully around her, he sealed their bodies together with her hands between them. Then he rolled onto his back again, bringing her up and on top of him. When she straightened in preparation for straddling him, he pushed her dress up to her waist. Earlier she'd hated having such little use of her hands, but now she loved the challenge.

Gripping her waist with both hands, he positioned her so his hard cock slid along her belly. Pushing his cock-cloth aside, she cradled him between her pelvis and palms, careful to keep her weight off his injured side.

"Lift your arms," he ordered.

When she did, he ran his hands up the inside of her dress and took possession of her breasts. Her nipples hardened, and he turned his attention to them, lightly but firmly gripping, drawing her downward. Not being allowed to touch him was nearly more than she could stand, and yet something about their helplessness fed her mind and heated her crotch.

Thinking to reposition herself to improve her balance, she supported her weight on her knees. When she came down, her wet cunt lips slid over his skin.

"Just like that?" he asked.

She rocked forward, threatening to squash his at-attention cock under her. "Just like that."

"Are you always like this, quick to be ready for sex?"

"No, never before." If she could have taken away her words, would she?

"I'm the difference?"

"I don't want to talk. About anything."

Afraid he'd probe, she spread her fingers over his chest. Strength rolled out of him and spoke to her of a power she'd never dreamed possible. Not allowing herself time to question what she was doing, she leaned forward until her breasts brushed his chest and kissed him.

The touch was like lightning, more unnerving than when he'd used the *club* on her. Scared, she broke off the contact, then again brushed her lips against his. Yes, like lightning. Like thunder and sunlight.

But much as she needed to explore the sensations, trying to keep her balance with such little use of her arms caused her shoulders and the back of her neck to ache. She slowly straightened, trying to comprehend his expression, but the night kept his secrets.

"I can't think when I'm around you," he said, and ran his hands from her waist to her buttocks. "Tell me one thing. When I do this"—he pressed a finger along the base of her spine—"can you think?"

"No." Squirming, she dug her nails into his flesh. "No."

"Scratch me, Nari. Leave your marks on me."

The notion of his fellow warriors teasing him about sex scratches made her laugh, and although she continued to rake him, she did so lightly.

His hands roamed over her, repeatedly claiming her waist, buttocks, hips, and thighs, and when he started working his way between their thighs, she widened her stance. Then he reached for her labia. Her breath whistling, she leaned back, exposing herself even more. Her hands trailed from his chest to the flat belly.

Suddenly he sat up, knocking her off balance so her back was now supported by his raised knees. She reached out to anchor herself but found his cock; she claimed it and held on. They hung like that.

After a moment, he chuckled. "There are no winners here, Nari. And no losers."

Laughing with him, she secured her hold. He started to tremble, which she took as proof that bracing both of them was taking its toll on him. Still, she wasn't ready when he lay back down, and she raked her nails over his belly to protest her displeasure.

He grunted. The grunt turned into a low laugh. Fingers tightened around her waist as he pushed her up and off him. Once more she reached for him, but this time only her fingertips made contact.

Then he brought her forward a little and she understood.

Pushing her pelvis forward, she went in search of his cock, found it. His organ slid along the front of her pelvis, prompting her to raise herself up as far as her legs and his assistance allowed. She came down again, exploring, moving to one side and the other until his tip pressed against her opening. Head back, concentrating, she sucked in air through her open mouth.

Down. Invasion increasing. Another sideways adjustment. His fingers hard on her hip bones and his cock plowing hard, going deeper, expanding her. Filling and fulfilling her.

In. Home.

While he created little circles on her belly, she slid her hands under her dress and did the same to her breasts. At first touching both at the same time was awkward, but she discovered that she could use the heels of her hands to push the mounds together. She loved being part of him, two bodies united, and explored the sensation by gripping him with her inner muscles. Whenever she did, he pushed up and into her. Otherwise, his cock remained quietly embedded.

Her breasts were like summer-ripe fruit, full and firm, heated from endless sunlight. The same heat had found its way to her cunt.

She was running her nails over her rocklike nipples when it

occurred to her that she'd made him her prisoner. Yes, he occasionally lifted his ass off the ground, but it took considerable effort. Yes, he could encourage her to move by pushing up and down on her waist, but she was in charge.

For the first and maybe the only time, she controlled the pace of their fucking.

Only time?

Don't think about that now. Don't!

The reasoning creature who'd tried to invade her world faded into nothing, leaving her free to be what she wanted to be tonight—his sex-chattel.

Now housing one breast in both hands, she fully embraced the words. *Sex-chattel.* A creature with one purpose, one role, a single goal.

Propelled by the thought, she twisted to one side and then the other, bringing his trapped cock with her. Gripping her forearms, he pulled her hands off her breasts, then directed them to his chest. Still working her body from side to side, she leaned forward.

Gripping his cock with hot, slick muscles, she rose as high as she could, taking him with her. As she did, he released her forearms and roughly ran his hands over her shoulders. Her flesh burned, but instead of trying to escape, she again leaned as far forward as she dared. Once more he gripped her buttocks, perhaps ready to punish her if she put his cock under too much strain, but she wouldn't do that to him. Ever.

Instead, she licked his wounded shoulder and then nipped the other.

Feeling the strain in her back, she straightened, laughing when he slapped her ass. Still laughing, she bit his healthy shoulder again, slightly harder this time.

He slapped her, hard, repeatedly.

"Stop it!" She reared up, gripping his cock with all her strength. "Or I'll hurt you."

"With those puny muscles?" He began working his hands around to her mons.

"Don't you dare." She started to lift herself off him, then stopped. "Displease me in any way and I'll make you beg."

"You?" One hand continued its march to her mons. The other dove under her tangled dress to grip a nipple. "Make me beg?"

"Scream, then. Scream and bellow."

She could do this. Wanted to do this. Needed it. Not caring what he might do or think or say, she rose a little more, but when his cock began sliding out of her, she came down again and welcomed him home. His hands were on her sides now, traveling over her ribs, gliding over her hips. Powered by him, she braced her arms and leveraged herself up and down. She started slow, experimenting with the sensations. Filling herself with him felt wonderful and frightening, a repeated surrender of her body to his. In contrast, lifting herself up and nearly off him was ever more frightening, and yet she wasn't truly afraid, ever.

This was right. Hot. Pumping the man who before had pumped her. Playing with his cock just as he'd played with her cunt.

Feeling him, everywhere. Pussy on fire, thigh muscles trembling, breasts flopping, nails burrowing into his skin, head back, and lungs hungry.

"Nari. Nari. Nari."

She tried to look at him, tried to find her way past the night. "Tarek!"

Startled by her voice, she pushed against his pelvis. She'd trap him under her, hold him down, imprison him. Feed off him.

But just as she took her first bite, he clamped his hands around her ass cheeks and drew them apart. Cool air found her crack.

"Stop!" she ordered, and ground her pussy muscles against him. "Stop it!"

"No." With that, he rounded his back and rolled up. For a moment they were face-to-face and breast-to-chest. Then he shoved into her and knocked her back. But she didn't fall because he caught her, his hands digging into her spine. "Off me. Turn around and then take me again," he ordered.

Although she wasn't sure what he had in mind, with his help she stood, turned her back to him, and straddled his hips. He guided her down until his cock kissed her entrance. *More! Now!*

Sweat broke out on her forehead and throat. Eyes shut, she opened herself, and he dove home, his heat gliding over hers. Reaching out, she found his inner thighs and then his balls and cradled his weight.

He drove up into her, nearly knocking her off balance and forcing her to release him. With her back straight and no way of bracing herself, she cupped her hands around her mons. When he drew away, she sank down with him, riding him as she sometimes rode a wilding.

Another powerful thrust followed by withdrawal. By putting what there was of her mind to it, she found his rhythm. With that accomplished, she concentrated heart and soul on her dance of surrender. Swirls of pleasure caressed her from breasts to thighs because he'd guided her into a hot, wet fog and was now bathing her with it. Fueled by the reckless need for release and relief, she worked to heighten the necessary friction of flesh against flesh.

Heat raked her nerves and fueled her muscles. As her frenzied movements increased, her flailing breasts felt as if they might tear themselves free, so she flattened them as best she could, knees grinding into the earth, thighs burning.

Just as the first wave of her climax rose in her, she lost her balance and started to slide off him. He caught her around the waist and held her, his cock pressed tight and possessively. Promising. Insisting.

She couldn't see him! Had to see him!

Ignoring his grunted protests, she twisted free and lifted herself off him. The instant her feet were under her, she spun around so she was again facing him and stood with her legs on either side of him. He stroked her calves, and now it didn't matter that he was lost in night shadows.

I want you, she'd told him.

I'll take you, now.

With that, she sank back onto her knees, hands searching. Finding his cock, she guided the soft-as-spring tip into her.

Yes! Again. Yes.

He was back where he belonged, housed inside her. *Hers!*

Then he grabbed her wrist restraints and yanked her down onto him. *His. I'm his.*

He hit her with a searing pass that forced a roar from both of them. She started melting, becoming lava, merging with him.

Another pass. Another roar from him, a scream from her this time.

She lived through her slick, tight flesh and the purple-veined shaft invading it. Hissed through several ragged breaths.

The cliff, the waterfall appeared in her mind's eye. A cry of tormented ecstasy tore her lungs. The waterfall became a wave and the wave a climax that crested hot and long.

Once more she screamed. The air captured the sound and held it, mixed it with his animal growls, turned it all into a single whole.

22

Tarek was deeply asleep.

Barely daring to move, Nari eased away and lay not breathing until she was sure she hadn't wakened him. Just a few moments ago she'd been lost in sleep herself, but her dream had been so vivid that she'd awakened in a cold sweat and gasping for breath.

Its intensity was already fading, but she still heard children screaming as they ran from the relentless motos. There'd been other screams as women fought the ropes encircling their bodies and the deeper cries of men locked in furious battle or bleeding from wounds caused by sun-sticks.

Black billowing smoke rose from deliberately set fires that destroyed homes and lives. Terrified wildings bucked and galloped, too many mares separated from their foals. Some were being chased by Centrois astride their motos.

But what truly filled her with hopeless rage were the collars being placed around the necks of the Centrois' new prisoners—their reclaimed chattel.

What a fool she'd been to put Tarek's body and her need for it ahead of her people's lives!

He hadn't untied her, but neither had he secured her to him. Either he'd been so worn out from their energetic sex while still recovering from his wounds that he'd fallen asleep without considering whether she'd try to escape or he'd believed she'd stay with him.

Looking at him, her skin still raw and heated from him, she wanted to. Her heart both beat like a young bird's and ached, and memories of the things they'd done enticed her to return to a place where only fucking and being fucked mattered.

But if the Centrois found the Baasta, her family would be destroyed.

Although she desperately wanted to at least leave Tarek with her taste on his lips, she didn't dare chance it. Fighting tears and the nearly impossible weight dragging her down, she rolled away. Then she sat up and pushed her dress down over her hips, covering the part of her that she'd joyfully and dangerously handed over to him.

Her tears broke free as she got to her feet, and she sagged, too weak to move. Then, knowing what she had to do, she ran her fingers over her collar, and the nightmare returned. The collar might be a symbol of something deep and personal between her and Tarek, but for the rest of her people, it represented one thing—imprisonment.

I'll never forget you, she told him. *When you discover what I've done, you'll hate me, but maybe a part of me will remain with you just as I'll carry some of you with me.*

With that, she slipped into the night.

Caught in the river's current, Tarek barely had time to throw out his hands before he struck the partly submerged boulder. He slid off it only to be caught in a whirlpool. Instead of fighting the powerful force, he went limp. A moment later, the whirlpool flung him back into the current. The banks beyond his reach looked so peaceful and were filled with flowers and sweet grass with small red deer grazing, but here there was only the powerful, roaring water.

Suddenly he was pulled under. Eyes open and searching desperately for something, anything, he fought the nearly colorless world he'd been thrust into. Despite his strength, the water tossed him about as if he weighed no more than a twig. His lungs burned. Terror clawed at him, barely held at bay by will and courage.

Just when he was certain his lungs would explode, he was hurtled to the surface. When he took in a breath, he inhaled water along with air, but at least he was no longer trapped in nightmare depths. The current lessened a little, giving him the opportunity to look around again.

He wasn't alone! Other Centrois warriors flowed and bobbed everywhere, all looking as unnerved as he felt.

How had they gotten here?

"Tarek. Tarek."

A jolt ran through him. Disoriented, he ran his hand over his eyes. When his vision cleared, he realized that Saka was kneeling beside him, shaking his shoulder. As he sat up, the nightmare peeled away, leaving behind only the memory of helplessness.

"She's gone," Saka said.

Although he might never tell anyone, he wasn't surprised. Was, in fact, glad.

"I saw her leave a few moments ago," Saka continued. "She hurried past where Reyna and I were. If she knew we were there, she didn't acknowledge us."

"What about the others? Do they know?"

Saka shook his head. The moon had made its appearance since he'd fallen asleep, making it possible for him to read his brother's expression. There was no anger or blame there. "Reyna begged me to simply let her go," Saka said, "but you needed to know."

Nodding, he scooted over to make room on the sleep-pelt. As he ran his hand over it, he noted that it no longer held her heat. "I knew," he admitted. "Knew she'd put her people first."

"Do you blame her?"

He wanted to. Damnation, he wanted to hate her so much that no other emotion could reach him, but it wasn't that simple. "We fucked. She told me she wanted me. It was the same for me." He took a deep breath. "And then she waited for me to fall asleep so she could escape."

Saka squeezed his arm. "Reyna, too, wants to warn her people."

"Did you tie her?"

"No. I hope . . . I hope I don't have to, but maybe that's the only way I can spare her from having to make the decision Nari did."

Rocking forward, Tarek studied the night. Darkness embraced Nari in the same way it had always welcomed him. Morning's sun warmed both of them while creeks and rivers provided them with water and animals and the earth fed them. And he craved her body just as she craved his.

They had those things and more in common, but in other ways they were predator and prey, hunter and hunted, free and chattel.

"Reyna cried while we were having sex," Saka said. "So did I because what brought us together will tear us apart. By all that's holy, I swore I'd never give my heart to another woman, especially someone who isn't of my breed! But I did."

Centrois men were taught not to show sympathy or compassion for each other because that weakened a warrior, but this was his brother, and he didn't care if anyone saw when he wrapped his arms around Saka.

"What are you going to do?" Saka asked after a long silence.
"What I have to."

Tarek was placing the last of his supplies on his moto a few minutes later when he heard approaching footsteps. Bit by bit the night gave up its secrets. Every one of the men he considered a part of himself were here. He acknowledged all of them, even Helki.

J'ron walked at the front of the group with his arms hanging at his sides. "*She* isn't there, is she?"

"No."

"Because she ran away."

"Yes."

He fully expected J'ron to call him a fool, even accuse him of letting her go. Instead, J'ron simply nodded.

"You aren't fully healed," A'tala said from his position to J'ron's right. Although the two had always been friends, A'tala frowned at J'ron, then turned his attention on Tarek. "In need of rest, not tracking her down. Why didn't you turn her over to one of us?"

Because she doesn't belong to me—or anyone. "I know what I have to do."

Grunting, Helki stepped forward. Where A'tala had appeared confused, Helki was obviously enraged, as evidenced by his clenched fists. "Find her? How? You don't know where she's gone. By the Divine Eternal, if she reaches the Baasta before we do, they'll be ready. Attack. This is a search for all of us, Tarek. We'll stop her—in whatever way it takes."

"No!" Fighting his conflicting emotions, Tarek forced himself to calm down. "This is between me and her, my duty."

Not just Helki but everyone was grim-faced and studying him as closely as the moon and stars allowed. "*Will* you do your duty?" Helki demanded. "Conduct yourself like a Centrois leader and warrior and not a man with a new sex-chattel?"

What he wanted was to dive into his dream river and let it carry him away, anywhere. Instead, he placed his fist over his chest. How proud he'd been when the hawk heads had been tattooed there! "This a Centrois heart. It beats only one way."

Helki spat. "You let her go."

"What happened was of her own doing."

"Because you didn't treat her like a hostage, a chattel."

No, I didn't. "She can't outrun a moto. I know what I have to do."

"But will—"

"Don't challenge me, Helki! I'm warlord, not you. As long as I wear this"—he rubbed the hawk heads—"certain decisions and tasks are mine."

His declaration apparently satisfied the others, although he wasn't sure about Helki; either that or no one was willing to argue with him. Whichever it was, after talking among themselves for a short while, the men shuffled away, all except for Helki and J'ron.

"Say it, Helki. Don't hide behind silence."

Although Helki stood his ground, he didn't assume a confrontational stance. "Right now I only have one thing to tell you. Don't fail your people. If you do—"

"I won't. I'm warlord."

Helki's head came up, but instead of questioning his statement, he looked at the retreating men. After a tense moment, he started after them, leaving just J'ron.

"What is it?" Tarek demanded. "What?" he repeated when J'ron didn't say anything.

"I wish you didn't have to do this."

"What are you saying?"

"She saved our lives, yours and mine."

"You believe that? Helki said—"

"He's wrong. You and I are alive because of her. I wish . . . I wish I'd thanked her."

"And maybe she has sealed our doom."

Clouds were building on the horizon, but so far there weren't enough to threaten rain. Keeping to a rapid walk, Nari put her mind to the need for rain despite the problems a storm would present. Wildings ignored a light rain, but if a brisk wind kicked up, they sought shelter. Given the suns' strength this morning, she was certain that they were barely moving as they fed.

Although she hadn't yet seen fresh sign of them, she was heading for an open stretch of land flanked by hills on one side and several narrow but deep cracks in the earth on the other. She'd revealed a great deal to Tarek, but she hadn't told him how well she knew this area. Not only had she come here a number of times for wildings, but she also knew the most direct route from there to the sheltered area where her people lived.

Exhaustion so deep it threatened to rob her of the will to breathe rose up to engulf her. It wasn't the first time. Neither did she expect it to be the last, because leaving the Centrois warlord had been the hardest thing she'd ever done.

Shaking her head made her dizzy, but that was the only way she could fight her exhaustion—if that's what it was. Self-control regained, she faced reality. The Centrois had to be tracking her.

She pressed her hand against her forehead, then ran her hand down her face until she reached her mouth. Her lips were dry, so she moistened them with her tongue, but doing so reminded her of how thirsty and hungry she was. She hadn't dared take the time to grab some food and water before running away, and she hadn't tried to sever the ropes around her wrists until coming across a sharp boulder as it was getting light.

Where was Tarek? How far behind her was he and was he

alone or had he brought the rest of his warriors with him? What about Reyna?

"I'm sorry," she muttered as an image of her cousin rose in her mind. "I wanted to bring you with me, but I was afraid Saka would wake—maybe you wouldn't have left him."

I don't want to be doing this, Tarek. Can you possibly understand?

Weariness again swirling around her, she put one heavy foot in front of the other. When she'd left him and his bed, she'd still been carrying Tarek's seed inside her. During those first moments of *freedom* when she felt as if she were dying, she'd kept her heart beating by reminding herself of the gift he'd given her—and of the possibility that she was carrying his child. But imagining his son or daughter at her breast brought searing pain because that son or daughter would grow up not knowing its father.

And her body would have to live with the memories.

Despite the hot tears pushing against her eyes, her mouth remained dry. If she put her fingers into her pussy, it might still be wet with him, but that single source of moisture wasn't enough. She had to nourish her body.

Walk. Square your shoulders and lift your head. You're a Baasta! Return to them. Warn them. Fight with them. Save them.

The three wildings at the bottom of the slope lifted their heads and watched her approach. One nervously swished its tail, but the others only pricked their ears forward. After coming a little closer, she started talking to them. Her chant was made up of nonsense sounds and unrelated words chosen because of their rhythm. This trio was no different from wildings she'd spoken to before, in that they seemed to enjoy and be fascinated by the sound.

Fortunately she'd come across a shaded pond a little while ago, and although there'd been a green scum on top, she'd brushed it away and drank as much as she dared put in her empty stomach. As a result, she was clearer-headed than she'd been earlier.

And single-minded.

"Don't worry, wild ones. Letting me on one of your backs won't change your lives. I only need you to take me home and then I'll let you go. I promise."

Walking slowly, she kept repeating herself, wondering when, and not if, the one who was twitching its tail would bolt. No matter how she presented herself, some wildings were so nervous that they weren't worth the effort. Fortunately, most had calmer temperaments.

"One day is all I ask. One day and you can run wild and free again."

She was now so close that she could see their eyelashes. Always before, she'd stopped and waited for a while so they could get used to her smell, but she didn't dare take the time. She'd looped what was left of her wrist restraints around her shoulder and planned to use that to guide the wilding once she'd mounted it. "I know. I'm a strange-looking creature, maybe the first thing you've ever seen on two legs but—"

With a squeal, the nervous wilding raced past her. Fortunately it didn't come so close that she had to jump out of the way, which might have caused the others to bolt. "There," she said once he was gone. "I guess he was in a hurry. Now, where was I?"

Catching a wilding. Getting far away from Tarek and everything he represents.

She'd chosen the smaller of the remaining two because it was female and probably of a quieter nature and because she was more densely muscled than the young male. After running her hands all over the female, Nari had spent precious time getting her accustomed to the rope's feel. At first the female had resisted having the rope on her, but now she stood next to a rotting log while Nari prepared her for accepting a rider by standing on the log and leaning on the wilding's back. The young male alternated between prancing just out of reach and nibbling on Nari's dress and hair. The male's hot breath reminded her of another breath.

Fear rose in her throat and threatened to cut off her ability to breathe. Until this moment she'd imagined Tarek wrapping her body in ropes, pushing the sun-powered cock deep inside her, maybe beating or even raping her. But she hadn't allowed herself to ask whether he might kill her.

Why not? The Centrois could be brutal. And she'd done the unforgivable by running away after begging him to fuck her, by trying to warn her people.

"I won't let anything bad happen to you," she promised the wilding. With that, she pushed off the log and onto the bony back. "If he aims his sun-stick, I'll stand between you and it."

The wilding reared, but because she expected her to, Nari grabbed the long neck hair and hung on. Her mount squealed. So did the other wilding.

By the time the two animals were done snorting, she'd managed an upright position, but although she needed to get her mount to start moving, she had to wait until it stopped shaking.

"I know it feels strange and frightening," she said soothingly, "but remember, I vowed I'll never hurt you. I need your speed for one day, just one day. Then you'll—"

Before she could finish, the male spun around and stared in the direction she'd come from. Both animals squealed again, but it didn't matter because she'd heard the sound.

A moto!

23

As he came over the rise, Tarek all but stood on his moto. However, although the prints had told him that wildings were around, he wasn't prepared for what he saw.

Nari, on a wild animal's back!

Moving slower now, he closed a little of the distance between them and then stopped. She was leaning forward on her mount, holding short ropes leading from the creature's head, staring at him. As he returned her stare, time slipped back to when he'd first seen her. He knew much more about her now than he had back then, and yet in the most fundamental of ways he didn't know her at all.

Hated her.

Maybe loved her.

The moto eased forward.

"No!" she screamed, and yanked on one of the ropes, turning the wilding around. The animal reared, then began a rough and uncertain run. Instead of taking off after it, he remained where he was, watching her hair stream out behind her and her healthy young body wedded to her mount. Maybe he'd let her go, tell the others he hadn't found her.

But he couldn't.

Cursing both of them and where they'd come from, he sped after her. Although she'd tried not to let him know, she'd clearly enjoyed being on his moto. Now he wished he was with her, feeling living muscle and speed.

Not wanting to put her safety at any more risk than he already had, he didn't try to overtake the wilding but hung back, thinking to wait until the animal had worn itself down. What concerned him the most was that it acted as if it had never been ridden and repeatedly tried to shake her off.

Urged on by its determined rider, the wilding headed downhill, but although Nari tried to slow it, it ran at full speed. The hill became steeper, and Nari leaned back, bracing herself. From where he was, he couldn't see the ground ahead of her but feared there were even more rocks there than beneath him.

Touching the brake, he slid to a stop. *Be careful! Slow down! Can't you see I'm no longer—*

Suddenly the wilding dug its hind legs into the ground. At the same time, it turned its head and front legs to the right in an attempt to change directions. Unfortunately, it lost its balance and rolled onto its side, landing heavily. Legs flailing behind it, it slid down the hill. Nari managed to jump free, but she, too, was tumbling, unable to stop. Instinct and fear kicked in, and he charged after them.

By the time he overtook her, she'd stopped rolling and lay with her arms and legs twisted under her. Not waiting for his moto to come to a complete stop, he jumped off. Just then she lifted her head. Her hair was filled with grass and debris, and she had a scratch on her cheek that extended to the collar he'd forced her to wear.

"Are you all right?" Much as he wanted to touch her, he didn't.

"Go away!"

"I can't."

Sighing, she rested her head on the ground. He couldn't tell whether she was deciding whether she was injured or resigning herself to his presence. Although he could have easily touched her sex, he gave it only passing thought. Her desperate race for freedom followed by the accident consumed him—that and the chasm that had opened up between them.

"Where are the others?" she asked, and sat up.

"Waiting for me to bring you back."

"Why didn't you kill me?" She nodded at his sun-stick in its carrying bag at his waist.

"Why did you run?"

Despite Tarek's hard question, Nari forced herself to return his gaze. She ached everywhere but was certain she hadn't broken any bones. Maybe it would have been easier if she'd been knocked unconscious or if the wilding had fallen on her and crushed her, but because those things hadn't happened, she had no choice but to look at the man who'd changed her life. The man she hated as she'd never hated before.

When he stepped closer and started to kneel down, she knew this was what it felt like to be a deer brought down by an arrow, spear, or a sun-stick. The deer might still be alive with memories of freedom, but it was helpless.

Doomed.

Screaming, she gathered herself and kicked, her heels striking his crotch. He grunted and tried to back away but lost his balance and landed on his buttocks. As he planted his hands on the ground, she scrambled to her feet, but she'd only taken a couple of steps when he grabbed an ankle and yanked her down with him. Strengthened by another scream, she spun around thinking to attack with everything she had, but before she could, he shoved her onto her belly and straddled her hips, pinning her. No matter how she struggled, his weight was too much. By his ragged breathing, she guessed her heels had connected where she'd aimed.

Her flailing fingers found his calves, and she dug in like a cougar determined to cripple a larger prey, but Tarek wasn't prey; he was predator. Although she managed to evade him the first time he tried to snag her wrists, he pressed his forearm against her shoulder blades and flattened her against the ground. Seizing a wrist, he jerked her arm behind her and forced it as high as it would go. Pain sparked everywhere, forcing her to stop struggling so she could pant through it.

A rope. Around her wrist.

Then her other arm being pressed against her spine and the rope circling that wrist not once or twice but three times.

Sucking in air, he released her. Her useless hands rested on her buttocks.

"You haven't learned, have you?" he demanded. "You'll never win a fight with me."

"Bastard! Belly crawler!"

"You're the one on her belly, not me, Nari."

She'd managed to turn her head to the side when he'd sat on her but still couldn't see what he was doing. He was obviously in no hurry to let her up.

Repositioning himself so less of his weight pressed down on her, he ran his knuckles along her fingers on his way to comforting his cock. Instead of relishing in this small measure of satisfaction, she went back in her mind to when she'd held him. Stroked him. Given him pleasure and helped guide him to climax.

Those times were behind her. She was his prisoner again, his hostage. His sex-chattel. And although she didn't want it, along with her fear came warm heat, swollen nipples, and a sweet grinding low in her belly.

"Our battle was short," he said, and slid down her until he

now rested lightly on her thighs. "If you were stronger, we could have made it last much longer, equal to equal, but you're back where we both knew you'd be, aren't you?"

She struggled to lift her upper body off the ground so she could glare at him, but the effort made her back throb. "I don't want this! How dare you think—"

A rough hand sliding between her thighs and pressing against her cunt silenced her. She barely gave thought to resisting.

"My chattel. My little sex beast." He ran his thumb along her labia, dipped into her, retreated. "You're wet, Nari. Oh yes, this is what you want."

"No!" She clamped her thighs as tightly together as she could, but instead of trying to free himself, he turned his attention to her clit. At his touch, her nub sent lightning throughout her.

"Yes, chattel, yes. I *will* have you. And when I'm done, you'll know what you are to me. Nothing."

Nothing? But why should she hate the word when she desperately needed him to be nothing to her?

To her horror, when he removed his hand, she came too close to begging. He ran his wet fingers over the back of her thighs, then tugged up on her dress hem until her buttocks were exposed.

"A woman's ass." He slapped her. "Made for punishment." More slaps, light but stinging, humiliating and yet—

"Stop! Stop it!" She twisted to the side, his crotch sliding along her thighs.

"Yes, chattel, yes."

He easily repositioned her on her belly and breasts, then went back to slapping her until she was certain her buttocks had turned bright red. Clenching her teeth to keep from cursing him, she felt herself falling into the relentless sensation. To have her ass subjected to *this* should be humiliating. Instead, she burrowed deep inside her helplessness.

He owned her ass. At the same time, her body fascinated him, held his attention, in a strange way owned him.

When he stopped, she lay limp and panting on the thankfully cool ground. And when he climbed off her, she couldn't rouse herself enough to watch him.

There. Touching her again. Only it wasn't his hand but a rope end trailing over her heated ass. She twitched with each pass.

"Ticklish?"

"No."

"You lie, Nari." The soft end barely stroked her abraded skin and yet freed a moan. "Don't lie to me."

Tarek hated her for escaping. Maybe he didn't care why she'd run and had simply been determined to lull her into believing he was human beneath the warrior. She'd weakened under his touches and the heady feel of his cock in her. She'd embraced his gratitude when she saved his life, but he was showing his true self now. This was Tarek the Centrois, the warlord, the keeper of sex-chattel, and the hunter of Baasta.

And because he was those things, she could hide the truth about herself to him. Distract him. Sell her body to him in exchange for her people's lives.

If she didn't, the Baasta were doomed.

He'd grabbed her ankle and was lifting it, bending her knee in the process. A rope looped around her ankle and started to tighten. She jerked, freeing her leg from his hand but not the rope.

"Stop fighting! You're going back with me. You *have* to."

At his words, she nearly lost touch with her desperate plan, but because she didn't dare, she forced herself to relax. By the time he was done, he'd hobbled her, leaving only a little space between her ankles. He'd done this to her before. She'd survived then, and she'd survive now. Somehow.

Taking hold of her shoulders, he hauled her to her feet. Then he brushed leaves off her dress and shook more leaves and twigs out of her hair. She nearly thanked him, belatedly reminded herself to hide behind her one weapon—silence.

When he stepped back, she nearly followed him. Fortunately, the ankle restraints kept her in place and served as an inescapable lesson. He glared at her. "I'm not going to touch you the way I did last night." Hooking a finger through the ring in her collar, he lifted her onto her toes. "There's only one thing left between us, chattel. Your use in my finding your people."

This was the Tarek she'd known when he first captured her, a hard and unfeeling man.

"I saved your life," she hissed.

"You shouldn't have."

24

His hold on the collar forced Nari to concentrate on her breathing, and she should loathe him for handling her this way, but she didn't. Perhaps there was something about helplessness that forced her attention on her body, on its unwanted response to his. He'd done what he'd wanted to her the other day, including forcing repeated climaxes on her. Maybe elements of those climaxes remained inside her like coals waiting to spring to life.

"You're wrong, Tarek," she finally thought to say. "Many things exist between us, secrets revealed, gentleness when neither of us expected or wanted it."

Letting go of the ring, he shoved, and she started to fall. At the last moment, he grabbed her around the waist and jerked her upright. They stood chest to breast, their eyes burning. His hard and heavy cock pressed against her, and although she was on fire, she forced her legs together.

"Damn you!" he growled, and threw her over his shoulder. She couldn't tell where he was carrying her, but what did it matter when she was at *his* mercy? She expected, wanted, him to run his hand between her legs, but all he did was wrap his arm around her legs to keep her from moving.

When he deposited her on the ground, she realized he'd brought her to his moto. *We're going back*, his action said. *Now.*

Where was her resolve, her insane plan to break through his defenses? She couldn't do anything, had been *his*.

He wouldn't have tied her legs if he'd intended to have her ride ahead of him, would he? That left only one thing—being thrown over the seat like a fresh kill.

"Do it," she hissed. "Do it and call yourself a man, if you can."

Instead of the slap she expected, he rubbed her shoulders. What was it she'd just called herself, a fresh kill? No. Not that. She simply belonged to him.

All signs of his recent wounding had faded, and the prime male she'd recognized from the moment she'd known he existed had returned. Once again his cock-cloth barely covered him. Once more her cunt begged to embrace the essence of that prime male. She'd been a fool, such a fool to think she could seduce him when all power lay with him.

Called to her.

Her nipples had become so sensitive that the weight of her dress against them was painful, and she hunched forward to lessen the pressure. He watched, his gaze focused on her breasts. The longer he studied her, the hotter his gaze burned until she was afraid she'd scream. She tried to set her spine in silent declaration of how little impact he was having on her, but something had stolen her strength. *I want you. By the spirits, I need you!*

With a low growl, he grabbed her dress and yanked it up, exposing her breasts. Growling herself, she arched her back and presented herself to him, surrendered. Another growl rolled out of him as he slapped one breast. Thinking he'd keep on slapping her, she drew into herself and waited for the molten sensation. Instead, he placed his hand on the top of her head and forced her to lean over, then hauled the dress over her head and down her arms until the soft hide caught against her bonds.

Naked.

Again naked.

His.

He'd run his hands under her breasts and was lifting them before she could prepare for this latest assault. Back still arched and mouth open, she presented herself to him.

"Witch," he muttered. "You're a witch."

Not her. He was the one with all the power.

"Why am I doing this?" Indicating the mounds cradled in his palms, he glared at her in confusion. "By all the spirits, I vowed I'd take you back, nothing else. That I wouldn't touch you."

"And I vowed that if you found me, I wouldn't touch you."

"You can't because that's the way I need it to be."

"Why? Are you afraid of me?" The moment the words were out of her mouth, she wished she could take them back because surely this battle-tested warrior didn't fear his prisoner. When he continued to hold her breasts, she accepted this as proof of his control.

"You've crawled under my skin and into my blood," he said after a lengthy silence. "I don't want you there."

His breath was hot on her cheeks, and more heat slid over her breasts. Energy unlike anything she'd ever experienced or known existed radiated out from him to coat her entire body. She was drowning in him, melting from nothing more than a touch—a touch and her helplessness.

Helpless, yes! A prisoner, not simply of this warlord but of her own hunger.

"I . . . my aunt told me that although she fled along with the others, part of her didn't want to leave."

"What?"

"She said she felt fulfilled when kneeling at her owner's feet. She didn't want it to be that way, wanted to take charge of and responsibility for her own body, but when she was fucking, nothing else mattered."

"What are you saying?"

She'd closed her eyes while speaking. Now she opened them and looked up into a face she both loved and hated. "That maybe it was like that for us."

"The past." His arms dropped to his side.

"Yes."

Eyes hardening, he turned his back on her. He was doing something to his moto, but she didn't care. She'd said too much, exposed herself in ways that went far beyond her nudity, but she sensed he felt the same way.

"What is it?" she asked around the hot lump in her throat and the equally hot ache between her legs.

Whirling around, he raked her with a dark gaze. "No sex-chattel would ever tell her master what you've told me. I can't believe a chattel feels that way."

"My aunt did."

"She was addicted to the sex, to cocks, not to the cock's owner."

Am I? "It isn't that simple. My aunt is a wise and warm woman who loves playing tricks on her grandchildren. She married not long after becoming free—but sex with her husband has always disappointed her."

"She told you this?"

If felt strange to be carrying on this conversation while standing there with her clothing bunched around her useless hands, but words kept piling up inside her. "Her husband is a hard-working and considerate man, a good father and grandfather, quiet. Dull."

"He's a good husband but not in bed?"

"Yes." Memories of the conversations she'd had with her aunt rolled over her in waves. She remembered, not so much the words but the woman's aching tone. The idea of winding up like her aunt, safe and settled and so restless it tore at her heart, had been with her every time she looked at a man.

Tarek had destroyed her own restlessness, had silenced the ache in her heart. For a brief period.

Fighting tears, she focused on him. It was more than his physical strength, more than the sure way he played her body, more even than the danger he represented. In many ways he was like a savage or wilding—primitively and supremely alive.

And as he closed some of the scant distance between them, she lost herself in images of predators stalking prey, only, unlike a deer, she wouldn't flee even if she could. "You bring out a part of me I don't understand, a side I didn't know lived in me until you came into my life," he said. Reaching around her, he took hold of her elbows.

"I . . . I feel the same way."

"For me, a sex-chattel existed to take care of my need to fuck so I could concentrate on what I needed to do as warlord. Fucking whenever I wanted was like being able to eat whenever I was hungry."

His features blurred, and her breasts again skimmed over the familiar territory of his chest. Familiar and yet ever new.

He continued. "From the beginning, it was different between us, and yet I thought I knew how to make you answer my questions, by treating you like a fresh chattel."

That terrified me and yet I loved it.

"But I didn't think of you as chattel. And you didn't feel like one to my body." Yanking her tight against him, he widened his stance so his legs bracketed hers. "Why? Damn it, why?"

His body heat flowed and became part of her, slid over her sex and sparked it with new life. "I don't know."

"Maybe. And maybe you *are* a witch."

"Stop it!" He'd become a great tree, a raging storm, a vast river, her world. "That isn't true. You know it."

"I know only one thing, Nari. And that's that I was wrong. I can't take you back yet. Not before . . ."

She didn't need words because his body was saying everything. So was hers. It was becoming softer and smaller with skin that absorbed his every touch, the incredible feeling of being whatever he wanted her to be. Last night, despite the ropes on her wrists, she'd been free to touch him as much and in every way she wanted, but this was different.

Prisoner and captor.

Vulnerable, eager flesh.

She'd dropped to her knees before she knew she was going to, nearly falling onto her face, his hands sliding over her as she went. His fingers in her hair kept her upright. Then he released her and stood there.

Waiting for her.

She tried to draw his cock-cloth aside with her teeth, but it kept falling back in place. Giving up, she suckled him through the rough material, but it filled too much of her mouth, forcing her to concentrate on his tip. His cock became mystery in her mind, a prize just out of reach, flesh-to-flesh contact denied. But even with her frustration, she loved taking possession of that much of him.

He leaned into her and then withdrew, perhaps teasing himself as much as he was her. Determined to do the same thing, she lightly closed her teeth around him and settled herself lower, taking his cock with her. He pushed his pelvis at her, at the same time looping a finger through her collar ring and pulling her closer, maybe challenging her to absorb him.

She did, nearly gagging on the material but determined to command. What did she need with her hands? Her mouth was enough. Hunger snaked through her, at first a mutter but now an insistent plea. Soon it would roar.

This wasn't enough! Where was his heated weight, the taste and feel of him?

Angry, she opened her mouth as wide as she could and whipped her head to the side, expelling him. "Take it off. Now!"

He slapped her cheek. "You, ordering me?"

"Yes. Damnation, yes!"

The second slap sent pain prickling through her other cheek. Pulling the sting into her, relishing it, she imagined what his hand striking her cunt would feel like.

Mastery and mastered.

"Hit me! Go on, hit me. And when you're done, it's my turn."

Sharp but light and teasing stings landed on her cheeks, shoulders, and breasts, and she leaned into every blow, moaning because they all found the route to her cunt. His fingers had lit a fire in her, and it kept growing, blowing hot over her entire body. She didn't try to stop panting or hold still; sound and movement intensified everything.

Suddenly he stopped. Thoughts still swirling, she fought to bring him into focus. Leaning low, he again caught her collar and hauled her up as far as possible while still on her knees. Only then did she see that he'd pulled off his cock-cloth.

"Fire woman!" he taunted. "Whore."

"Yes!"

"Then I'll treat you like one."

When he released the collar, she remained where he'd positioned her. An ache like nothing she'd ever imagined stormed into her cunt. She was burning up, pain and pleasure slamming together when he hadn't yet touched her sex.

Growling as he had earlier, he seized her shoulders and forced her down. She just managed to turn her head to the side so her cheek and not her forehead rested on the ground. Maybe she could sit back up without use of her hands, but she didn't try. Instead, she thought about her buttocks sticking up in the air, waiting . . .

A quick blow to her right ass cheek made her jump. Then, although she was ready for one to her left, she jumped at it too. She imagined him standing behind her while he studied her offered ass.

Her heart continued to beat. She even remembered to breathe, and still he didn't touch her. Anticipation made her pussy flow.

"My cunt." He ran his hand along her labia, collecting her juice as he went. "My poor, helpless cunt."

"Yes!"

"What do you want?" He wiped his fingers on her hanging breast. "Tell me, cunt. What do you want?"

"For you to fuck me."

After replenishing his supply of her juice, he deposited it between her shoulder blades. "What did you say, chattel? Surely this isn't an order like last night. Today you must be begging."

"Begging! Begging! Please, fuck me."

"How?" He ran something, maybe a leaf or twig, between her ass cheeks. When he was done, the object stayed there. "With what?"

"Not that. You!"

"What's that, bitch?" He pressed on the small of her back as if trying to drive her into the ground. "Are you ordering me?"

"No. No. Please. Oh, please."

"Please what?"

Because of the position he'd placed her in, she drooled when she spoke, but it didn't matter. Nothing mattered beyond this moment and him and her screaming need. "Please fuck me, master."

This time he touched her with his fingertips, a bare brushing that sped to her pussy. "Master. Is that what you called me?"

"Yes. Oh, please."

Dropping to his knees, he planted his hands on her buttocks. Feeling his cock slide along her cunt, she tried to spread her legs, but his were outside hers, stopping her.

She could wait, had to wait. He was her master.

Master. The word pounded against her skull. By the time she'd forced it away, he'd reached under her and spread his hand over her belly. He pressed, forcing her to arch her back, then shoved his groin against her. If not for his grip, she would have been knocked off balance.

Caught by him. Owned.

Something softened in her, a now familiar melting down she craved as much as she did life. Nothing mattered beyond this moment and him, and because he'd become her everything, she pushed back. His cock, there, so close! Pressing up against her nether lips, probing. If only she could use her hands to guide him home.

Don't beg. Whatever it takes, keep something of yourself.

Sensing movement and then pressure, she held her breath. There. Him. In her.

Despite the shared awkwardness, they worked together to make the fit strong and sure. Knowing they were in harmony about this one thing added to the sense that she was flowing into him. Giving up so much ownership was dangerous, but did she have a choice? Did she want one?

Instead of pounding into her, he remained still. Waiting, maybe sharing a single experience with him, she closed her eyes. She no longer thought of herself as a separate human being, was no longer a member of a proud people.

Her body had become a restless beast, hungry and determined. And in the end, it overruled her mind, forcing movement and sound out of her. Awash in heat, she worked herself back toward him. He answered with a forceful thrust that slapped his balls against her ass. Eyes closed because everything in her demanded attention to the act of fucking, she nevertheless carried an image of the powerful warrior who was pummeling her, his ass tightening and relaxing, tightening again. Each movement drove his cock deeper and stole even more of her.

His rapid-paced attack was too much. Even with his hands on her belly to keep her in place, she kept sliding along the ground, skinning her knees and the side of her head.

"Ah, no!"

Masterful hands seized her forearms and yanked her upright, their union slackening but still holding. Moving her hands to the side, she again lifted her ass, desperate not to lose him. How wise he was! How wise to press one arm against her collarbone while the other slid over her mons, anchoring her, anchoring them.

His sex dance changed tempo, quick, short thrusts replacing the earlier long and strong glides. Although it was centered in her cock-stuffed pussy, exquisite heat boiled through her.

"Yes, yes, yes!"

"Whore. Bitch."

"Night beast."

"Where's your fight, Nari? Why aren't you running away?"

"You have me. Have me. Ah!"

Hot in the wake of her curse, he pushed her forward and down again, but not as they'd been before. Instead, still driven deep in her, he rolled both of them onto their sides. Using his grip on her breast for leverage, he straightened her. Bending her knees, she fought her ankle restraints and scratched what she could reach of his chest.

There! Attacking her cunt again. Sliding along the ground, his upper leg raised while the other provided necessary leverage.

She dug her nails into his chest. "Night beast!"

"Damnation!" he bellowed. Still powering into her, he raked from her breast to her belly. Once there, he all but buried a finger in her navel.

"Do it!" she hissed. "By the spirits, do it!"

"What?"

Had she spoken? Did he expect a reply? A sensation like sharp claws began running down her spine. By the time it reached the small of her back, it had spread to her breasts and groin. Maybe, like a flaming tree in a wildfire, she'd explode.

What?

Belatedly, she realized he was trying to sit up, again bringing her with him. Judging by his sweat-stained body and trembling muscles, she guessed he was close to exhaustion. Panting and lightheaded, she worked with him so they were back on their knees and upright, still mating. He took a deep and shaky breath, one she echoed.

"More?" he asked.

"More! Yes, more!"

Pummeling her again, bodies slapping, his hand between her legs in front, finding her clit, teasing, touching, forcing strangled cries out of her. She couldn't reach his balls but, yes, there was the place where groin and cock joined, which she stroked and lightly pinched. When he rubbed her labia, she closed her fingers around the base of his cock and answered with a like movement.

Happening! Oh yes, happening! "I'm coming! Coming!"

"Shit, shit, shit! Ahh."

A man climaxing was both powerful and helpless, precious fluid leaving him and becoming part of a woman. Her.

"Coming," she chanted. "Coming."

"Ahh!"

25

When he'd recovered enough to move, Tarek untied Nari and shared his water with her. Then, not looking for a way through his silence, he placed her in front of him on the moto. As they traveled, he guided the moto with one hand while the other remained around her waist. She'd put her dress back on, which he was thankful for because he needed space between himself and her skin—between the two of them in every possible way.

If she tried to escape now, what would he do?

After covering what he estimated to be half the distance back to his fellow warriors, he stopped so they could stretch their muscles but was careful to remain close to her.

"I'm not going to run," she said.

"Why not?"

"I've been thinking about this since . . . maybe since you caught up with me. By the spirits, why does this have to be so hard? My trying to convince my people to hide isn't right."

"Why not?"

"Tarek, sooner or later, your people and mine must stand face-to-face."

"That isn't what the Centrois want."

"I know." Touching a bruise on the side of her neck, she indicated his reddened knees. "Your men will know we fucked again."

"Yes."

"Not that you demanded your rights but that we wanted the same thing."

"And that will give Helki even more reason to try to become warlord. No one, except maybe Saka and Reyna, will understand."

"Do you?"

Don't ask me that! "I don't want to try. Do you?"

"No," she whispered, and looked down. "Tarek, I have to ask you something."

"What?"

"Do . . . do you still need to punish your father's killer?"

"Need? I can't answer that until I'm standing face-to-face with him."

"Then you, too, believe our people must meet?"

I don't know. "Let me ask you something. Do you still hate and fear the Centrois?"

"Fear, yes. But not hate." She sank to the ground, a small yet strong figure communicating with the earth. "Being with you has changed so much."

Could he say the same thing? But even if he could, he'd only be speaking for himself. "We can't change what was set in place when we were children."

"No, we can't."

"And maybe all we have in common is the way our bodies speak to each other."

She started to nod, then stared up at him. Had her eyes ever been so deep or dark? "Do you believe that?"

He'd never felt more naked, more exposed or less sure of himself, and it was her doing! In many ways she could strip him down until he became a small, unwise boy. "Around you, I don't know what I believe. Or feel." Stunned by his admission, he spun away. But then, because he didn't know how to be anything except a warrior, he turned back around. She'd stood and was watching him with those incredible eyes, and yet he couldn't sense what she was thinking. Maybe it was better that way.

"And more talking between us now won't change anything," he said.

"No, it won't."

Although she'd promised that her time of trying to escape was over, he'd tethered Nari before they returned to camp because as long as he marked her as his, Helki or others wouldn't touch her. Maybe.

Although it nearly tore him apart to tell his fellow warriors this, he announced that they'd continue their search for the Baasta. Saka, and to his surprise J'ron, countered that the savages presented the immediate danger, but the others were pleased with Tarek's decision, undoubtedly because Helki had influenced them.

As he spoke, he studied Helki, who obviously hadn't expected him to say this without fresh argument. But what Helki didn't and couldn't understand unless he became warlord was that it didn't matter what a single Centrois wanted. Maybe Nari didn't either.

From there the discussion shifted to the search. Everyone lamented that their attempts to locate the Baasta had been unsuccessful, and he wasn't surprised when Helki insisted, as he had before, that Nari and Reyna needed to have the truth forced out of them.

"No!" he snapped, interrupting Helki. "As long as I'm warlord, they will *not* be tortured."

"She has weakened you," Helki shot back. "Cast a spell over you and your cock."

"She and her cousin saved two Centrois lives."

"Maybe."

He calmly returned Helki's glare. "Say what you want, but I want you to remember one thing: We're warriors, not wolves or coyotes. A Centrois warrior doesn't run down, cripple, and tear apart helpless prey."

"He's right," J'ron said before Helki could speak. "When I face the Divine Eternal, I want him to be pleased with me."

"What about Reyna?" Tarek asked his brother later as the two sat by themselves. "You gave her no opportunity to escape?"

"I couldn't call myself a warrior if I did."

Was he still a warrior? *Yes*, he wanted to shout because that was the only thing he'd ever been or wanted to be, the only role he'd been trained for. *No*, he nearly admitted, because his seed still rested inside the *enemy* and even now he wanted to add to it. "Have the two of you talked?"

Saka shook his head. "I was careful not to be near her, and I think that's what she wanted. I've renewed my vow, brother." He pressed his hand against his forehead. "To keep my heart hidden, safe."

Is that possible? Instead, because it was easier, he pondered the recent change in J'ron. J'ron had always been eager to attack other breeds. J'ron's father, Aali, was also quick to anger and lacking in patience. In addition, Aali used his hands and sometimes his fists on his children and wife. Tarek would never forget the day J'ron had wrenched the stick Aali was beating him with out of his father's hands and thrown Aali to the ground. From then on Aali had left his eldest son alone.

"He's changed," Saka agreed. "It's as if he's looking at his world with new eyes, and he speaks with a patience I've never heard from him."

"Maybe because he's never come that close to death."

"I thought about that. Those he hated saved his life."

That's what Nari did for me, and now I'm leading the hunt for her people.

The wind always blew through the canyon they were in, and today its relentless power added to Nari's exhaustion and dread. Because she'd ridden behind Tarek for the past two days, and he hadn't come near her at night, she shouldn't be that tired, but she'd learned that fear had a way of wearing her down. Having to keep her balance with her hands secured to her waist had taken its toll on her muscles, but that only had a little to do with why she could hardly wait to get through the canyon.

Although Tarek had insisted he wouldn't force her and Reyna to reveal where the Baasta lived, the others were growing more and more impatient. Thank goodness the Baasta had been careful to select a long, wide mountain ledge above Hevassen's rich, vast valley for their home. No one, not even the savages, had found it, and so far, none of the Centrois scouts had come across so much as a footprint. The canyon was a half day's ride from the village and at present, the Centrois weren't heading in that direction.

But this riding and searching wouldn't last indefinitely. Sooner or later, the Centrois would either find what they were looking for, or Helki would try to wrench leadership from Tarek. If he succeeded . . .

The sight of a rapidly approaching moto brought her upright. Tense, she waited for the scout to reach them. The narrow canyon had forced the Centrois to ride no more than two abreast, but they were now all crowding as best they could into a circle. At a signal from Tarek, everyone silenced their motos.

"Savages!" the scout exclaimed, and pointed behind him. "Moving rapidly, stalking."

"Stalking what?" Helki demanded.

"I didn't try to find out, not by myself."

"How many are there?" Tarek asked. "What arc they armed with?"

The scout had counted at least ten savages, all armed with spears and clubs. "They aren't after animals." Tarek's tone was grim. "If they were hunting, they'd use arrows."

My people!

Now acknowledging her presence, Tarek began issuing orders. About half would ride with him and Saka with the rest following closer than they had during the last confrontation with savages.

"Baasta," Helki said. "It *has* to be them."

Tarek nodded.

"Finally! Finally we have them!"

"Not if the savages get to them first."

Fear weakened her, and she started to rest her head against Tarek's back, then caught herself.

"What about *them?*" Helki indicated her and Reyna.

"They're coming with us."

A few moments later, those Tarek had selected were following the scout out of the canyon. Before taking off, he'd gagged her while Saka did the same to Reyna. Then he'd warned her not to try anything because he'd leave her behind if she did. She desperately wanted to at least lock eyes with her cousin, but Saka and Reyna were bringing up the rear while she and Tarek rode just behind the scout. At least Helki wasn't with him; Tarek had selected him to lead the second group.

She'd never been on a moto going this fast, and Tarek's ability to concentrate should have seized her attention, but only one thing mattered—how this would end.

At a signal from the scout, everyone stopped. "Over that rise." He pointed. "That's where I saw them."

"What direction were they moving?"

"Toward the setting suns, running as if they'd never grow tired."

"Listen to me," Tarek announced. "We'll stay close together, riding abreast instead of single file. When we spot them, but before we get too close, we'll stop and plan our attack."

Looking every bit the hunter, he started moving again. They were going slower now, and Nari kept looking around Tarek while trying not to think about the width of his back or the sun-stick at his waist. Most of all she fought to distance her thoughts from her people.

Could she have prevented this from happening?

The Centrois paused at the top of the rise, but she couldn't see enough to know what they were looking at. Most likely the savages had gone into the brush at the bottom of the slope. As the Centrois approached the brush, she saw that the growth wasn't as abundant as she'd thought, which made it possible for the motos to keep a steady pace. Bushes kept slipping behind her, and she grew slightly dizzy from the sensation. Concerned that one might strike her if she leaned to the side too much, she hunched behind Tarek, trusting him to keep her safe.

Trusting him?

Straightening suddenly, he touched the brakes. Then she heard it. Distant and yet sharp male voices. High-pitched bellows.

"They're attacking!" With that, Tarek started moving again. The rapid pace frightened her. If only she could hold on!

Even with the increased moto sounds, she understood the sounds of battle. Yet no matter how much she strained, she couldn't make sense of the cries and yells and had no way of guessing how many savages and others were involved. Tarek's tension flowed into her and, she became him—a Centrois warlord riding into battle.

Once more he stopped, causing her to slam into his back.

Then he was off his moto, leaving her to keep it upright. As one, the others did the same, joining him as he crouched behind a grassy mound. Saka and J'ron flanked him. She still couldn't see what they were looking at, but the cries and yells chilled her. Gnawing into her gag, she jumped free of the moto. As it fell to the ground, she hurried to join Tarek.

Ignoring him and J'ron, who was so close the young warrior could have grabbed her, she stared. At first she couldn't make sense of the turmoil beyond the chilling sight of naked, hairy savages. No matter how many times she'd seen them, the creatures made her shudder. Their shrieks raked over her skin, and even from this distance, she half believed she could smell them. They were swarming around something like feeding wolves. Only when two who'd been close together moved apart did she see who they'd surrounded.

Red hair. Baasta men, at least three.

"No!" she screamed into her gag.

She'd only taken a couple of steps when Tarek grabbed her and hauled her back with him. He yanked off her gag. "No!" he ordered.

"They'll kill . . . please, they'll kill—"

"No, they won't."

Before she could demand an explanation, he addressed his fellow warriors. "The savages are holding back, waiting. Whatever their reasons, this is our chance."

"What are we going to do?" J'ron asked.

Speaking with a confidence born of long experience, he explained that they were to close in on the savages but keep an eye on their surroundings in case other savages were hiding. "Unless you have no choice, don't fight hand to hand. Instead, wait until you're sure you won't miss and then fire your sunsticks. They won't know what to think of the sound. They might try to run away, but don't let them."

Positioning himself beside his brother, Saka raised his arm

so everyone could see that he was holding his sun-stick. "This is our time," he announced. "The savages will taste our revenge."

Nari couldn't keep her eyes off the distant action. Tarek was right. Despite the aggressive movement, the savages were keeping distance between themselves and the Baasta they'd surrounded. Once again she took a step only to have Tarek stop her.

"Stay here," he ordered. He took off at a trot, the others behind him. Watching, it was all she could do not to scream at them to stop. What if, once they'd killed or chased off the savages, they turned their rage on her people? A muffled exclamation distracted her, and she turned to see a still-gagged Reyna right behind her. Giving little thought to the consequences, she brought her hands to Reyna's bonds and untied her. Reyna did the same for her, only then yanking off her gag.

"I can't stay here," Reyna blurted.

"Neither can I."

Without that, they took off after the men. Because they were running instead of matching the warriors' more cautious pace, it didn't take them long to close the distance. Then they slowed, and Nari prayed that neither Tarek nor Saka would look behind them. Even with fear numbing her muscles, she admired the Centrois' single-minded determination, and if they were afraid, they showed no sign. To a man, they'd committed themselves to defeating the savages. They'd do what had to be done. The possibility for injury or death didn't matter; at least, they refused to admit it.

Tarek stopped and crouched, and the others immediately followed suit. She and Reyna had started to do the same when Tarek swung around in her direction. *Be quiet,* his eyes commanded.

A heartbeat later he'd turned his attention back to the savages and the Baasta. Pulling out his sun-stick, he gripped it with both hands. All around him, his companions were doing the same. Nari held her breath. Time slowed, stopped, and still she didn't breathe.

Crack!

The sound was still ringing in the air when the others fired. One savage started to turn in the direction of the repeated blasts but fell before he could finish. Another was shrieking while yet another started coughing. Seeing that he was coughing up blood, Nari clamped her hand over her mouth but didn't turn away. There was so much movement that she couldn't tell how many savages had been hit. Several had dropped to the ground, but maybe they were trying to protect themselves.

A rapid *thunk, thunk, thunk* caught her attention. There. A savage at a slight distance from the others, sitting with his legs outstretched and his arms braced behind him, his feet repeatedly pounding the ground while blood erupted from a thigh wound.

She expected the Centrois to charge, but although they stood and yelled at the savages, they remained where they were. When they'd gotten the savages' attention—at least those capable of concentrating—they again aimed their sun-sticks. The moment they did, several of the savages threw up their hands as if that could protect them. One, short and with a massive chest, started running toward the Centrois, but he'd only taken a few steps when someone yelled at him, and he stopped.

"Now!" Tarek ordered. Sun-stick aimed at the savages, he began walking toward them.

No, please don't! Nari wanted to scream, but he was a warrior. The large-chested savage stared at Tarek, his mouth hanging open.

"Fear me, dung of dung," Tarek snapped. "Feel my wrath and the wrath of my fellow fighters." He indicated those who'd joined him in the slow, steady march. "You're going to die today. Think about that. You'll be dead before the suns set."

Whether the savages understood him or not didn't matter because the impact had been made. Reminding her of wildings fleeing predators, the savages who were still standing started running in every direction except toward the Centrois. Now that they'd separated, she could see that there were only six able-bodied savages while four remained on the ground. One was screaming something at those who were fleeing, but the other three were silent, dead or dying.

"Nari," Reyna gasped. "Your father."

26

Movement out of the corner of his eye wrenched Tarek's attention off the fleeing savages. Recognizing Nari, his first thought was that she was trying to escape again, but she was running *toward* something, not away. Leaping over a fallen savage, she threw herself into the arms of one of the Baasta.

They clung to each other, both crying, and he was taken back to when his father used to hold him, and from there to that final time when he'd eased his father's journey into the afterlife. Shaking off the painful image, he studied the two. Had she thrown herself at someone she'd fucked? Instead of anger and a sense of betrayal, loneliness settled over him. Although the others were boasting about how easily they'd defeated the savages, he couldn't concentrate on that.

As Tarek approached, the man drew Nari to his side. The knife the Baasta had been using in a desperate attempt to keep the savages at a distance was now pointed at Tarek's chest. "You're Centrois," the man said.

Tarek drew out his own knife.

"Tarek, please, no!" Nari gasped.

Without taking his attention off Tarek, the man shook his head at Nari, and as they stood looking at each other, Tarek took note of the lines around the Baasta's eyes. His hair was gray but still rich, his gray-dusted chest broad and strong-looking. "Who is he?" he asked Nari.

"My father."

Another wave of loss washed over him. When it retreated enough for him to think, he concentrated on the relationship between the two. They doubtlessly loved each other deeply. "What are you doing here?" he asked the man, although he already knew the answer.

"Looking for her." Nari's father gave her a quick, hard hug. "It's all I've done since she failed to return." His voice cracked.

The rest of his warriors had gathered around. Giving no sign that they felt overwhelmed, the Baasta glared in return, spears and knives at the ready. No wonder the savages had held back.

"What are you going to do?" Nari demanded. "Four Baasta against a Centrois war party? Is that what it takes for your need for revenge to become reality?"

This was his captive, someone he'd once intended to turn into his sex-chattel? It would be like trying to tame an eagle. He was still staring at Nari when Reyna threw herself into the arms of another Baasta. "Father!" she sobbed. "I was afraid I'd never see you again."

As Nari's father had done, Reyna's father managed to embrace his daughter while warily watching the Centrois. It occurred to Tarek that nothing, really, had changed for the Baasta in the last few moments. They might no longer be confronted by savages, but was this any better? Maybe it was worse.

"Why did you capture them?" Nari's father asked. "Why not kill them?"

Maybe I should have. But even as the thought broke loose, he knew he couldn't have killed defenseless women. Still, how much less complex his life would be without Nari in it—less complex and hollow.

"Where's your gratitude, Baasta?" he shot back. "If we hadn't come, the savages would have killed you."

"My name is Ojo, father of Nari. And I would be grateful if you weren't responsible for *this.*" He touched Nari's collar, glaring at it as if he'd never hated anything more. "How this takes me back to when the Centrois believed they owned our bodies and hearts. Nari, did he—"

"Don't, please," she interrupted, and in her eyes Tarek saw not regret for handing her body to him, but acknowledgment of what she couldn't change or explain. He felt the same way, and yet maybe his emotions ran even deeper. "I'm all right, all right."

Another image at odds with the old memory of his father's violent death rose in Tarek's mind. Now he saw himself putting away his weapons and turning his back on Nari and her father, walking away, returning to the life he'd known before she'd come into it.

Then he heard more approaching motos, and the image died.

Ojo's eyes widened at the sight of so many more Centrois, and he and his companions crowded even closer together; but they still struck Tarek as warriors, not a defeated foe.

"Praise the Divine Eternal!" Helki shouted as he dismounted. "Baasta. Finally." He pointed at the old chattel brand on Ojo's shoulder. "What's she doing with him?" he demanded of Tarek. "She should—"

"He's my father."

Even surrounded by his fellow warriors, Tarek felt isolated. Against all reason, he wanted to be alone with Nari and for none of this to have happened. He needed her body against his, but not just so they could fuck. She'd taken him someplace he'd never been, had forced him to look at himself in ways he'd never done, question what he'd never questioned before, and he needed to do that again because otherwise how could he make the decisions he needed to today?

"What is this?" Helki demanded. "The Baasta should be on their knees, or dead. How can you call yourself warlord?"

Suddenly furious, Tarek whirled and knocked Helki to the ground. As one, the Centrois gasped and backed away from him, even his brother.

Staring at Tarek, Nari struggled to find the man she'd spent the last few nights with, but his eyes had never been this stormy. He'd never struck another Centrois or looked this apart from the others. Although Helki had propped himself up on his elbow, he made no attempt to stand, maybe because he was afraid of Tarek.

Was she?

Again her father hugged her, but, like her, he kept his attention on Tarek.

"I *am* warlord," Tarek finally said. "And what happens here is *my* decision."

The Centrois began muttering among themselves. Saka was looking at Reyna, but she couldn't read his expression. Neither did she understand her own thoughts.

"We can't fight you," her father said, his tone low and somber and yet proud. "We had a chance against the savages, but if you choose to kill us, we can't stop you."

Don't say that, please! But her father had always been a realist.

"Dead, you have no value," Helki said, and got to his feet. Keeping a careful distance from Tarek, he slipped closer to the rest of the Centrois warriors. "But as chattel—"

"No! Never again."

There was a note of finality to her father's words she'd never doubt or forget, and as one moment slid into two, she believed

Tarek had heard the same tone. What would happen if these two strong, proud men could talk without the weight of what they'd been and were now coming between them? Would her father understand why she'd fucked Tarek? And would Tarek find something of his own father in hers?

Shaking her head to rid herself of the heavy questions, she again turned her full attention to Tarek. If he was aware that everyone was waiting for him to speak, he gave no indication. Instead, he continued to study her and her father. What was he seeing? An aging warrior, yes, and the daughter who'd made a lie of her people's determination to be free by having sex with a Centrois, but was there more to it than that?

Tarek's tattoos rose and fell with his every breath, and the sunstick he'd returned to its carrying bag rested on his right hip, the weight pulling down on his belt and exposing too much of his belly. She was grateful for the cock-cloth, but it couldn't hide a certain reality. Tarek was aroused.

Of course. Danger and fighting could do that to a man.

As could looking at a woman he desired.

I don't want it to be like this between us, she told him.

Neither do I, he replied. *I want it to be yesterday and for us to be alone, exploring each other, touching, learning the difference between a gentle caress and strength.*

Strength, yes. I became excited when you struck me.

Just as running my hands, tongue, and cock over your naked and helpless body excites me.

Yes, oh yes!

Ah, Nari, I want that and more. To taste your sex, slipping my tongue into your opening, drinking of your offering.

By the Divine Eternal, yes! To hold you in my mouth again, to have you come so I can feed off your seed!

My seed? Is it still inside you?

Yes.

Like a storm cloud covering the moon, the silent communication died, and she belatedly noticed that Helki had gathered several warriors around him. Now, eyes determined and remote, they stepped toward Tarek. "What is it going to be?" Helki demanded. "Are you still warlord, or has *she* turned you into *her* sex-chattel?"

"Warlord. Heart and soul, warlord."

"Then kill—"

"Enough! There's so much more to leadership than spilling our enemies' blood! Will you never understand that? There's walking on this land the Divine Eternal created and the Baasta call Hevassen and asking it to accept us."

Helki snorted. "Today isn't about land, no matter how rich it is. Today we can finally avenge the greatest wrong ever done to the Centrois."

"Centrois?" Nari blurted, unable to remain silent. Although her father tried to hold on to her, she wrenched free and stalked toward Helki. "Is that all you ever think about? What about the other breeds the Divine Eternal created?"

"Be quiet!"

"No. No. Can't you understand that an even greater wrong was done to the Baasta?" Determined to prove her point, she grabbed her collar. "Wear this, Helki. Only then will you understand what your breed did to ours."

Eyes lowered to slits, Helki jabbed his knife at her. "Be silent, chattel! If you don't, I'll kill you."

The blade hadn't come so close that she was in danger, but when Saka and J'ron flanked Helki, it was clear they'd sensed the potential. Only when Helki acknowledged the two young men did she look at Tarek again.

Instead of confronting Helki, Tarek was staring at her father, his body so tense she wondered if he might shatter. Helki was saying something, but she didn't care because Tarek had changed from the forceful man she knew, and in his place stood a shocked and hurting child.

"What is it?" she asked.

Tarek's attention remained on her father. "The scar." He spoke so softly she barely heard him. "I know that scar."

"Do you?" her father asked.

27

_____

Her attention snagged by her father's somber tone, Nari turned toward him. He was fingering the old slash on his side, and like Tarek's, his expression was unlike any she'd ever seen. No matter how desperately she needed an explanation, she understood that this was between her father and Tarek.

"*You* killed him." Tarek's shoulders slumped, then squared. "Because of you, *my* father bled to death in my arms."

No! No. Oh please—

"Your father," Ojo muttered with a slight nod. "I was fighting for my freedom with the only weapon I had."

"*Your* weapon. It was *my* father's knife."

Even with the threat of death surrounding him, Ojo closed his eyes. She'd never loved or hurt for him more. "I remember a boy," he whispered. "You?"

"Yes, me."

Tarek, I'm so sorry.

When her father opened his eyes, she found sorrow and resignation. "When I saw you standing there, I wanted to tell you how much I regretted what I'd done, to try to make you understand that I had no choice. But if I'd stayed, your people would have robbed me of my only chance at freedom, killed me."

"Kill him!" Helki fairly shrieked, his words shattering her already splintered mind. "Now, finally, destroy your father's murderer."

More afraid and yet more determined than she'd been in her life, Nari stood in front of Tarek. The longer she looked up at the tense and silent warrior, the less aware she was of the others, even her father, who was right behind her. His love and concern seeped into her, and she prayed he could feel her love for him. Soon, maybe, she'd be able to tell him everything that had happened since she'd last seen him, but these moments were for Tarek. Maybe for both of them.

"I didn't know," she whispered.

"Your father killed mine."

Hurting, she placed her palm over his tattoos. To her relief, he didn't flinch or knock her hand away. "But if he hadn't, your father would have killed mine."

"Don't let her touch you!" Helki yelled. "Don't let her weaken—"

"Silence! You have no idea what's happening here." Tearing his gaze off her, Tarek locked eyes with one after the other of his fellow warriors. "The time for a decision has come," he said when he'd finally finished. "Who do you want for your warlord, him or me?"

"Tarek?" J'ron blurted. "What are you saying?"

"Helki believes this woman has made me less of a warrior, and I'm no longer capable of leading. If you agree, say so now."

Tarek's boldness and honesty in putting the question to everyone awed her. They deserved a leader who thought like them, one they respected, but if Helki became warlord, he'd certainly order the Centrois to either kill or capture her father and the others. And after they'd accomplished that, they'd hunt down and attack the rest of the Baasta.

Her hand sliding off Tarek's chest, she looked around for her cousin and found her standing near Saka. Reyna's eyes were tear-filled, and Nari understood how deeply she hurt for Saka because, like Tarek, Saka had just come face-to-face with his father's murderer.

Birds were singing in a nearby tree, and wasn't that a distant coyote cry? The wind was gentle and lazy today, barely disturbing the trees and grasses. If not for the humans here, it would be a peaceful place.

Peaceful. No one speaking.

"Hear me!" Helki shouted. "The Centrois are warriors, not chattel! We *must* right an old wrong, we *must.*"

Holding her breath, Nari waited, but instead of the agreement Helki had demanded, the birds continued to sing while first J'ron and then the rest of the Centrois stepped back from Helki and put their weapons away.

Shaking and suddenly pale, Helki stood with his knife still clenched by white knuckles.

"You have your answer," J'ron said at length. "*You* are our leader, Tarek, not *him*. What do you want us to do?"

J'ron had never looked or sounded so mature, and if Tarek's answer hadn't meant so much, she would have told the young warrior that she was glad she'd been able to save his life.

"Nothing, yet," Tarek said after a too-long silence. With that, he took her hand in his too-cool one.

Before Tarek could take a step, her father grabbed Tarek's arm. "What are you doing?"

Although she wanted to warn her father to release Tarek, she didn't; this was between the two men. "I don't know, yet," Tarek whispered.

"It's all right," she told her father. "I want to go with him. I have to."

At first just walking next to Tarek with her feet touching ground she'd grown up on was all she could concentrate on. He

no longer held her hand, and although their fingers occasionally brushed, he didn't acknowledge her presence. It was better
this way. Silence allowed her to get in touch with her emotions,
to guess at what was going through him, to ask herself whether
and how she might reach him, to mourn Tarek's father, to acknowledge the burden her father had carried for so long.

As her surroundings and memories became clear, she changed
direction. After a moment, Tarek followed her to a low hill and
the level area beyond it. Dropping to her knees, she brushed
aside the long summer grasses.

"In spring, the ground here is covered with tiny, sweet-
smelling purple flowers," she told him. "When I first saw them,
I picked as many as I could hold and took them to my mother,
but she told me not to do that again so flowers would continue
to grow. I learned so many things here, Tarek, things I wouldn't
have if I'd grown up as a chattel."

"Your father—"

"Killed yours, yes. Tarek, I didn't know," she said, and
stood up. "If I had . . . if I had, I don't know what I would have
done, whether I would have told you."

"Maybe you would have done more to keep me away from
him."

"Maybe." Was he aware of the warm and gentle breeze, and
could he hear the birds and coyote?

"So much has happened today," he muttered. "So much has
changed."

He hadn't met her gaze since they'd stopped walking, but
although it was easier for both of them this way, it couldn't
continue—not with what she had to say. "Now that you've
found us, will you and the others return home? Maybe those
you left behind won't think the way you and your warriors do.
They might still want revenge."

"Revenge? I'm so tired of the word."

"Are you? It controlled you for many years."

"Just as the Baasta's past as chattel controlled them."

How wise you are. "Yes. Tarek, revenge is one thing, hatred another. I need to know something. Do you hate my father?"

Instead of answering, he ran his foot over the grass as if looking for tiny purple flowers. "Summer is nearing its end. Once it starts snowing, the motos won't be able to get through the mountains."

"No, they won't."

On a sigh, he turned his attention to her. How beautiful his eyes were, beautiful and remote and deep. He'd touched her with lightning before, so shouldn't she know what it felt like? But today he was also whipping her body with energy and life —only today might be the last time she'd ever experience it.

"I don't know when we'll leave. The decision—"

"You didn't answer me. Do you hate my father?" His eyes narrowed as he looked up at the sky. She did the same, using a hand to block the sun's glare. "He's told me so much of what happened that day believing I should know about our past, but he never said a word about . . ."

"About murdering a man?"

"No. Maybe he would have if he wasn't carrying your memory."

"Maybe." Lowering his head, he again studied their surroundings. "This is a beautiful place, lush and peaceful."

"Except for the savages."

"Except for the savages. No, Nari, I don't hate your father, just as I hope you don't hate mine."

"Yours? Why—"

"He was one of those who enslaved your people."

"Yes, he was."

"I'm sorry."

Two simple words. So much depth and meaning. Taking his hand, she lifted it so she could kiss his knuckles and palm, then placed his hand over her breast. "Do you hear my heart? If you can, you know what matters to me. You."

Sliding his hand under her breast, he lifted and cradled it in the palm she'd just kissed.

Tears burned and spilled over, but she didn't try to brush them away. Instead, she asked the Divine Eternal for new strength and courage. "I don't want our parents or people to be part of what's between us," she managed. "Later, yes, but not right now."

"What do you want?"

"For you to listen to what I have to say. Tarek, I'm . . . I'm fertile, at least I was when we started fucking."

He might have only taken a quick breath, but maybe it was a sob. Releasing her, he stepped back. Slow, so slow that she thought she might burst into flames with the waiting, he studied her from her red Baasta hair down to her earth-hardened feet. He gave her neck and arms and ankles the same consideration he did her breasts and crotch—at least as much as her dress allowed.

"You're carrying my child?"

"I don't know yet, but maybe."

"I should have considered—will your people reject it?"

"No! No. All children are precious to us."

Naked relief spread over him. "What about you?"

What about you, Tarek? Do you want a child by me? "An infant is a new life, part of what existed between us."

"Existed? No longer?"

"You're leaving, Tarek." She forced the words. "Going home."

Taking hold of her dress, he lifted it over her head so she stood naked before him. Then he ran his fingers over her stomach, and fresh tears tracked down her cheeks. "My child."

And mine. "If . . . if I'm pregnant, it won't be the way it was between your brother and the chattel he loved. No one is going to sell me. No one has a right to beat me, and you won't bury my name. My infant will suckle at *my* breast, not a stranger's."

"*Our* child will grow up half-Centrois and half-Baasta."

Our. "Yes."

When he reached for his knife, it didn't register what he was doing, but then he held it up, and her breathing stopped. Then he extended his free hand toward her, and her throat loosened. More importantly, her instant of fear had already died because she believed with all her being that the man she'd given her body and heart to would never hurt her.

Her tears had dried by the time he'd finished severing her collar. Taking it from him, she threw it as far as she could, laughing at her awkwardness. She was still laughing when he wrapped his arms around her and drew her into his heated embrace. "You're right," he muttered. "I have to go back home. As warlord—"

"I know." Her heart ached. *Good-bye.*

"But I'll return."

"You . . . you will?"

"Maybe alone."

You'd give up your people for me?

"Maybe with the rest of the Centrois."

"They might come here?"

"When I tell them about wildings and mild winters and no floods and rich earth and learning from the Baasta who already understand this land, yes."

"What about the savages? Your people don't know—"

It was his turn to laugh, the sound easing into and igniting her. "Together, the Centrois and Baasta will end that threat."

"You believe your people and mine can work as one?"

When he didn't answer, she forced herself to pull away a little. He was looking down at her, the darkness gone from his eyes. In its place was an expression she'd never seen on him, a softness. Peace.

"You and I came together, Nari."

Yes. Yes.

Acknowledging that everything that had once made them enemies hadn't been washed away, she nevertheless embraced this moment by reaching behind him and untying his cock-cloth. She sent it flying after her collar, then cupped his cock between her palms and sank onto her knees. As she did, he laced his fingers through her hair and thrust his pelvis at her. She lightly closed her teeth around the tip of his cock and leaned back, watching his expression. To her delight, he smiled.

"What is this, *chattel?* Do you think you can turn me into your possession?"

Yes! Yes. And when I'm done, you'll do the same to me.

"Maybe you can," he said. "After all, I was your teacher."

"You still are."

Realizing she'd released his cock in order to speak, she opened her mouth again, but he was already kneeling, leaning over her, encouraging her to plant her arms behind her, arch her back, and thrust her breasts at him. "What is this, Nari? Who is in control now?"

"You."

As fire licked through her and his life force caressed her skin, she braced herself so she was ready when he nudged her knees apart with his own. As his cock flattened against her belly, she clamped her arms around his neck. He threw himself to the side to keep from squashing her under him, and she rolled with him, and kept on rolling until she was on top of him. He helped her position her legs on either side of him, and she rested her cunt on his belly. "Who's in control now?" she demanded.

His smile bloomed. "You." With that, he gripped her waist and lifted her up, up, until she all but hung over him. When he started to lower her, she reached between her legs and guided his cock into her core.

"Both of us," she whispered. *Ride him. Ride and give and receive pleasure.*

"Together."

Then he started lightly pinching her thighs and hips and she forgot how to talk. Thought only of the hot energy inside her.

And their future.

Turn the page for
a tantalizing preview of
MIDNIGHT CONFESSIONS II.
On sale now!

1

Faye Grantham placed her cheek next to the smooth pine planking of the wall and peered through a peephole set at eye level. The angle of the hole gave her a perfect view of the bed in the next room. Odd how she already knew it would look like this. The walls were in shadow, with the bed spotlighted.

All she could see was the bed and a couple standing beside it. Their faces were obscured. The woman wore her long blond hair in a fall of cascading white and cream. Faye couldn't make out her face behind the curtain of lustrous hair.

She fingered her own shoulder-length waves. Hers were shorter, but the color was similar.

The man's upper face was in shadow. His jaw, strong and lightly bristled, glowed from the odd lighting. His mouth, mobile and hard, dipped in and out of the light so Faye couldn't see it clearly. A mystery couple about to do unmysterious things.

The man untied the laces at the bodice of the woman's nightgown to let it drift and skim down her body to her feet. White, cotton, chaste, the nightgown gave no clue to what era they were in.

The man wore trousers, but his chest was bare. Suspenders dangled at his hips. His erection strained for freedom until the woman guided it to peek out the top of his waistband.

Yum. Great chest, slim hips, hard belly, and a wide head on his cock. Faye responded as if she were the one cupping his balls and feeling his hot thumbs swirl across her nipples.

Odd, but pleasurable, the sensation of his callused hands aroused her.

Hot! She was suddenly aroused beyond tolerance by the seductively slow foreplay she witnessed through the peephole. She slid her hand to her crotch and pressed a fingertip to her clit through her thin silk nightie. She was wet and needy and the finger pressure made it better, but she still couldn't ease her need. She pressed harder, rubbed.

The narrow passageway she stood in closed in around her as she caught her breath. The man, naked now and gloriously hard, pressed the woman's shoulders down. She sank to her knees and took him into her mouth. Drew him in deep.

Faye's mouth worked in conjunction as she watched the woman suck him deep into her throat. Faye tasted hot manflesh and swirled her tongue around her mouth, feeling him.

Slowly, carefully, the man pumped into her mouth while the woman continued to lick. He was big and she had to adjust, but eventually, she took most of his full length.

The man's face was still in shadow and he hadn't spoken. Silent but for the sound of mouth-work, lit from a spotlight, the two performed while Faye watched through the bullet-sized hole. The man pumped harder; the woman's head bobbed more quickly. Tension rose around the silent couple, while Faye's arousal deepened.

Faye closed her eyes in passion while she worked to bring herself closer to climax. Next time she could focus, the couple had climbed onto the bed and were writhing together, with deep kisses and rough and ready hands. Still, no sounds came to Faye. No bedsprings, no sighs or moans torn from the amorous pair.

The woman's pale calves flashed in the dim light from the bedside lamps, as she raised them to offer herself to her lover.

Was this *her* room? Was she watching herself with Liam?

The long, slick invasion stretched her wide and she felt the man enter her, knew what the woman knew. The man's heated scent, the feel of his weight on her chest, the incredible stretch of his cock as he pressed her deep into the mattress.

Faye rolled her hips in acceptance and began the dance of need.

Vaguely, she understood she was dreaming. In Perdition House, anything could happen, and often did. She lived with ghosts who saw nothing wrong with siphoning off her orgasms, inciting her to sex with strangers, and causing wild, insatiable desires to bubble under her skin.

Pleasure rose under her hand as she played voyeur and rubbed at her pussy. Suddenly, her nightie slid off her shoulders and drifted away on a breeze that caressed her heated flesh as she watched the lovers, moaned along with them, and felt every sensation they did.

She fought the rising tide, trying to see whose room they were in. As she focused her eyes away from the couple, the details of the room came clearer. Past the bed, light shone on a wallpaper design decades old.

With no French doors, no staircase to a widow's walk on the roof, it wasn't her room. Hers was larger, airier, prettier.

Comforted, she settled in to watch, unable to tear her eyes away even though the couple deserved their privacy. After all, the man had paid for it.

The light in the room dimmed, but still the wall danced with the lovers' shadow, grotesquely erotic. A woman prone, her legs raised, the man's head at her crotch. Finally, she heard sucking and licking sounds as the man pleasured the woman.

The lover's lips and tongue slid harder against her tender flesh, wilder and wilder until the woman crested and moaned, eyes closed, in a low, deep, delicious orgasm that pulsed out in waves from her lowest reaches. Faye rode out the come, closed her eyes and melted and shook along with the lovers.

A sudden scream rent the air, ripping into Faye. The piercing wail came through the wall, clear as a chime and full of terror.

Faye opened her eyes and tried to see what had happened, who had screamed, but the light in the room was suddenly bright as a cloudless day and hurt her eyes. She could see nothing, and all sound faded.

She rolled over and woke, fading pulses the only proof that she'd dreamed again.

A nap—it had all happened during a nap. Groggy and sated from the still-pulsing orgasm, she rose to her elbow to look at the bedside clock. She had two hours. Lots of time.

She stretched, still shaken by what she'd heard. This dream was different from her usually pleasant unfolding stories. She could hardly make sense of it.

The narrow, secret passageway ran between two bedrooms on the second floor. She'd been in there once. The peepholes were installed by the original madam who built the house. She and a troupe of intrepid women had come to Seattle from Butte, Montana. They'd operated an exclusive men's retreat that catered only to the very wealthy and powerful.

Retreat being a polite word for the country's most expensive whorehouse of the last century. Completed in 1911, Perdition House was now hers, left to her by her great-aunt, Mae Grantham, who in turn had inherited it from the original madam, Belle Grantham.

Faye had decided to sell and cash in on her inheritance.

The only obstacle to that decision—Belle still lived here, as did the original four prostitutes. Salacious spirits, the five of them wreaked havoc on Faye's libido.

Not that she minded all that much. What red-blooded woman wouldn't want three or four orgasms a day, she reasoned.

Faye had moved into the mansion and discovered Perdition House was a place of sin, sex, and secrets.

Faye loved every minute of living here.

Logic dictated that the screamer in this dream was one of the women who'd worked here. She hadn't recognized the woman, though, except that the color of her hair was so similar to Faye's.

She couldn't trust anything she'd seen in a dream anyway. Her great-aunt Belle would have done anything to keep Perdition House going when she was alive. Now that she was dead, she was even more determined. Belle manipulated everyone who came here with sexual need and sleight-of-hand.

"Are you sure what you heard was a frightened scream? It might have just been a rapturous climax," Belle, her dead-for-decades great-great aunt, suggested.

For the moment, the beautiful spirit was perched on the staircase to the widow's walk, one of her favorite spots to sit.

"I don't know," Faye said, no longer fazed by speaking with a long-dead madam. "Maybe it was just a lusty come. Why not tell me what happened? Why the secrecy?"

Stupid question. The keeping of secrets was the backbone of Perdition House. Its whole structure was propped up by secrets.

"Oh, Faye, if I told you everything at once, we'd never have any fun." Her aunt's serene smile said it all. The woman enjoyed sending Faye dreams of tantalizing bits and pieces of the lives lived in Perdition. They unfolded like story lines out of a confession magazine: "How I Found Myself Working in a Whorehouse and Loving It."

Belle had reasons for everything she did, and if she wanted

to keep the story behind the screaming woman to herself for a while, so be it. Her aunt didn't have an impulsive bone in her long-dead body. All Faye had to do was wait. Eventually, Belle would tire of playing with her and the truth would come out.

"Smart girl," Belle said with a slight lift to her lips.

Faye blew her a raspberry and threw off the covers. She padded through to the adjoining bathroom to get ready for her date with the deliciously sexy and accommodating Mark.

She hadn't meant to nap, but when the spirits insisted, she couldn't refuse. The dreams had turned her into a prurient hedonist with two lovers—Mark, a down-and-dirty businessman from Denver, and Liam, a lawyer in her auntie's law firm.

Two lovers were down from three, but her repressed, boring ex-fiancé, Colin, hardly counted in the sexual satisfaction department. It still bothered her that he'd been boffing his slut of a receptionist while she'd been convinced their ho-hum sex life was her fault.

She set those thoughts aside. No point dwelling on her disappointments. Not when life had taken such an interesting turn. "Still," she said, "living with a bunch of horny spirits is a pain." She spoke to the empty bathroom.

At least she assumed it was empty. There hadn't been any cold drafts or shadowy movement behind her yet and Belle hadn't followed her. "But I love you all," she amended, meaning it.

She showered quickly, mentally picking out her outfit for her date with Mark, the first man with whom she'd released her inner sex imp.

She'd found him in a hotel bar on a night she'd planned as a one-night stand with a stranger to discover whether her sexual inadequacies were actually hers. Turns out, they weren't.

Mark had taught her to enjoy her sexuality, to revel in wild abandon and have fun with the act. Colin the pencil-dick had nearly convinced her she was a sexual dud. Mark's attentions had cleared the path for a rebirth inside Faye. The new woman she was owed him a lot.

She was afraid their one-night stand would turn into more.

Which would be fabulous, if she wasn't already sleeping with Liam Watson, of Watson, Watson and Sloane, the law firm that had handled Auntie Mae's estate. Watson the Elder had been her aunt's lawyer. Liam had been electrically hot at first sight.

She filled her toothbrush with paste and hit the button. Around the vibrating buzz, she considered her options. Sex with Mark was incredibly intense and liberating. He'd taught her more in one night than she'd ever known.

He was supposed to be back home in Denver, fading into a luscious memory while she enjoyed herself with Liam.

But in the farce she was now calling her life, he'd decided to go into retail outlets with his wholesale business—starting with Seattle. Which had brought him straight back into her life.

His expression when he looked at her was warm and affectionate. She liked Mark, admired his business acumen, and loved his sexual prowess.

She hit the shower and washed her hair in record time, then couldn't decide what to wear. With an entire vintage clothing store to pick from, she most often dressed in Hollywood castoffs. Clothes that had once belonged to the blond bombshells of the 50s and 60s suited her fair hair and heavy breasts best, but there were times she liked to play with a retro-hippie look.

Sunset-orange light beamed in through the lacy white curtains as she combed out her damp hair. She wanted long, straight hair tonight, parted in the middle. Straight bangs, too.

Belle appeared, preening prettily in the mirror Faye used. She frowned and peered closely at Faye from the mirror. "Straight hair? That's unusual."

Faye stuck out her tongue. "Yes, as long as it doesn't rain or get damp, it'll be straight."

"This is Seattle, honey, it won't be straight for long. What will Mark think?" Belle asked with a teasing glint in her eye.

"I have no idea. He loves it when I go with a fifties look, and I do so enjoy playing the sex kitten." She pouted her lips into a kiss. "Mohair sweaters and cantilevered bras, platform slingbacks and tight knee-length skirts make me feel sexy and available. But this mini-skirt makes me feel young and hot." She smoothed the wide white belt at her waist.

"Young, hot, and ready." Belle's smile turned sultry.

Faye was ready all the time these days.

Ready. Willing. Available.

Faye cleared her throat. "Thanks to you and the others, I'm a far cry from the repressed woman I was before I moved into the mansion. But that doesn't give you the right to keep pushing my libido into overdrive."

Rather than invite Mark here, she preferred to see him at his hotel. Except for Belle, who could tap into Faye no matter where she was, the spirits' influence decreased the farther away she was from the mansion.

"So," Belle chimed in, "what's on for tonight? Dancing? Dinner?"

"Dinner and then, with any luck he'll love this style so much he won't be able to keep his hands off me."

The madame enjoyed a spicy orgasm through Faye once in a while. All the spirits did. "I hope the outfit works, too," Belle murmured.

"The sex-kitten look is sultry, but I wanted to go for fun tonight. It's good to keep a man guessing." Especially Mark, who'd shocked the hell out of her by calling out of the blue.

She finished straightening her hair and slicked on a heavy black eyeliner, making sure to give it an upward lift at the outer corner of each eyelid. Catty.

Belle gave her a final inspection. "I like it."

"Great, now would you mind getting out of the mirror? I can't see to check my eyebrows. It's disconcerting to lean in close to the glass and have you looking back at me." She shooed at the mirror. "I need to check my brows, not yours."

Belle obliged by floating beside her instead.

"Thanks."

"You're welcome."

Faye continued to prepare for Mark, thinking of his hands, his lips, his teeth scraping lightly over her nipples. He so loved her breasts. She softened between her legs and felt the telltale slide of moisture that came with thoughts of him.

Their brief affair should have faded into a pleasant memory, but it looked as if it was off to a roaring start.

"I never thought Mark would fade away," said Belle, responding to Faye's inner dialogue. A habit that proved living with horny spirits was a pain. "He likes you too much."

"Maybe it would have been better if he'd decided against expanding his business and moving to Seattle. I wouldn't have to choose between him and Watson the Younger."

"Liam Watson's a lovely man: well-built, well-hung, and isn't afraid to show his kind heart. I'm impressed that he takes on hard-luck cases."

"This comment from a woman who prefers bad boys?" she asked, with a smirk at her dead lookalike.

For a lawyer, Liam Watson was a kind, compassionate man. A man Faye could fall for.

"You don't need to choose between them, Faye. A woman's entitled to take her time and more than entitled to take a second lover if one man isn't enough."

"If I wasn't providing all of you with your orgasms, one man would be enough!" Perhaps Belle was right. There was no reason to rush to a decision.

She wasn't committed to either man. Neither had they made

any commitment to her. Mark had slept with her knowing she was engaged. Besides, she was having fun with each of them.

Liam, soft-hearted and more open to fun sex and maybe even to the spirits, was a great guy.

But something dark in Mark appealed to her too. He was more intense, harder, brisker, and she admired his business sense and sharp intelligence. In truth, she didn't know enough about either man to make a choice.

She decided to keep things light. That way, no one would get hurt. If things got serious with either Mark or Liam, she'd tread carefully.

"I'm just out of a five-year relationship," she said to Belle. "I'm not ready for commitment." Not to anything more than opening a new store to help pay for the repairs to the mansion.

That had to be her priority.

Belle smirked. Faye glared back and slicked on a pale pink lip gloss. She pouted into the mirror to see if it caught the light and made her lips more kissable.

Belle didn't need an explanation—she could read Faye's thoughts—but still, Faye needed to vent. "Liam's a sweetie. And I like that he already has a sense that you're here. He responded very well when he heard Lizzie laughing out in the trees by the gazebo. I think he might even come to accept you're all here some day."

"But you're not sure about Mark's reaction?"

"Exactly. Sooner or later he's going to want to see the house. I don't know how to handle that unless you promise to leave him alone."

Belle rolled her eyes. "I can only speak for myself."

"Yeah, right."

She never knew when one of the spirits would act up or get cute. They loved men and loved sex. And Lizzie, in particular, enjoyed turning up the heat.

"How much does Liam know?" Belle asked.

"He's intrigued by the house, by what he senses here. He liked it when Lizzie got us hot and bothered out in the ga-zebo."

"We all liked that. It took, what, all of thirty seconds to have you writhing on the floor? I must say Liam's size was quite a shock."

She and Liam had been so hot for each other they'd barely had time for hello. Since then, their friendship had developed. She'd visited him in his office for another round, then he'd stayed with her in the mansion overnight. The man was a bull in the manly-endowments department. Her mouth watered just thinking about him.

Faye turned and leaned against the sink and crossed her arms. "He heard Lizzie giggling but didn't care that we might have an audience. Then, the next day in his office he told me he has sex whenever and wherever the need strikes." A pearl of de-sire slid low in her body. "I've been thinking of testing that statement."

The room chilled as more of the spirits joined Faye and Belle. They could ice up a room in no time. Faye had taken to keeping sweaters all over the house, in spite of the warm spring they were having.

Felicity, pretty in green velvet with her lustrous brown hair swept into a Gibson Girl hairdo, drifted into the bathroom from the adjoining bedroom. At least she arrived through doorways. Annie, a tomboy at heart, sometimes jumped down from the ceiling, scaring the hell out of Faye.

And Hope, the most tenderhearted of the troupe, often smelled of cinnamon, cloves, and apples. All she'd ever wanted was to be a wife and mother. She filled her time with household chores like baking and doing laundry. Not in the real world, but on the spirit plane.

Felicity grinned and perched on the side of the claw-footed tub.

"I always loved sex outside," she said, picking up on the conversation. "We'd dance in the gazebo, then I'd take my man out to the swing Annie built for me in the trees. I had this hole in the seat, you see, and my man would sit just so in front of the swing." She laughed and clasped her cheeks. "I did love my contraptions!"

Faye cocked an eyebrow. "Did you? Am I going to see these contraptions?"

Felicity laughed. "Of course! In due time."

More dreams. "I'll look forward to it." The dreams made her hot and needy. Most times she woke with her hand on her pussy and had to take the edge off. The way things were, she did need two lovers.

"Of course you need both men, Faye. Just like you need another store. Two's always better than one."

"A second location will help, but only time will tell if two stores will be enough to keep this place going." She'd given up millions of dollars to stay here and keep the girls in the house.

None of them, Faye included, wanted to see the beautiful grounds plowed under for multi-family housing. But the pressure would only increase. The house, north of Seattle, overlooked lovely Shilshole Bay and Bainbridge Island. Oceanfront acres would always be under the watchful eye of developers. If she ran into financial trouble, the vultures would circle.

Faye held their fates in her hand. She took the responsibility seriously, as had Auntie Mae Grantham.

Sometimes she thought Belle had tweaked her thoughts to go in that direction. Other times, she thought her need to keep the house going came from inside herself. A need for family? Her own was distant and cool. Her parents' volatile marriage, while passionate, left little room for grown children.

"There are a lot of neglected areas around the house and I don't want to settle for scraping by," she said, returning to the conversation. "I want to prosper. Now that my marriage is off, I have to rethink my future."

"Spoken like a true Grantham woman. And that marriage was no loss, honey," Belle drawled.

"I know. It's just that I haven't had to worry overmuch about profits in the store for the last few months. Now, I've got to gear up again."

"Your staff will help?" Felicity asked.

"Of course. Kim and Willa are great. That reminds me, Belle, I want to check out the attic to see if there are any clothes or shoes up there. I saw some photos from the 1940s in your trunk. I love the open-toed slingbacks from that era."

Hope glided in, bringing in the delicious homey smell of apple pies baking. "What in the world are you wearing?" she asked at her first sight of Faye.

Faye smoothed the mini-skirt and felt a rush of desire trill a need deep inside. "Like it?" She lifted her skirt a half inch to show she'd neglected to put on panties.

"Very sexy," agreed Hope.

Belle chuckled. "That's our Faye." To Faye, she said, "We'll see the attic tomorrow."

Felicity nodded. "You'll need inventory if you open a second location and the attic's stuffed full. You'll see." She beamed a smile. Felicity's assurance made Faye feel more hope that things would work out. She'd been the house's finance manager and had a good head for accounting.

"Give us a twirl, Faye," Felicity begged. "I haven't dressed for a man in so long, I've forgotten what it's like."

Faye obliged and pirouetted. Felicity laughed and clapped her hands. "Gorgeous! What era?"

"Sixties." The clothes had been worn by a hip young TV actress. "The mini-skirt, wide white belt and go-go boots are a dead giveaway."

"Maybe to you, but that's after our time."

* * *

"A go-go girl?" Mark grinned. His hazel eyes glowed with heat at Faye's appearance. "That's hot. Love the boots." He opened his arms and Faye walked straight into them, ignoring the bustling hum and buzz of the hotel lobby.

"You smell so good," she said. The sizzle of arousal skipped along her muscles and ligaments as he gathered her to his chest. Her heart picked up speed, and her blood rushed to her deepest core, warming as it moved through her body.

Bellmen pushed luggage carts every which way, cell phones rang incessantly, and the elevator arrival bells chimed a steady beat. Business people came and went and lined up for check-in. Welcome signs for a conference sat on easels all over the lobby.

None of the hustle around them interfered with the deep sexual need simmering under her skin. The need she read in Mark's eyes. She lightly rubbed her softer skin along his hard, bristly jawline. She wanted him and needed to know this came from her, not the girls' influence.

His hands dropped to her ass and he clasped both cheeks as he pulled her tight into his hips.

"Food? Or dessert?" he asked, letting her know what he wanted first.

"I'm hoping dessert has nothing to do with food."

He growled into her ear. "Damn straight." He glanced up. "Shit, let's get out of here. There's an old friend I don't want to share you with just yet." He took her hand and stepped toward the exit.

She held back. "Share me with?" Fanciful thoughts skipped through her mind. Thoughts that wouldn't normally be hers. Damn that Belle!

"I don't want—damn—he's seen us. Man's a bloodhound when it comes to beautiful women." His eyes turned wary as he looked over her shoulder.

She turned. The man who approached with an appraising

eye must be the friend. Handsome in an angular way, taller than Mark but thinner. She saw a bit of tall, thin Adrian Brody in his shoulders and long limbs.

"Grant Johnson, Faye Grantham. Sorry, we're out of here."

"Whoa, you sure about that, buddy? I mean, Faye here wouldn't want a man to eat a lonely bowl of soup in a hotel café, now, would she?" He stuck out his hand to Faye.

She clasped it. He pulled her close and kissed her cheek. Then he lifted her hand and kissed her palm for good measure. She felt the tingle to her toes. Very warm. Hot even.

She smiled, enjoying the sensation.